DAWN of TIME

DAWN of TIME

PREHISTORY THROUGH SCIENCE FICTION

edited by

Martin Harry Greenberg
Joseph Olander
Robert Silverberg

Elsevier/Nelson Books
New York

No character in this book is intended to represent any actual person; all the incidents of the stories are entirely fictional in nature.

Library of Congress Cataloging in Publication Data
Main entry under title:

Dawn of time.

    CONTENTS: De Camp, L. S. A gun for dinosaur.—Miller, P. S. The sands of time.—Olsen, R. R. Paleontology.—Thomas, T. The doctor.—Cartmill, C. The link. [etc.]
    1. Science fiction, American. I. Silverberg, Robert. II. Greenberg, Martin Harry. III. Olander, Joseph D.
PZ1.D2687   [PS648.S3]   813'.0876   79-1254
ISBN 0-525-66624-9

Published in the United States by Elsevier/Nelson Books, a division of Elsevier-Dutton Publishing Company, Inc., New York. Published simultaneously in Don Mills, Ontario, by Thomas Nelson and Sons (Canada) Limited.

Printed in the U.S.A.   First Edition
10 9 8 7 6 5 4 3 2 1

ACKNOWLEDGMENTS

"A Gun for Dinosaur," by L. Sprague de Camp. Copyright © 1956 by Galaxy Publishing Corporation. Reprinted by permission of the author.

"The Sands of Time," by P. Schuyler Miller. Copyright 1937 by Street & Smith Publications, Inc. Reprinted by permission of Mrs. Mary E. Drake for the author's estate.

"Paleontology: An Experimental Science," by Robert R. Olsen. Copyright © 1974 by Condé Nast Publications, Inc. Reprinted by permission of the author.

"The Doctor," by Ted Thomas. Copyright © 1967 by Damon Knight. Reprinted by permission of the author.

"The Link," by Cleve Cartmill. Copyright 1942 by Street & Smith Publications, Inc. (copyright renewed © 1970 by Condé Nast Publications, Inc.) Reprinted by permission of Forrest J. Ackerman on behalf of the author's heir, Matt Cartmill, Ph.D.

"The Day Is Done," by Lester del Rey. Copyright 1939 by Street & Smith Publications, Inc. Reprinted by permission of the author and the author's agents, Scott Meredith Literary Agency, Inc.

"The Gnarly Man," by L. Sprague de Camp. Copyright 1939 by Street & Smith Publications, Inc. (Copyright renewed © 1966 by L. Sprague de Camp.) Reprinted by permission of the author.

"Brave New Word," by J. Francis McComas. Copyright

CONTENTS

INTRODUCTION

SCIENCE FICTION is generally thought to be fiction about the future. But that is very much an oversimplification. Science fiction is, in Robert A. Heinlein's phrase, *speculative* fiction; and, though it is perhaps more natural to speculate about the future than the past, times gone by are just as fertile grounds for science-fictional speculations as times to come. And so, although most science fiction does happen to take place in the future, a substantial and significant portion of the literature examines the past. What science fiction primarily does, after all, is to carry the reader into an unknown situation and explore a realm of strangeness in meticulous and logical detail—and why is the Mars of A.D. 2500 any more strange, any less accessible to our experience, than the Earth of sixty million B.C.? Both are distant, bizarre, alien places, and our only hope of "knowing" them is through imaginative reconstruction of scientific projection.

Ever since the days of H. G. Wells, science-fiction writers have delighted in returning to the primordial past for the scenes of their stories. John Taine's novel *Before the Dawn* (1934) provided a dazzling view of the age of dinosaurs. Stanley Waterloo's *The Story of Ab* (1897) was one of the first books to dramatize the life of the Stone Age; another was Jack London's *Before Adam* (1906). A. Conan Doyle's *The Lost World* (1912) carried prehistory into the twentieth century by imagining a hidden plateau in South America where Jurassic dinosaurs have managed to survive. H. P. Lovecraft's *At the Mountains of Madness* and *The Shadow out of Time* (1936) suggested, in horrifying fashion, the occupation of Earth by intelligent alien visitors millions of years ago. Such stories as those, vivid and compelling even today, are much too long for inclusion in this book; but there is a rich trove of shorter science fiction from which to draw, and we have chosen ten of the finest for this collection, offering a spectrum of imaginative views of prehistory from the era of dinosaurs down to the last days of the Paleolithic era in Europe. These stories generally have attempted to work within established scientific knowledge, bringing the past to life by using paleontological and anthropological data as the foundation for imaginative speculations. Once again, then, science fiction serves as our time machine. We can never directly experience the Cretaceous or the Pleistocene or even the late Paleolithic, any more than we can visit the world of a million years hence; but we can make vicarious journeys of the imagination to those far harbors of time, and come away enriched, stimulated, aware of the texture and quality of those other worlds of time, and heightened in our perceptions not only of our own era but of those that went before.

—*Robert Silverberg*
Martin Harry Greenberg
Joseph D. Olander

A GUN FOR DINOSAUR

L. Sprague de Camp

L. Sprague de Camp is a man born out of his proper time. Tall, athletic-looking, of erect military bearing, with a neatly trimmed little beard and the glint of formidable erudition in his eyes, he looks like one of those nineteenth-century British scholar-adventurers who tracked the Nile to its source or hunted lost cities in the Himalayan foothills. Fate brought him into the world a little too late for that, but he has done his best to cope, leaving his quiet suburban home near Philadelphia from time to time and trekking off to explore the remote Sahara or the bazaars of Bombay. For more than forty years he had been a professional writer, both in fiction and nonfiction, producing on the one hand such classics of science fiction and fantasy as Lest Darkness Fall *and* The Wheels of If, *and on the other a host of splendid scholarly books on historical and scientific themes, such as* The Ancient Engineers *and* The Day of the Dinosaur *(the latter written in collaboration with his wife Catherine).*

So there are few writers better qualified to take us on a tour of the era of the dinosaurs—as in this hunting expedition to the Cretaceous, the third of the three great periods of the Mesozoic Era. The Mesozoic, the age of the mighty reptiles, began some 225 million years ago with what is known as the Triassic period; the relatively small dinosaurs of the Triassic developed, in the Jurassic that succeeded it, into the great creatures that so stir our imaginations, the brontosaurus and stegosaurus and allosaurus, and then, in the Cretaceous, the peak of dinosaur evolution—but let L. Sprague de Camp tell us that.

No, Mr. Seligman, I won't take you hunting late-Mesozoic dinosaur.

Why not? How much d'you weigh? A hundred and thirty? Let's see, that's under ten stone, which is my lower limit.

I'll take you to any period in the Cenozoic. I'll get you a shot at an entelodont or a titanothere or a uintathere. They've all got fine heads.

I'll even stretch a point and take you to the Pleistocene, where you can try for one of the mammoths or the mastodon.

I'll take you back to the Triassic, where you can shoot one of the smaller ancestral dinosaur.

But I will not—will jolly well not—take you to the Jurassic or Cretaceous. You're just too small.

No offense, of course.

What's your weight got to do with it?

Look here, old boy, what did you think you were going to shoot them with?

You hadn't thought, eh?

Well, sit there a minute. . . .

Here you are, my own private gun for that work, a Continental .600. Does look like a shotgun, doesn't it? But it's rifled, as you can see by looking through the barrels. Shoots a pair of .600 nitro express cartridges the size of bananas; weighs fourteen and a half pounds and has a muzzle energy of over seven thousand foot-pounds. Costs fourteen hundred and fifty dollars. Lot of money for a gun, what?

I have some spares I rent to the sahibs. Designed for knocking down elephant. Not just wounding them, knocking them base-over-apex. That's why they don't make guns like this in America, though I suppose they will if hunting parties keep going back in time through Prochaska's machine.

I've been guiding hunting parties for twenty years. Guided 'em in Africa until the game gave out there except on the preserves. That just about ended the world's real big-game hunting.

My point is, all that time I've never known a man your size who could handle the six-nought-nought. It knocks 'em

over. Even when they stay on their feet, they get so scared of
the bloody cannon after a few shots that they flinch. Can't hit
an elephant at spitting range. And they find the gun too heavy
to drag around rough Mesozoic country. Wears 'em out.

It's true, lots of people have killed elephant with lighter
guns: the .500, .475, and .465 doubles, for instances, or
even .375 magnum repeaters. The difference is that with a
.375 you have to hit something vital, preferably the heart,
and can't depend on simple shock power.

An elephant weighs—let's see—four to six tons. You're
planning to shoot reptiles weighing two or three times as
much as an elephant and with much greater tenacity of life.
That's why the syndicate decided to take no more people
dinosaur-hunting unless they could handle the .600. We
learned the hard way, as you Americans say. There were
some unfortunate incidents. . . .

I'll tell you, Mr. Seligman. It's after seventeen hundred.
Time I closed the office. Why don't we stop at the bar on our
way out while I tell you the story?

It was about the Raja's and my fifth safari. The Raja? Oh,
he's the Aiyar half of Rivers & Aiyar. I call him the Raja
because he's the hereditary monarch of Janpur. Means nothing nowadays, of course. Knew him in India and ran into him
in New York running the Indian tourist agency. That dark
chap in the photograph on my office wall, the one with his
foot on the dead saber-tooth.

Well, the Raja was fed up with handing out brochures
about the Taj Mahal and wanted to do a bit of hunting again.
I was at loose ends when we hard of Professor Prochaska's
time machine at Washington University.

Where is the Raja? Out on safari in the early Oligocene,
after titanothere, while I run the office. We take turns about
now, but the first few times we went out together.

Anyhow, we caught the next plane to St. Louis. To our
mortification, we found we weren't the first.

Lord, no! There were other hunting guides and no end of

scientists, each with his own idea of the right use for the machine.

We scraped off the historians and archeologists right at the start.

Seems the bloody machine won't work for periods more recent than a hundred thousand years ago. From there, up to about a billion years.

Why? Oh, I'm no four-dimensional thinker, but as I understand it, if people could go back to a more recent time, their actions would affect our own history, which would be a paradox or contradiction of facts. Can't have that in a well-run universe. But before one hundred thousand B.C., more or less, the actions of the expeditions are lost in the stream of time before human history begins. At that, once a stretch of past time has been used, say the month of January, one million B.C., you can't use that stretch over again by sending another party into it. Paradoxes again.

But the professor isn't worried; with a billion years to exploit, he won't soon run out of eras.

Another limitation of the machine is the matter of size. For technical reasons, Prochaska had to build the transition chamber just big enough to hold four men with their personal gear, plus the chamber-wallah. Larger parties have to be sent through in relays. That means, you see, it's not practical to take jeeps, boats, aircraft, or other powered vehicles.

On the other hand, since you're going to periods without human beings, there's no whistling up a hundred native bearers to trot along with your gear on their heads. So we usually take a train of asses—burros, they call them here. Most periods have enough natural forage to get you where you want to go.

As I say, everybody had his own idea for using the machine. The scientists looked down their noses at us hunters and said it would be a crime to waste the machine's time pandering to our sadistic amusements.

We brought up another angle. The machine cost a cool thirty million. I understand this came from the Rockefeller

Board and such people, but that only accounted for the original cost, not the cost of operation. And the thing uses fantastic amounts of power. Most of the scientists' projects, while worthy as worthy could be, were run on a shoestring, financially speaking.

Now we guides catered to people with money, a species with which America seems overstocked. No offense, old boy. Most of these could afford a substantial fee for passing through the machine to the past. Thus we could help finance the operation of the machine for scientific purposes, provided we got a fair share of its time.

Won't go into the details, but in the end the guides formed a syndicate of eight members, one member being the partnership of Rivers & Aiyar, to apportion the machine's time.

We had rush business from the start. Our wives—the Raja's and mine—raised bloody hell with us. They'd hoped when the big game gave out they'd never have to share us with lions and things again, but you know how women are. Can't realize hunting's not really dangerous if you keep your head and take precautions.

On the fifth expedition, we had two sahibs to wet-nurse: both Americans and in their thirties, both physically sound, and both solvent. Otherwise they were as different as different can be.

Courtney James was what you chaps call a playboy: a rich young man from New York who'd always had his own way and didn't see why that agreeable condition shouldn't continue. A big bloke, almost as big as I am; handsome in a florid way, but beginning to run to fat. He was on his fourth wife, and when he showed up at the office with a blonde with "model" written all over her, I assumed this was the fourth Mrs. James.

"Miss Bartram," she corrected me, with an embarrassed giggle.

"She's not my wife," James explained. "My wife is in

Mexico, I think, getting a divorce. But Bunny here would like to go along—"

"Sorry," I said, "we don't take ladies. At least not to the late Mesozoic."

This wasn't strictly true, but I felt we were running enough risks, going after a little-known fauna, without dragging in people's domestic entanglements. Nothing against sex, you understand. Marvelous institution and all that, but not where it interferes with my living.

"Oh, nonsense," said James. "If she wants to go, she'll go. She skis and flies my airplane, so why shouldn't she—"

"Against the firm's policy."

"She can keep out of the way when we run up against the dangerous ones."

"No, sorry."

"Damn it," said he, getting red. "After all, I'm paying you a goodly sum and I'm entitled to take who I please."

"You can't hire me to do anything against my best judgment," I said. "If that's how you feel, get another guide."

"All right, I will. And I'll tell all my friends you're a goddamn—" Well, he said a lot of things I won't repeat. It ended with my telling him to get out of the office or I'd throw him out.

I was sitting in the office thinking sadly of all that lovely money James would have paid me if I hadn't been so stiff-necked, when in came my other lamb, one August Holtzinger. This was a little slim pale chap with glasses, polite and formal where the other had been breezily self-confident to the point of obnoxiousness.

Holtzinger sat on the edge of his chair and said: "Uh—Mr. Rivers, I don't want you to think I'm here under false pretenses. I'm really not much of an outdoorsman and I'll probably be scared to death when I see a real dinosaur. But I'm determined to hang a dinosaur head over my fireplace or die in the attempt."

"Most of us are frightened at first," I soothed him, and little by little I got the story out of him.

While James had always been wallowing in money, Holtzinger was a local product who'd only lately come into the real thing. He'd had a little business here in St. Louis and just about made ends meet when an uncle cashed in his chips somewhere and left little Augie the pile. He'd never been married but had a fiancee. He was building a big house, and when it was finished, they'd be married and move into it. And one furnishing he demanded was a ceratopsian head over the fireplace. Those are the ones with the big horned heads with a parrot-beak and frill over the neck, you know. You have to think twice about collecting them, because if you put a seven-foot triceratops head into a small living room, there's apt to be no room left for anything else.

We were talking about this when in came a girl, a small girl in her twenties, quite ordinary-looking, and crying. "Augie!" she wept. "You can't! You mustn't! You'll be killed!" She grabbed him round and said to me: "Mr. Rivers, you mustn't take him! He's all I've got! He'll never stand the hardships!"

"My dear young lady," I said, "I should hate to cause you distress, but it's up to Mr. Holtzinger to decide whether he wishes to retain my services."

"It's no use, Claire," said Holtzinger. "I'm going, though I'll probably hate every minute of it."

"What's that, old boy?" I asked. "If you hate it, why go? Did you lose a bet or something?"

"No," said Holtzinger. "It's this way. Uh—I'm a completely undistinguished kind of guy. I'm just an ordinary Midwestern small businessman. You never even notice me at Rotary luncheons, I fit in so perfectly. But that doesn't say I'm satisfied. I've always hankered to go to far places and do big things. I'd like to be a glamorous, adventurous sort of guy. Like you, Mr. Rivers."

"Oh, come," I protested. "Professional hunting may seem glamorous to you, but to me it's just a living."

He shook his head. "Nope. You know what I mean. Well,

now I've got this legacy, I could settle down to play bridge
and golf the rest of my life and try to act like I wasn't bored.
But I'm determined to do something big for once. Since
there's no more real big-game hunting, I'm gonna shoot a dinosaur and hang his head over my mantel. I'll never be
happy otherwise.''

Well, Holtzinger and his girl, whose name was Roche,
argued, but he wouldn't give in. She made me swear to take
the best care of her Augie and departed, sniffling.

When Holtzinger had left, who should come in but my
vile-tempered friend Courtney James. He apologized for in-
sulting me, though you could hardly say he groveled.

"I don't actually have a bad temper,'' he said, "except
when people won't cooperate with me. Then I sometimes get
mad. But so long as they're cooperative, I'm not hard to get
along with.''

I knew that by "cooperate'' he meant to do whatever
Courtney James wanted, but I didn't press the point. "How
about Miss Bartram?'' I asked.

"We had a row,'' he said. "I'm through with women. So
if there's no hard feelings, let's go on from where we left
off.''

"Absolutely,'' I agreed, business being business.

The Raja and I decided to make it a joint safari to eighty-
five million years ago: the early upper Cretaceous, or the
middle Cretaceous, as some American geologists call it. It's
about the best period for dinosaur in Missouri. You'll find
some individual species a little larger in the late upper Cretaceous, but the period we were going to gives a wider variety.

Now, as to our equipment, the Raja and I each had a Continental .600 like the one I showed you and a few smaller
guns. At this time, we hadn't worked up much capital and
had no spare .600s to rent.

August Holtzinger said he would rent a gun, as he expected this to be his only safari and there was no point in

spending over a thousand dollars for a gun he'd shoot only a few times. But since we had no spare .600s, his choice was between buying one of those and renting one of our smaller pieces.

We drove into the country to let him try the .600. We set up a target. Holtzinger heaved up the gun as if it weighed a ton and let fly. He missed completely and the kick knocked him flat on his back with his legs in the air.

He got up, looking paler than ever, and handed me back the gun, saying: "Uh—I think I'd better try something smaller."

When his shoulder stopped being sore, I tried him out on the smaller rifles. He took a fancy to my Winchester 70, chambered for the .375 magnum cartridge. It's an excellent all-round gun—

What's it like? A conventional magazine rifle with a Mauser-type bolt action. It's perfect for the big cats and bears, but a little light for elephant and very definitely light for dinosaur. I should never have given in, but I was in a hurry and it might have taken months to get him a new .600. They're made to order, you know, and James was getting impatient. James already had a gun, a Holland & Holland .500 double express. With 5700 foot-pounds of muzzle energy, it's almost in a class with the .600.

Both sahibs had done a bit of shooting so I didn't worry about their accuracy. Shooting dinosaur is not a matter of extreme accuracy but of sound judgment and smooth coordination so you shan't catch twigs in the mechanism of your gun, or fall into holes, or climb a small tree the dinosaur can pluck you out of, or blow your guide's head off.

People used to hunting mammals sometimes try to shoot a dinosaur in the brain. That's the silliest thing you can do, because dinosaur haven't got any. To be exact, they have a little lump of tissue about the size of a tennis ball on the front end of their spines, and how are you doing to hit that when it's imbedded in a moving six-foot skull?

The only safe rule with dinosaur is—always try for a heart

shot. They have big hearts, over a hundred pounds in the largest species, and a couple of .600 slugs through the heart will kill them just as dead as a smaller beast. The problem is to get the slugs through that mountain of muscle and armor around it.

Well, we appeared at Prochaska's laboratory one rainy morning: James and Holtzinger, the Raja and I, our herder Beauregard Black, three helpers, a cook, and twelve jacks. Burros, that is.

The transition chamber is a little cubbyhole the size of a small lift. My routine is for the men with the guns to go first in case a hungry theropod might be standing in front of the machine when it arrived. So the two sahibs, the Raja and I crowded into the chamber with our guns and packs. The operator squeezed in after us, closed the door, and fiddled with his dials. He set the thing for April twenty-fourth, eighty-five million B.C., and pressed the red button.

The lights went out, leaving the chamber lit by a little battery-operated lamp. James and Holtzinger looked pretty green, but that may have been the dim lighting. The Raja and I had been through all this before, so the vibration and vertigo didn't bother us.

I could see the little black hands of the dials spinning round, some slowly and some so fast they were a blur. Then they slowed down and stopped. The operator looked at his ground-level gauge and turned a hand-wheel that raised the chamber so it shouldn't materialize underground. Then he pressed another button and the door slid open.

No matter how often I do it, I get a frightful thrill out of stepping into a bygone era. The operator had raised the chamber a foot above ground level, so I jumped down, my gun ready. The others came after. We looked back at the chamber, a big shiny cube hanging in mid-air a foot off the ground, with this little liftdoor in front.

"Right-ho," I told the chamber-wallah, and he closed the door. The chamber disappeared and we looked around. The scene hadn't changed from my last expedition to this era, which had ended, in Cretaceous time, five days before this one began. There weren't any dinosaur in sight, nothing but lizards.

In this period, the chamber materializes on top of a rocky rise from which you can see in all directions as far as the haze will let you. To the west, you see the arm of the Kansas Sea that reaches across Missouri and the big swamp around the bayhead where the sauropods live. It used to be thought the sauropods became extinct before the Cretaceous, but that's not so. They were more limited in range because swamps and lagoons didn't cover so much of the world, but there were plenty of them if you knew where to look. To the north is a low range that the Raja named the Janpur Hills after the little Indian kingdom his forebears had ruled. To the east, the land slopes up to a plateau, good for ceratopsians, while to the south is flat country with more sauropod swamps and lots of ornithopods: duckbills and iguanodonts.

The finest thing about the Cretaceous is the climate: balmy, like the South Sea Islands, with little seasonal change, but not so muggy as most Jurassic climates. We happened to be there in spring, with dwarf magnolias in bloom all over, but the air feels like spring almost any time of year.

A thing about this landscape is that it combines a fairly high rainfall with an open type of vegetation cover. That is, the grasses hadn't yet evolved to the point of forming solid carpets over all open ground, so the ground is thick with laurel, sassafras and other shrubs, with bare ground between. There are big thickets of palmettos and ferns. The trees round the hill are mostly cycads, standing singly and in copses. Most people call them palms, though my scientific friends tell me they're not true palms.

Down toward the Kansas Sea are more cycads and willows, while the uplands are covered with screw-pine and gingkos.

Now I'm no bloody poet—the Raja writes the stuff, not

me—but I can appreciate a beautiful scene. One of the helpers had come through the machine with two of the jacks and was pegging them out, and I was looking through the haze and sniffing the air, when a gun went off behind me— bang! bang!

I turned round and there was Courtney James with his .500 and an ornithomime legging it for cover fifty yards away. The ornithomimes are medium-sized running dinosaurs, slender things with long necks and legs, like a cross between a lizard and an ostrich. This kind is about seven feet tall and weighs as much as a man. The beggar had wandered out of the nearest copse and James gave him both barrels. Missed.

I was a bit upset, as trigger-happy sahibs are as much a menace as those who get panicky and freeze or bolt. I yelled:

"Damn it, you idiot, I thought you weren't to shoot without a word from me!"

"And who the hell are you to tell me when I'll shoot my own gun?" he demanded.

We had a rare old row until Holtzinger and the Raja got us calmed down.

I explained: "Look here, Mr. James, I've got reasons. If you shoot off all your ammunition before the trip's over, your gun won't be available in a pinch and it's the only one of its caliber. Second, it you empty both barrels at an unimportant target, what would happen if a big theropod charged before you could reload? Finally, it's not sporting to shoot everything in sight. I'll shoot for meat, or for trophies, or to defend myself, but not just to hear the gun go off. If more people had exercised moderation in killing, there'd still be decent sport in our own era. Understand?"

"Yeah, I guess so," he said. Mercurial sort of bloke.

The rest of the party came through the machine and we pitched our camp a safe distance from the materializing place. Our first task was to get fresh meat. For a twenty-one-day safari like this, we calculate our food requirements closely so we can make out on tinned stuff and concentrates if we must, but we count on killing at least one piece of meat.

When that's butchered, we go on a short tour, stopping at four or five camping places to hunt and arriving back at base a few days before the chamber is due to appear.

Holtzinger, as I said, wanted a ceratopsian head, any kind. James insisted on just one head: a tyrannosaur. Then everybody'd think he'd shot the most dangerous game of all time.

Fact is, the tyrannosaur's overrated. He's more a carrion-eater than an active predator, though he'll snap you up if he gets the chance. He's less dangerous than some of the other theropods—the flesh eaters—such as the big saurophagus of the Jurassic, or even the smaller gorgosaurus from the period we were in. But everybody's read about the tyrant lizard and he does have the biggest head of the theropods.

The one in our period isn't the rex, which is later and a little bigger and more specialized. It's the trionyches with the forelimbs not reduced to quite such little vestiges, though they're too small for anything but picking the brute's teeth after a meal.

When camp was pitched, we still had the afternoon, so the Raja and I took our sahibs on their first hunt. We already had a map of the local terrain from previous trips. The Raja and I have worked out a system for dinosaur hunting. We split into two groups of two men and walk parallel from twenty to forty yards apart. Each group consists of one sahib in front and one guide following and telling the sahib where to go.

We tell the sahibs we put them in front so they shall have first shot, which is true, but another reason is they're always tripping and falling with their guns cocked, and if the guide were in front, he'd get shot.

The reason for two groups is that if a dinosaur starts for one, the other gets a good heart shot from the side.

As we walked, there was the usual rustle of lizards scuttling out of the way: little fellows, quick as a flash and colored like all the jewels in Tiffany's, and big gray ones that hiss and plod off. There were tortoises and a few little snakes. Birds with beaks full of teeth flapped off squawking.

And always that marvelous mild Cretacean air. Makes a chap want to take his clothes off and dance with vine-leaves in his hair, if you know what I mean. Not that I'd ever do such a thing, you understand.

Our sahibs soon found that Mesozoic country is cut up into millions of nullahs—gullies, you'd call them. Walking is one long scramble, up and down, up and down.

We'd been scrambling for an hour and the sahibs were soaked with sweat and had their tongues hanging out, when the Raja whistled. He'd spotted a group of bonehead feeding on cycad shoots.

These are the troödonts, small ornithopods about the size of men with a bulge on top of their heads that makes them look quite intelligent. Means nothing, because the bulge is solid bone and the brain is as small as in other dinosaur, hence the name. The males butt each other with these heads in fighting over the females. They would drop down to all fours, munch a shoot, then stand up and look round. They're warier than most dinosaur because they're the favorite food of the big theropods.

People sometimes assume that because dinosaur are so stupid, their senses must be dim, but it's not so. Some, like the sauropods, are pretty dim-sensed, but most have good smell and eyesight and fair hearing. Their weakness is that, having no minds, they have no memories; hence, out of sight, out of mind. When a big theropod comes slavering after you, your best defense is to hide in a nullah or behind a bush, and if he can neither see nor smell you, he'll just forget all about you and wander off.

We sneaked up behind a patch of palmetto downwind from the bonehead. I whispered to James: "You've had a shot already today. Hold your fire until Holtzinger shoots and then shoot only if he misses or if the beast is getting away wounded."

"Uh-huh," said James and we separated, he with the Raja and Holtzinger with me. This got to be our regular arrangement. James and I got on each other's nerves, but the Raja, once you forget that Oriental-potentate rot, is a friendly, sentimental sort of bloke nobody can help liking.

Well, we crawled round the palmetto patch on opposite sides and Holtzinger got up to shoot. You daren't shoot a heavy-caliber rifle prone. There's not enough give and the kick can break your shoulder.

Holtzinger sighted round the last few fronds of palmetto. I saw his barrel wobbling and weaving and then off went James's gun, both barrels again. The biggest bonehead went down, rolling and thrashing, and the others ran on their hindlegs in great leaps, their heads jerking and their tails sticking up behind.

"Put your gun on safety," I said to Holtzinger, who'd started forward. By the time we got to the bonehead, James was standing over it, breaking open his gun and blowing out the barrels. He looked as smug as if he'd inherited another million and he was asking the Raja to take his picture with his foot on the game. His first shot had been excellent, right through the heart. His second had missed because the first knocked the beast down. James couldn't resist that second shot even when there was nothing to shoot at.

I said: "I thought you were to give Holtzinger first shot."

"Hell, I waited," he said, "and he took so long, I thought something must have gone wrong. If we stood around long enough, they'd see us or smell us."

There was something in what he said, but his way of saying it got me angry. I said: "If that sort of thing happens just once more, we'll leave you in camp the next time we go out."

"Now, gentlemen," said the Raja. "After all, Reggie, these aren't experienced hunters."

"What now?" asked Holtzinger. "Haul the beast back ourselves or send out the men?"

"I think we can sling him under the pole," I said. "He weighs under two hundred." The pole was a telescoping aluminum carrying pole I had in my pack, with yokes on the ends with sponge-rubber padding. I brought it along because in such eras you can't always count on finding saplings strong enough for proper poles on the spot. The Raja and I cleaned our bonehead, to lighten him, and tied him to the pole. The flies began to light on the offal by the thousands. Scientists say they're not true flies in the modern sense, but they look and act like them. There's one conspicuous kind of carrion fly, a big four-winged insect with a distinctive deep note as it flies.

The rest of the afternoon, we sweated under that pole. We took turns about, one pair carrying the beast while the other two carried the guns. The lizards scuttled out of the way and the flies buzzed round the carcass.

When we got to camp, it was nearly sunset. We felt as if we could eat the whole bonehead at one meal. The boys had the camp running smoothly, so we sat down for our tot of whiskey feeling like lords of creation while the cook broiled bonehead steaks.

Holtzinger said: "Uh—if I kill a ceratopsian, how do we get his head back?"

I explained: "If the ground permits, we lash it to the patent aluminum roller-frame and sled it in."

"How much does a head like that weigh?" he asked.

"Depends on the age and the species," I told him. "The biggest weigh over a ton, but most run between five hundred and a thousand pounds."

"And all the ground's rough like today?"

"Most of it. You see, it's the combination of the open vegetation cover and the high rainfall. Erosion is frightfully rapid."

"And who hauls the head on its little sled?"

"Everybody with a hand. A big head would need every ounce of muscle in this party and even then we might not succeed. On such a job, there's no place for sides."

"Oh," said Holtzinger. I could see him wondering whether a ceratopsian head would be worth the effort.

The next couple of days, we trekked round the neighborhood. Nothing worth shooting; only a herd of fifty-odd or-nithomimes who went bounding off like a lot of bloody ballet dancers. Otherwise there were only the usual lizards and pterosaurs and birds and insects. There's a big lace-winged fly that bites dinosaurs, so you can imagine its beak makes nothing of a human skin. One made Holtzinger leap into the air when it bit through his shirt. James joshed him about it, saying: "What's all this fuss over one little bug?"

The second night, during the Raja's watch, James gave a yell that brought us all out of our tents with rifles. All that had happened was that a dinosaur tick had crawled in with him and started drilling into his armpit. Since it's as big as your thumb even when it hasn't fed, he was understandably startled. Luckily he got it before it had taken its pint of blood. He'd pulled Holtzinger's leg pretty hard about the fly bite, so now Holtzinger repeated: "What's all the fuss over one little bug, buddy?"

James squashed the tick underfoot and grunted. He didn't like being twitted with his own words.

We packed up and started on our circuit. We meant to take them first to the borders of the sauropod swamp, more to see the wild-life than to collect anything.

From where the transition chamber materializes, the sauro-pod swamp looks like a couple of hours' walk, but it's an all-day scramble. The first part is easy, as it's downhill and the brush isn't heavy. But as you get near the swamp, the cycads and willows grow so thickly, you have to worm your way among them.

There was a sandy ridge on the border of the swamp that I led the party to, for it's pretty bare of vegetation and affords a fine view. When we got to the ridge, the Sun was about to go down. A couple of crocs slipped off into the water. The sahibs were so exhausted, being soft yet, that they flopped down in the sand as if dead.

The haze is thick round the swamp, so the Sun was deep red and distorted by the atmospheric layers—pinched in at various levels. There was a high layer of clouds reflecting the red and gold, too, so altogether it was something for the Raja to write one of his poems about. Only your modern poet prefers to write about a rainy day in a garbage dump. A few little pterosaur were wheeling overhead like bats, only they don't flutter like bats. They swoop and soar after the big night-flying insects.

Beauregard Black collected firewood and lit a fire. We'd started on our steaks, and that pagoda-shaped Sun was just slipping below the horizon, and something back in the trees was making a noise like a rusty hinge, when a sauropod breathed out in the water. If Mother Earth were to sigh over the misdeeds of her children, it would sound just about like that.

The sahibs jumped up, waving and shouting: "Where is he? Where is he?"

I said: "That black spot in the water, just to the left and this side of that point."

They yammered while the sauropod filled its lungs and disappeared. "Is that all?" yelped James. "Won't we see any more of him?"

Holtzinger said: "I read they never come out of the water because they're too heavy."

"No," I explained. "They can walk perfectly well and often do, for egg-laying and moving from one swamp to another. But most of the time they spend in the water, like hippopotamus. They eat eight hundred pounds of soft swamp plants a day, all with those little heads. So they wander about the bottoms of lakes and swamps, chomping away, and stick their heads up to breathe every quarter-hour or so. It's getting dark, so this fellow will soon come out and lie down in the shallows to sleep."

"Can we shoot one?" demanded James.

"I wouldn't," said I.

"Why not?"

I said: "There's no point in it and it's not sporting. First, they're even harder to hit in the brain than other dinosaurs because of the way they sway their heads about on those long necks and their hearts are too deeply buried in tissue to reach unless you're awfully lucky. Then, if you kill one in the water, he sinks and can't be recovered. If you kill one on land, the only trophy is that little head. You can't bring the whole beast back because he weighs thirty tons or more. We don't need thirty tons of meat.''

Holtzinger said: ''That museum in New York got one.''

''Yes,'' I agreed. ''The American Museum of Natural History sent a party of forty-eight to the early Cretaceous, with a fifty-caliber machine gun. They assembled the gun on the edge of a swamp, killed a sauropod—and spent two solid months skinning it and hacking the carcass apart and dragging it to the time machine. I know the chap in charge of that project and he still has nightmares in which he smells decomposing dinosaur. They also had to kill a dozen big theropods who were attracted by the stench and refused to be frightened off, so they had *them* lying round and rotting, too. And the theropods ate three men of the party despite the big gun.''

Next morning, we were finishing breakfast when one of the helpers called: ''Look, Mr. Rivers! Up there!''

He pointed along the shoreline. There were six big duck-bill feeding in the shallows. They were the kind called parasaurolophus, with a crest consisting of a long spike of bone sticking out the back of their heads, like the horn of an oryx, and a web of skin connecting this with the back of their neck.

''Keep your voices down,'' I said. The duckbill, like the other ornithopods, are wary beasts because they have no armor or weapons against the theropods. The duckbill feed on the margins of lakes and swamps, and when a gorgosaur rushes out of the trees, they plunge into deep water and swim off. Then when phobosuchus, the super-crocodile, goes for them in the water, they flee to the land. A hectic sort of life, what?

Holtzinger said: ''Uh—Reggie, I've been thinking over

what you said about ceratopsian heads. If I could get one of those yonder, I'd be satisfied. It would look big enough in my house, wouldn't it?''

''I'm sure of it, old boy,'' I said. ''Now look here. I could take you on a detour to come out on the shore near there, but we should have to plow through half a mile of muck and brush, up to our knees in water, and they'd hear us coming. Or we can creep up to the north end of this sand spit, from which it's four or five hundred yards—a long shot, but not impossible. Think you could do it?''

''With my 'scope sight and a sitting position—yes, I'll try it.''

''You stay here,'' I said to James. ''This is Augie's head and I don't want any argument over your having fired first.''

James grunted while Holtzinger clamped his 'scope to his rifle. We crouched our way up the spit, keeping the sand ridge between us and the duckbills. When we got to the end where there was no more cover, we crept along on hands and knees, moving slowly. If you move slowly directly toward or away from a dinosaur, it probably won't notice you.

The duckbills continued to grub about on all fours, every few seconds rising to look round. Holtzinger eased himself into the sitting position, cocked his piece, and aimed through the 'scope. And then—

Bang! bang! went a big rifle back at the camp.

Holtzinger jumped. The duckbills jerked up their heads and leaped for the deep water, splashing like mad. Holtzinger fired once and missed. I took a shot at the last duckbill before it disappeared. I missed, too: the .600 isn't designed for long ranges.

Holtzinger and I started back toward the camp, for it had struck us that our party might be in theropod trouble and need reinforcements.

What happened was that a big sauropod, probably the one we'd heard the night before, had wandered down past the camp under water, feeding as it went. Now the water shoaled

about a hundred yards offshore from our spit, halfway over to
the edge of the swamp on the other side. The sauropod had
ambled up the slope until its body was almost all out of
water, weaving its head from side to side and looking for
anything green to gobble. This kind looks like the well-
known brontosaurus, but a little bigger. Scientists argue
whether it ought to be included in the genus camarasaurus or
a separate genus with an even longer name.

When I came in sight of the camp, the sauropod was turning round to go back the way it had come, making horrid
groans. It disappeared into deep water, all but its head and
ten or twenty feet of neck, which wove about for some time
before they vanished into the haze.

When we came up to the camp, James was arguing with
the Raja. Holtzinger burst out: "You bastard! That's the second time you've spoiled my shots!" Strong language for little
August.

"Don't be a fool," said James. "I couldn't let him wander
into camp and stamp everything flat."

"There was no danger of that," objected the Raja politely.
"You can see the water is deep offshore. It is just that our
trigger-happee Mr. James cannot see any animal without
shooting."

"I said: "If it did get close, all you needed to do was
throw a stick of firewood at it. They're perfectly harmless."
This wasn't strictly true. When the Comte de Lautree ran
after one for a close shot, the sauropod looked back at him,
gave a flick of its tail, and took off the Comte's head as
neatly as if he'd been axed in the Tower.

"How was I to know?" yelled James, getting purple.
"You're all against me. What the hell are we on this goddamn trip for except to shoot things? You call yourselves
hunters, but I'm the only one who's hit anything!"

I got pretty wrothy and said he was just an excitable young
skite with more money than brains, whom I should never
have brought along.

"If that's how you feel," he said, "give me a burro and some food and I'll go back to the base by myself. I won't pollute your air with my loathsome presence!"

"Don't be a bigger ass than you can help," I snapped. "That's quite impossible."

"Then I'll go all alone!" He grabbed his knapsack, thrust a couple of tins of beans and an opener into it, and started off with his rifle.

Beauregard Black spoke up: "Mr. Rivers, we cain't let him go off like that by hisself. He'll git lost and starve or be et by a theropod."

"I'll fetch him back," said the Raja and started after the runaway. He caught up as James was disappearing into the cycads. We could see them arguing and waving their hands, but couldn't make out what they said. After a while, they started back with arms around each other's necks like old school pals. I simply don't know how the Raja does it.

This shows the trouble we get into if we make mistakes in planning such a do. Having once got back into the past, we had to make the best of our bargain. We always must, you see.

I don't want to give the impression Courtney James was only a pain in the rump. He had his good points. He got over these rows quickly and next day would be as cheerful as ever. He was helpful with the general work of the camp—when he felt like it, at any rate. He sang well and had an endless fund of dirty stories to keep us amused.

We stayed two more days at the camp. We saw crocodiles, the small kind, and plenty of sauropod—as many as five at once—but no more duckbill. Nor any of those fifty-foot super-crocodiles.

So on the first of May, we broke camp and headed north toward the Janpur Hills. My sahibs were beginning to harden up and were getting impatient. We'd been in the Cretaceous a week and no trophies.

I won't go into details of the next leg. Nothing in the way of a trophy, save a glimpse of a gorgosaur out of range and some tracks indicating a whooping big iguanodont, twenty-five or thirty feet high. We pitched camp at the base of the hills.

We'd finished off the bonehead, so the first thing was to shoot fresh meat. With an eye to trophies, too, of course. We got ready the morning of the third.

I told James: "See here, old boy, no more of your tricks. The Raja will tell you when to shoot."

"Uh-huh, I get you," he said, meek as Moses. Never could tell how the chap would act.

We marched off, the four of us, into the foothills. We were looking for bonehead, but we'd take an ornithomime. There was also a good chance of getting Holtzinger his ceratopsian. We'd seen a couple on the way up, but mere calves without decent horns.

It was hot and sticky and we were soon panting and sweating like horses. We'd hiked and scrambled all morning without seeing a thing except lizards, when I picked up the smell of carrion. I stopped the party and sniffed. We were in an open glade cut up by these little dry nullahs. The nullahs ran together into a couple of deeper gorges that cut through a slight depression choked with a denser growth, cycad and screw-pine. When I listened, I heard the thrum of carrion flies.

"This way," I said. "Something ought to be dead—ah, here it is!"

And there it was: the remains of a huge ceratopsian lying in a little hollow on the edge of the copse. Must have weighed six or eight tons alive; a three-horned variety, perhaps the penultimate species of Triceratops. It was hard to tell because most of the hide on the upper surface had been ripped off and many bones had been pulled loose and lay scattered about.

Holtzinger said: "Oh, hell! Why couldn't I have gotten to him before he died? That would have been a darn fine head."

Associating with us rough types had made little August profane, you 'll observe.

I said: "On your toes, chaps. A theropod's been at this carcass and is probably nearby."

"How d'you know?" James challenged, with the sweat running off his round red face. He spoke in what was for him a low voice, because a nearby theropod is a sobering thought even to the flightiest.

I sniffed again and thought I could detect the distinctive rank odor of theropod. But I couldn't be sure because the stench of the carcass was so strong. My sahibs were turning green at the sight and smell of the cadaver.

I told James: "It's seldom even the biggest theropod will attack a full-grown ceratopsian. Those horns are too much for them. But they love a dead or dying one. They'll hang round a dead ceratopsian for weeks, gorging and then sleeping their meals off for days at a time. They usually take cover in the heat of the day anyhow, because they can't stand much direct hot sunlight. You'll find them lying in copses like this or in hollows, anywhere there's shade."

"What'll we do?" asked Holtzinger.

"We'll make our first cast through this copse, in two pairs as usual. Whatever you do, don't get impulsive or panicky."

I looked at Courtney James, but he looked right back and then merely checked his gun.

"Should I still carry this broken?" he wanted to know.

"No; close it, but keep the safety on till you're ready to shoot," I said. It's risky carrying a double closed like that, especially in brush, but with a theropod nearby, it would have been a greater risk to carry it open and perhaps catch a twig in it when one tried to close it.

"We'll keep closer than usual, to be in sight of each other," I said. "Start off at that angle, Raja. Go slowly and stop to listen between steps."

We pushed through the edge of the copse, leaving the carcass but not its stink behind us. For a few feet, we couldn't see a thing. It opened out as we got in under the trees, which shaded out some of the brush. The Sun slanted down through the trees. I could hear nothing but the hum of insects and the scuttle of lizards and the squawks of toothed birds in a treetop. I thought I could be sure of the theropod smell, but told myself that might be imagination. The theropod might be any of several species, large or small, and the beast itself might be anywhere within a half-mile radius.

"Go on," I whispered to Holtzinger, for I could hear James and the Raja pushing ahead on my right and see the palm-fronds and ferns lashing about as they disturbed them. I suppose they were trying to move quietly, but to me they sounded like an earthquake in a crockery shop.

"A little closer," I called, and presently they appeared slanting in toward me.

We dropped into a gully filled with ferns and clambered up the other side, then found our way blocked by a big clump of palmetto.

"You go round that side: we'll go round this," I said, and we started off, stopping to listen and smell. Our positions were exactly the same as on that first day when James killed the bonehead.

I judge we'd gone two thirds of the way round our half of the palmetto when I heard a noise ahead on our left. Holtzinger heard it and pushed off his safety. I put my thumb on mine and stepped to one side to have a clear field.

The clatter grew louder. I raised my gun to aim at about the height a big theropod's heart would be at the distance it would appear to us out of the greenery. There was a movement in the foliage—and a six-foot-high bonehead stepped into view, walking solemnly across our front from left to right, jerking its head with each step like a giant pigeon.

I heard Holtzinger let out a breath and had to keep myself from laughing. Holtzinger said: "Uh—"

"Quiet," I whispered. "The theropod might still—"

That was as far as I got when that damned gun of James's went off, bang! bang! I had a glimpse of the bonehead knocked arsy-varsy with its tail and hindlegs flying.

"Got him!" yelled James, and I heard him run forward.

"My God, if he hasn't done it again!" I groaned. Then there was a great swishing, not made by the dying bonehead, and a wild yell from James. Something heaved up and out of the shrubbery and I saw the head of the biggest of the local flesh-eaters, tyrannosaurus trionyches himself.

The scientists can insist that rex is bigger than trionyches, but I'll swear this tyrannosaur was bigger than any rex ever hatched. It must have stood twenty feet high and been fifty feet long. I could see its bright eye and six-inch teeth and the big dewlap that hangs down from its chin to its chest.

The second of the nullahs that cut through the copse ran athwart our path on the far side of the palmetto clump. Perhaps six feet deep. The tyrannosaur had been lying in this, sleeping off its last meal. Where its back struck up above ground level, the ferns on the edge of the nullah masked it. James had fired both barrels over the theropod's head and woke it up. Then James, to compound his folly, ran forward without reloading. Another twenty feet and he'd have stepped on the tyrannosaur's back.

James understandably stopped when this thing popped up in front of him. He remembered his gun was empty and he'd left the Raja too far behind to get a clear shot.

James kept his nerve at first. He broke open his gun, took two rounds from his belt and plugged them into the barrels. But in his haste to snap the gun shut, he caught his right hand between the barrels and the action—the fleshy part between his thumb and palm. It was a painful pinch and so startled James that he dropped his gun. That made him go to pieces and he bolted.

His timing couldn't have been worse. The Raja was running up with his gun at high port, ready to snap it to his shoulder the instant he got a clear view of the tyrannosaur. When he saw James running headlong toward him, it made him hesitate, as he didn't want to shoot James. The latter plunged ahead and, before the Raja could jump aside, blundered into him and sent them both sprawling among the ferns. The tyrannosaur collected what little wits it had and crashed after to snap them up.

And how about Holtzinger and me on the other side of the palmettos? Well, the instant James yelled and the tyrannosaur's head appeared, Holtzinger darted forward like a rabbit. I'd brought my gun up for a shot at the tyrannosaur's head, in hope of getting at least an eye, but before I could find it in my sights, the head was out of sight behind the palmettos. Perhaps I should have shot at where I thought it was, but all my experience is against wild shots.

When I looked back in front of me, Holtzinger had already disappeared round the curve of the palmetto clump. I'm pretty heavily built, as you can see, but I started after him with a good turn of speed, when I heard his rifle and the click of the bolt between shots: bang—click-click—bang—click-click, like that.

He'd come up on the tyrannosaur's quarter as the brute started to stoop for James and the Raja. With his muzzle twenty feet from the tyrannosaur's hide, he began pumping .375s into the beast's body. He got off three shots when the tyrannosaur gave a tremendous booming grunt and wheeled round to see what was stinging it. The jaws came open and the head swung round and down again.

Holtzinger got off one more shot and tried to leap to one side. He was standing on a narrow place between the palmetto clump and the nullah. So he fell into the nullah. The tyrannosaur continued its lunge and caught him, either as he was falling or after he struck bottom. The jaws went chomp and up came the head with poor Holtzinger in them, screaming like a damned soul.

I came up just then and aimed at the brute's face. Then I realized its jaws were full of my friend and I'd be shooting him. As the head went up, like the business end of a big power shovel, I fired a shot at the heart. But the tyrannosaur was already turning away and I suspect the ball just glanced along the ribs.

The beast took a couple of steps away when I gave it the

other barrel in the back. It staggered on its next step but kept on. Another step and it was nearly out of sight among the trees, when the Raja fired twice. The stout fellow had untangled himself from James, got up, picked up his gun and let the tyrannosaur have it.

The double wallop knocked the brute over with a tremendous smash. It fell into a dwarf magnolia and I saw one of its hindlegs waving in the midst of a shower of incongruously pretty pink-and-white petals.

Can you imagine the leg of a bird of prey enlarged and thickened until it's as big round as the leg of an elephant?

But the tyrannosaur got up again and blundered off without even dropping its victim. The last I saw of it was Holtzinger's legs dangling out one side of its jaws (by now he'd stopped screaming) and its big tail banging against the treetrunks as it swung from side to side.

The Raja and I reloaded and ran after the brute for all we were worth. I tripped and fell once, but jumped up again and didn't notice my skinned elbow till later. When we burst out of the copse, the tyrannosaur was already at the far end of the glade. I took a quick shot, but probably missed, and it was out of sight before I could fire another.

We ran on, following the tracks and spatters of blood, until we had to stop from exhaustion. Their movements look slow and ponderous, but with those tremendous legs, they don't have to step very fast to work up considerable speed.

When we'd finished gasping and mopping our foreheads, we tried to track the tyrannosaur, on the theory that it might be dying and we should come up to it. But the spoor faded out and left us at a loss. We circled round hoping to pick it up, but no luck.

Hours later, we gave up and went back to the glade, feeling very dismal.

Courtney James was sitting with his back against a tree, holding his rifle and Holtzinger's. His right hand was swollen and blue where he'd pinched it, but still usable.

His first words were: "Where the hell have you been? You shouldn't have gone off and left me; another of those things might have come along. Isn't it bad enough to lose one hunter through your stupidity without risking another one?"

I'd been preparing a pretty warm wigging for James, but his attack so astonished me, I could only bleat: "We lost—?"

"Sure," he said. "You put us in front of you, so if anybody gets eaten it's us. You send a guy up against these animals undergunned. You—"

"You stinking little swine," I began and went on from there. I learned later he'd spent his time working out an elaborate theory according to which this disaster was all our fault—Holtzinger's, the Raja's and mine. Nothing about James's firing out of turn or panicking or Holtzinger's saving his worthless life. Oh, dear, no. It was the Raja's fault for not jumping out of his way, et cetera.

Well, I've led a rough life and can express myself quite eloquently. The Raja tried to keep up with me, but ran out of English and was reduced to cursing James in Hindustani.

I could see by the purple color on James's face that I was getting home. If I'd stopped to think, I should have known better than to revile a man with a gun. Presently James put down Holtzinger's rifle and raised his own, saying: "Nobody calls me things like that and gets away with it. I'll just say the tyrannosaur ate you, too."

The Raja and I were standing with our guns broken open, under our arms, so it would take a good part of a second to snap them shut and bring them up to fire. Moreover, you don't shoot a .600 holding it loosely in your hands, not if you know what's good for you. Next thing, James was setting the butt of his .500 against his shoulder, with the barrels pointed at my face. Looked like a pair of blooming vehicular tunnels.

The Raja saw what was happening before I did. As the beggar brought his gun up, he stepped forward with a tremendous kick. Used to play football as a young chap, you see. He knocked the .500 up and it went off so the bullet missed my head by an inch and the explosion jolly well near broke my eardrums.

The butt had been punted away from James's shoulder when the gun went off, so it came back like the kick of a horse. It spun him half round.

The Raja dropped his own gun, grabbed the barrels and twisted it out of James's hands, nearly breaking the bloke's trigger finger. He meant to hit James with the butt, but I rapped James across the head with my own barrels, then bowled him over and began punching the stuffing out of him. He was a good-sized lad, but with my sixteen stone, he had no chance.

When his face was properly discolored, I stopped. We turned him over, took a strap out of his knapsack and tied his wrists behind him. We agreed there was no safety for us unless we kept him under guard every minute until we got him back to our time. Once a man has tried to kill you, don't give him another opportunity. Of course he might never try again, but why risk it?

We marched James back to camp and told the crew what we were up against. James cursed everybody and dared us to kill him.

"You'd better, you sons of bitches, or I'll kill you some day," he said. "Why don't you? Because you know somebody'd give you away, don't you? Ha-ha!"

The rest of that safari was dismal. We spent three days combing the country for that tyrannosaur. No luck. It might have been lying in any of those nullahs, dead or convalescing, and we should never see it unless we blundered on top of it. But we felt it wouldn't have been cricket not to make a good try at recovering Holtzinger's remains, if any.

After we got back to our main camp, it rained. When it wasn't raining, we collected small reptiles and things for our scientific friends. When the transition chamber materialized, we fell over one another getting into it.

The Raja and I had discussed the question of legal proceedings by or against Courtney James. We decided there was no precedent for punishing crimes committed eighty-five million years before, which would presumably be outlawed by the statute of limitations. We therefore untied him and pushed him into the chamber after all the others but us had gone through.

When we came out in the present, we handed him his gun—empty—and his other effects. As we expected, he walked off without a word, his arms full of gear. At that point, Holtzinger's girl, Claire Roche, rushed up crying: "Where is he? Where's August?".

I won't go over the painful scene except to say it was distressing in spite of the Raja's skill at that sort of thing.

We took our men and beasts down to the old laboratory building that Washington University has fitted up as a serai for expeditions to the past. We paid everybody off and found we were nearly broke. The advance payments from Holtzinger and James didn't cover our expenses and we should have damned little chance of collecting the rest of our fees from James or from Holtzinger's estate.

And speaking of James, d'you know what the blighter was doing all this time? He went home, got more ammunition and came back to the university. He hunted up Professor Prochaska and asked him:

"Professor, I'd like you to send me back to the Cretaceous for a quick trip. If you can work me into your schedule right now, you can just about name your own price. I'll offer five thousand to begin with. I want to go to April twenty-third, eighty-five million B.C."

Prochaska answered: "Vot do you vant to go back again so soon so badly for?"

"I lost my wallet in the Cretaceous," said James. "I figure if I go back to the day before I arrived in that era on my last trip, I'll watch myself when I arrived on that trip and follow myself till I see myself lose the wallet."

"Five thousand is a lot for a valet."

"It's got some things in it I can't replace. Suppose you let me worry about whether it's worth my while."

"Vell," said Prochaska, thinking, "the party that vas supposed to go out this morning has phoned that they vould be late, so maybe I can vork you in. I have alvays vondered vot vould happen vhen the same man occupied the same time tvice."

So James wrote out a check and Prochaska took him to the chamber and saw him off. James's idea, it seems, was to sit behind a bush a few yards from where the transition chamber would appear and pot the Raja and me as we emerged.

Hours later, we'd changed into our street clothes and phoned our wives to come get us. We were standing on Forsythe Boulevard waiting for them when there was a loud crack, like an explosion or a close-by clap of thunder, and a flash of light not fifty feet from us. The shock-wave staggered us and broke windows in quite a number of buildings.

We ran toward the place and got there just as a policeman and several citizens came up. On the boulevard, just off the curb, lay a human body. At least it had been that, but it looked as if every bone in it had been pulverized and every blood vessel burst. The clothes it had been wearing were shredded, but I recognized an H. & H. .500 double-barreled express rifle. The wood was scorched and the metal pitted, but it was Courtney James's gun. No doubt whatever.

Skipping the investigations and the milling about, what had happened was this: Nobody had shot us as we emerged on the twenty-fourth and that, of course, couldn't be changed. For that matter, the instant James started to do anything that would make a visible change in the world of eighty-five million B.C., the space-time forces would snap him forward to the present to prevent a paradox.

Now that this is better understood, the professor won't send anybody to a period less than five hundred years prior to the time that some time traveler has already explored, because it would be too easy to do some act, like chopping down a tree or losing some durable artifact, that would affect the later world. Over long periods, he tells me, such changes average out and are lost in the stream of time.

We had a bloody rough time after that, with the bad publicity and all, though we did collect a fee from James's estate. The disaster hadn't been entirely James's fault. I shouldn't have taken him when I knew what a spoiled, unstable sort he was. And if Holtzinger could have used a heavy gun, he'd probably have knocked the tyrannosaur down, even if he didn't kill it, and so given the rest of us a chance to finish it.

So that's why I won't take you to that period to hunt. There are plenty of other eras, and if you think them over, I'm sure you'll find—

Good Lord, look at the time! Must run, old boy; my wife'll skin me. Good night!

THE SANDS OF TIME

P. Schuyler Miller

The late P. Schuyler Miller successfully combined science and fiction in his own life. He worked for a large engineering firm in the Pittsburgh area, but his avocation was archaeology, and he spent most of his free time out on digs, exploring the sites of Paleolithic human settlement in the northeastern United States. He also loved science fiction, and published his first stories in 1930, when he was still a schoolboy; for the next ten or fifteen years he was one of the best, and most popular, of science-fiction writers, and he retained an active and sympathetic interest in the field until his death a few years ago.

Perhaps his most famous story is this one, first published in 1937 and just as fresh and exciting as when it originally appeared. Like L. Sprague de Camp, he sweeps us back in time to the Cretaceous, to the climax and grand finale of the hundred-million-plus-years-long epoch of the dinosaurs. But Miller does not take us quite so deep into the Cretaceous; his story takes place some 25 million years later, when the dinosaurs still rule but at a time when the earliest birds fly overhead and tiny mouselike mammals, forerunners of much that is to come, lurk in the underbrush.

A LONG SHADOW FELL across the ledge. I laid down the curved blade with which I was chipping at the soft sandstone, and squinted up into the glare of the afternoon sun. A man was sitting on the edge of the pit, his legs dangling over the side. He raised a hand in salutation.

"Hi!"

He hunched forward to jump. My shout stopped him.

"Look out! You'll smash them!"

He peered down at me, considering the matter. He had no hat, and the sun made a halo of his blond, curly hair.

"They're fossils, aren't they?" he objected. "Fossils I've seen were stone, and stone is hard. What do you mean—I'll smash 'em?"

"I mean what I said. This sandstone is soft and the bones in it are softer. Also, they're old. Digging out dinosaurs is no pick-and-shovel job nowadays."

"Um-m-m." He rubbed his nose thoughtfully. "How old would you say they were?"

I got wearily to my feet and began to slap the dust out of my breeches. Evidently I was in for another siege of questions. He might be a reporter, or he might be any one of the twenty-odd farmers in the surrounding section. It would make a difference what I told him.

"Come on down here where we can talk," I invited. "We'll be more comfortable. There's a trail about a hundred yards up the draw."

"I'm all right." He leaned back on braced arms. "What is it? What did it look like?"

I know when I'm beaten. I leaned against the wall of the quarry, out of the sun, and began to fill my pipe. I waved the packet of tobacco courteously at him, but he shook his head.

"Thanks. Cigarette." He lighted one. "You're Professor Belden, aren't you? E. J. Belden. 'E' stands for Ephratah, or some such. Doesn't affect your digging any, though." He exhaled a cloud of smoke. "What's that thing you were using?"

I held it up. "It's a special knife for working out bones like these. The museum's model. When I was your age we used butcher knives and railroad spikes—anything we could get our hands on. There weren't any railroads out here then."

He nodded. "I know. My father dug for 'em. Hobby of his, for a while. Changed over to stamps when he lost his leg." Then, with an air of changing the subject, "That thing

you're digging out—what did it look like? Alive, I mean."
I had about half of the skeleton worked out. I traced its
outline for him with the knife. "There's the skull; there's the
neck and spine, and what's left of the tail; this was its left
foreleg. You can see the remains of the crest along the top of
the skull, and the flat snout like a duck's beak. It's one of
many species of trachodon—the duckbilled aquatic dinosaurs. They fed along the shore lines, on water plants and
general browse, and some of them were bogged down and
drowned."

"I get it. Big bruiser—little front legs and husky hind ones
with a tail like a kangaroo. Sat on it when he got tired. Fin
on his head like a fish, and a face like a duck. Did he have
scales?"

"I doubt it," I told him. "More likely warts like a toad, or
armor plates like an alligator. We've found skin impressions
of some of this one's cousins, south of here, and that's what
they were like."

He nodded again—that all-knowing nod that gets my eternal goat. He fumbled inside his coat and brought out a little
leather folder or wallet, and leafed through its contents. He
leaned forward and something white came scaling down at
my feet.

"Like that?" he asked.

I picked it up. It was a photograph, enlarged from a minia-
ture camera shot. It showed the edge of a reedy lake or river,
with a narrow, sandy strip of beach and a background of
feathery foliage that looked like tree ferns. Thigh-deep in the
water, lush lily stalks trailing from its flat jaws, stood a rep-
lica of the creature whose skeleton was embedded in the rock
at my feet—a trachodon. It was a perfect likeness—the
heavy, frilled crest, and glistening skin with its uneven
patches of dark tubercles, the small, webbed forepaws on
skinny arms.

"Nice job," I admitted. "Is it one of Knight's new ones?"

"Knight?" He seemed puzzled. "Oh—the Museum of
Natural History. No—I made it myself."

"You're to be congratulated," I assured him. "I don't know when I've seen a nicer model. What's it for—the movies?"

"Movies?" He sounded exasperated. "I'm not making movies. I made the picture—the photograph. Took it myself—here—or pretty close to here. The thing was alive, and is still for all I know. It chased me."

That was the last straw. "See here," I said, "If you're trying to talk me into backing some crazy publicity stunt, you can guess again. I wasn't born yesterday, and I cut my teeth on a lot harder and straighter science than your crazy newspaper syndicates dish out. I worked these beds before you were born, or your father, either, and there were no trachodons wandering around chasing smart photographers with the d.t.s, and no lakes or tree ferns for 'em to wander in. If you're after a testimonial for someone's model of Cretaceous fauna, say so. That is an excellent piece of work, and if you're responsible you have every right to be proud of it. Only stop this blither about photographing dinosaurs that have been fossils for sixty million years."

The fellow was stubborn. "It's no hoax," he insisted doggedly. "There's no newspaper involved and I'm not peddling dolls. I took that photograph. Your trachodon chased me and I ran. And I have more of the same to prove it! Here."

The folder landed with a thump at my feet. It was crammed with prints like the first—enlargements of Leica negatives—and for sheer realism I have never seen anything like them.

"I had thirty shots," he told me. "I used 'em all, and they were all beauties. And I can do it again!"

Those prints! I can see them now: landscapes that vanished from this planet millions of years before the first furry tree shrew scurried among the branches of the first temperate forests, and became the ancestor of mankind; monsters whose buried bones and fossil footprints are the only mementos of a race of giants vaster than any other creatures that ever walked the earth; there were more of the trachodons—a whole herd of them, it seemed, browsing along the shore of a lake or large river, and they had that individuality that marks the work of the true artist; they were Corythosaurs, like the one I was working on—one of the better-known genera of the great family of Trachodons. But the man who had restored them had used his imagination to show details of markings and fleshy structure that I was sure had never been shown by any recorded fossils.

Nor was that all. There were close-ups of plants—trees and low bushes—that were masterpieces of minute detail, even to the point of showing withered fronds, and the insects that walked and stalked and crawled over them. There were vistas of rank marshland scummed over with stringy algae and lush with tall grasses and taller reeds, among which saurian giants wallowed. There were two or three other varieties of trachodon that I could see, and a few smaller dinosaurs, with a massive bulk in what passed for the distance that might have been a Brontosaurus hangover from the Jurassic of a few million years before. I pointed to it.

"You slipped up there," I said. "We've found no traces of that creature so late in the Age of Reptiles. It's a very common mistake; every fantastic novelist makes it when he tries to write a time-traveling story. Tyrannosaurus eats Brontosaurus and is then gored to death by Triceratops. The trouble with it is that it couldn't happen."

The boy ground his cigarette butt into the sand. "I don't know about that," he said. "It was there—I photographed it—and that's all there was to it. Tyrannosaurus I didn't see—and I'm not sorry. I've read those yarns you're so supercilious about. Good stuff—they arouse your curiosity and make you think. Triceratops—if he's the chunky devil with three big horns sticking out of his head and snout—I got in profusion. You haven't come to him yet. Go down about three more."

I humored him. Sure enough, there was a vast expanse of low, rolling plains with some lumpy hills in the distance. The thing was planned very poorly—any student would have laid it out looking toward the typical Cretaceous forest, rather than away from it—but it had the same startling naturalness that the others had. And there were indeed Triceratops in plenty—a hundred or more, grazing stolidly in little family groups of three or four, on a rank prairie grass that grew in great tufts from the sandy soil.

I guffawed. "Who told you that was right?" I demanded. "Your stuff is good—the best I've ever seen—but it is careless slips like that that spoil everything for the real scientist. Reptiles never herd, and dinosaurs were nothing but overgrown reptiles. Go on—take your pictures to someone who has the time to be amused. I don't find them funny or even interesting."

I stuffed them into the folder and tossed it to him. He made no attempt to catch it. For a moment he sat staring down at me, then in a shower of sand he was beside me. One hob-nailed boot gouged viciously across the femur of my dinosaur and the other crashed down among its brittle ribs. I felt the blood go out of my face with anger, then come rushing back. If I had been twenty years younger I would have knocked him off his feet and dared him to come back for more. But he was as red as I.

"Damn it," he cried, "no bald-headed old fuzzy-wuzzy is going to call me a liar twice! You may know a lot about dead bones, but your education with regard to living things has been sadly neglected. So reptiles never herd? What about alligators? What about the Galápagos iguanas? What about snakes? Bah—you can't see any farther than your own nose and never will! When I show you photographs of living dinosaurs, taken with this very camera twenty-four hours ago, not more than three or four miles from where we're standing— well, it's high time you scrap your hide-bound, bone-dry theories and listen to a branch of science that's real and living, and always will be. I photographed those dinosaurs! I can do it again—any time I like. I will do it."

He stopped for breath. I simply looked at him. It's the best way, when some crank gets violent. He colored and grinned sheepishly, then picked up the wallet from where it had fallen at the base of the quarry cut. There was an inner compartment with a covering flap which I had not touched. He rummaged in it with a finger and thumb and brought out a scrap of leathery-looking stuff, porous and coated with a kind of shiny, dried mucus.

"Put a name to it," he demanded.

I turned it over in my palm and examine it carefully. It was a bit of eggshell—undoubtely a reptilian egg, and a rather large one—but I could tell nothing more.

"It might be an alligator or crocodile egg, or it might have been laid by one of the large oviparous snakes," I told him. "That would depend on where you found it. I suppose that you will claim that it is a dinosur egg—a fresh egg."

"I claim nothing," he retorted. "That's for you to say. You're the expert on dinosaurs, not I. But if you don't like that—what about this?"

He had on a hunting jacket and corduroy breeches like mine. From the big side pocket he drew two eggs about the length of my palm—misshapen and gray-white in color, with that leathery texture so characteristic of reptile eggs. He held them up between himself and the sun.

"This one's fresh," he said. "The sand was still moist around the nest. This other is from the place where I got the shell. There's something in it. If you want to, you can open it."

I took it. It was heavy and somewhat discolored at the larger end, where something had pierced the shell. As he had said, there was evidently something inside. I hesitated. I felt that I would be losing face if I took him at his word to open it. And yet—

I squatted down and, laying the egg on a block of sandstone beside the weird, crested skull of the Corythosaur, I ripped its leathery shell from end to end.

The stench nearly felled me. The inside was a mass of greenish-yellow matter such as only a very long-dead egg can create. The embryo was well advanced, and as I poked around in the noisome mess it began to take definite form. I dropped the knife and with my fingers wiped away the last of the putrid ooze from the twisted, jellylike thing that remained. I rose slowly to my feet and looked him squarely in the eye.

"Where did you get that egg?"

He smiled—that maddening, slow smile. "I told you," he said. "I found it over there, a mile or so, beyond the belt of jungle that fringes the marshes. There were dozens of them—mounds like those that turtles make, in the warm sand. I opened two. One was fresh; the other was full of broken shells—and this." He eyed me quizzically. "And what does the great Professor Belden make of it?"

What he said had given me an idea. "Turtles," I mused aloud. "It could be a turtle—some rare species—maybe a mutation or freak that never developed far enough to really take shape. It must be!"

He sounded weary. "Yes," he said flatly, "it could be a turtle. It isn't but that doesn't matter to you. Those photographs could be fakes, and none-too-clever fakes at that. They show things that couldn't happen—that your damned dry-bone science says are wrong. All right—you've got me. It's your round. But I'm coming back, and I'm coming to bring proof that will convince you and every other stiff-necked old fuzz-buzz in the world that I, Terence Michael Aloysius Donovan, have stepped over the traces into the middle of the Cretaceous era and lived there, comfortably and happily, sixty million years before I was born!"

He walked away. I heard his footsteps receding up the draw, and the rattle of small stones as he climbed to the level of the prairie. I stood staring down at the greenish mess that was frying in the hot sun on the bright -red sandstone. It could have been a turtle, malformed in the embryo so that its carapace formed a sort of rudimentary, flaring shield behind the beaked skull. Or it could be—something else.

If it was that something, all the sanity and logic had gone

out of the world, and a boy's mad, pseudoscientific dream became a reality that could not possibly be real. Paradox within paradox—contradiction upon contradiction. I gathered up my tools and started back for camp.

During the days that followed we worked out the skeleton of the Corythosaur and swathed it in plaster-soaked burlap for its long journey by wagon, truck and train back to the museum. I had perhaps a week left to use as I saw fit. But somehow, try as I would, I could not forget the young, blond figure of Terry Donovan, and the two strange eggs that he had pulled out of his pocket.

About a mile up the draw from our camp I found the remains of what had been a beach in Cretaceous times. Where it had not weathered away, every ripple mark and worm burrow was intact. There were tracks—remarkable fine ones—of which any museum would be proud. Dinosaurs, big and little, had come this way, millions of years ego, and left the mark of their passing in the moist sand, to be buried and preserved to arouse the apish curiosity of a race whose tiny, hairy ancestors were still scrambling on all fours.

Beyond the beach had been marshes and a quicksand. Crumbling white bones protruded from the stone in incalculable profusion, massed and jumbled into a tangle that would require years of careful study to unravel. I stood with a bit of crumbling bone in my hand, staring at the mottled rock. A step sounded on the talus below me. It was Donovan.

Some of the cocksure exuberance had gone out of him. He was thinner, and his face was covered with a stubbly growth of beard. He wore shorts and a tattered shirt, and his left arm was strapped to his side with bands of some gleaming metallic cloth. Dangling from the fingers of his good hand was the strangest bird I have ever seen.

He flung it down at my feet. It was purplish-black with a naked red head and wattled neck. Its tail was feathered as a sumac is leafed, with stubby feathers sprouting in pairs from a naked, ratty shaft. Its wings had little three-fingered hands at the joints. And its head was long and narrow, like a lizard's snout, with great, round, lidless eyes and a mouthful of tiny yellow teeth.

I looked from the bird to him. There was no smile on his lips now. He was starting at the footprints of the rock.

"So you've found the beach." His voice was a weary monotone.

"It was a sort of sandy spit, between the marshes and the sea, where they came to feed and be fed on. Dog eat dog. Sometimes they would blunder into the quicksands and flounder and bleat until they drowned. You see—I was there. That bird was there—alive when those dead, crumbling bones were alive—not only in the same geological age but in the same year, the same month—the same day! You've got proof now—proof that you can't talk away! examine it. Cut it up. Do anything you want with it. But by the powers, this time you've got to believe me! This time you've got to help!"

I stooped and picked the thing up by its long, scaly legs. No bird like it had lived, or could have lived, on this planet for millions of years. I thought of those thirty photographs of the incredible—of the eggs he had had, one of them fresh, one with an embryo that might, conceivably, have been an unknown genus of turtle.

"All right," I said. "I'll come. What do you want?"

He lived three miles away across the open prairie. The house was a modernistic metal box set among towering cottonwoods at the edge of a small reservoir. A power house at the dam furnished light and electricity—all that he needed to bring civilized comfort out of the desert.

One wing of the house was windowless and sheer-walled, with blower vents at intervals on the sloping roof. A laboratory, I guessed. Donovan unlocked a steel door in the wall and pushed it open. I stepped past him into the room.

It was bare. A flat-topped desk stood in the corner near the main house, with a shelf of books over it. A big switchboard

covered the opposite wall, flanked by two huge D.C. generators. There were cupboards and a long worktable littered with
small apparatus. But a good half of the room was empty save
for the machine that squatted in the middle of the concrete
floor.

It was like a round lead egg, ten feet high and half as
broad. It was set in a cradle of steel girders, raised on massive insulators. Part of it stood open like a door, revealing the
inside—a chamber barely large enough to hold a man, with a
host of dials and switches set in an insulated panel in the
leaden wall, and a flat Bakelite floor. Heavy cables came out
of that floor to the instrument board, and two huge, copper
bus bars were clamped to the steel base. The laboratory was
filled with the drone of the generators, charging some hidden
battery, and there was a faint tang of ozone in the air.

Donovan shut and locked the door. "That's the Egg," he
said. "I'll show it to you later, after you've heard me out.
Will you help me with this arm of mine, first?"

I cut the shirt away and unwrapped the metallic gauze that
held the arm tight against his body. Both bones of the
forearm were splintered and the flesh gashed as though by
jagged knives. The wound had been cleaned, and treated with
some bright-green antiseptic whose odor I did not recognize.
The bleeding had stopped, and there was none of the inflam-
mation that I should have expected.

He answered my unspoken question. "She fixed it up—
Lana. One of your little playmates—the kind I didn't see the
first time—wanted to eat me." He was rummaging in the
bottom drawer of the desk. "There's no clean cloth here,"
he said. "I haven't time to look in the house. You'll have to
use that again."

"Look here," I protested, "you can't let a wound like that
go untreated. It's serious. You must have a doctor."

He shook his head. "No time. It would take a doctor two
hours to get out here from town. He'd need another hour, or
more, to fool around with me. In just forty minutes my accumulators will be charged to capacity, and in forty-one I'll

be gone—back there. Make a couple of splints out of that orange crate in the corner and tie me up again. It'll do—for as long as I'll be needing it.''

I split the thin boards and made splints, made sure that the bones were set properly and bound them tightly with the strange silvery cloth, then lopped the loose ends in a sling around his neck. I went into the house to get him clean clothes. When I returned he was stripped, scrubbing himself at the laboratory sink. I helped him clamber into underwear, a shirt and breeches, pull on high-top shoes. I plugged in an electric razor and sat watching him as he ran it over his angular jaw.

He was grinning now. "You're all right, Professor," he told me. "Not a question out of you, and I'll bet you've been on edge all the while. Well—I'll tell you everything. Then you can take it or leave it.

"Look there on the bench behind you—that coiled spring. It's a helix—a spiral made up of two-dimensional cross sections twisted in a third dimension. If you make two marks on it, you can go from one to the other by traveling along the spring, round and round for about six inches. Or you can cut across from one spiral to the next. Suppose your two marks come right together—so. They're two inches apart, along the spring—and no distance at all if you cut across.

"So much for that. You know Einstein's picture of the universe—space and time tied up together in some kind of four-dimensional continuum that's warped and bent in all sorts of weird ways by the presence of matter. Maybe closed and maybe not. Maybe expanding like a balloon and maybe shrinking like a melting hailstone. Well—I know what that shape is. I've proved it. It's spiraled like that spring— spiraled in time!

"See what that means? Look—I'll show you. This first scratch, here on the spring, is today—now. Here will be tomorrow, a little further along the wire. Here's next year. And here is some still later time, one full turn of the coil away, directly above the first mark.

"Now watch. I can go from today to tomorrow—to next year—like this by traveling with time along the spring. That's what the world is doing. Only by the laws of physics—entropy and all that—there's no going back. It's one-way traffic. And you can't get ahead any faster than time wants to take you. That's if you follow the spring. But you can cut across!

"Look—here are the two marks I just made, now and two years from now. They're two inches apart, along the coiled wire, but when you compress the spring they are together—nothing between them but the surface of the two coils. You can stretch a bridge across from one to the other, so to speak, and walk across—into a time two years from now. Or you can go the other way, two years into the past.

"That's all there is to it. Time is coiled like a spring. Some other age in earth's history lies next to ours, separated only by an intangible boundary, a focus of forces that keeps us from seeing into it and falling into it. Past time—present time—future time, side by side. Only it's not two years, or three, or a hundred. It's sixty million years from now to then, the long way around!

"I said you could get from one coil of time to the next one if you built a bridge across. I built that bridge—the Egg. I set up a field of forces in it—no matter how—that dissolve the invisible barrier between our time and the next. I give it an electromagnetic shove that sends it in the right direction, forward or back. And I land sixty million years in the past, in the age of dinosaurs."

He paused, as if to give me a chance to challenge him. I didn't try. I am no physicist, and if it was as he said—if time was really a spiral, with adjacent coils lying side by side, and if his leaden Egg could bridge the gap between—then the pictures and the eggs and the bird were possible things. And they were more than possible. I had seen them.

"You can see that the usual paradoxes don't come in at all," Donovan went on. "About killing your grandfather, and being two places at once—that kind of thing. The time screw has a sixty-million-year pitch. You can slide from coil to coil, sixty million years at a time, but you can't cover any shorter distance without living it. If I go back or ahead sixty million years, and live there four days, I'll get back here next Tuesday, four days from now. As for going ahead and learning all the scientific wonders of the future, then coming back to change the destiny of humanity, sixty million years is a long time. I doubt that there'll be anything human living then. And if there is—if I do learn their secrets and come back—it will be because their future civilization was built on the fact that I did so. Screwy as it sounds, that's how it is.''

He stopped and sat staring at the dull-gray mass of the Egg. He was looking back sixty million years, into an age when giant dinosaurs ruled the earth. He was watching herds of Triceratops grazing on the Cretaceous prairie—seeing unsuspected survivors of the genus that produced Brontosaurus and his kin, wallowing in some protected swamp—seeing rat-tailed, purple-black Archaeopteryx squawking in the tree ferns. And he was seeing more!

"I'll tell you the whole story,'' he said. "You can believe it or not, as you like. Then I'll go back. After that—well, maybe you'll write the end, and maybe not. Sixty million years is a long time!''

He told me: how he hit on his theory of spiraled time; how he monkeyed around with the mathematics of the thing until it hung together—built little models of machines that swooped into nothingness and disappeared; how he made the Egg, big enough to hold a man, yet not too big for his generators to provide the power to lift it and him across the boundary between the coils of time—and back again; how he stepped out of the close, cramped chamber of the Egg into a world of steaming swamps and desert plains, sixty million years before mankind!

That was when he took the pictures. It was when the Corythosaur chased him, bleating and bellowing like a monster cow, when he disturbed its feeding. He lost it among the tree ferns, and wandered warily through the bizarre, luxurious jungle, batting at great mosquitoes the size of horseflies and ducking when giant dragonflies zoomed down and seized them in midair. He watched a small hornless dinosaur scratch a hole in the warm sand at the edge of the jungle and ponderously lay a clutch of twenty eggs. When she had waddled away, he took one—the fresh one he had shown me—and scratched out another from a nest that had already hatched. He had photographs—he had specimens—and the sun was getting low. Some of the noises from the salt marshes along the seashore were not very reassuring. So he came back. And I laughed at him and his proofs, and called him a crazy fake!

He went back. He had a rifle along this time—a huge thing that his father had used on elephants in Africa. I don't know what he expected to do with it. Shoot a Triceratops, maybe— since I wouldn't accept his photographs—and hack off its ungainly, three-horned head for a trophy. He could never have brought it back, of course, because it was a tight enough squeeze as it was to get himself and the big rifle into the Egg. He had food and water in a pack—he didn't much like the look of the water that he had found ''over there'' —and he was in a mood to stay until he found something that I and every one like me would have to accept.

Inland, the ground rose to a range of low hills along the horizon. Back there, he reasoned, there would be creatures a little smaller than the things he had seen buoying up their massive hulks in the sea and marshes. So, shutting the door of the Egg and heaping cycad fronds over it to hide it from inquisitive dinosaurs, he set out across the plain toward the west.

The Triceratops herds paid not the slightest attention to him. He doubted that they could see him unless he came very close, and then they ignored him. They were herbivorous, and anything his size could not be an enemy. Only once, when he practically fell over a tiny, eight-foot calf napping in the tall grass, did one of the old ones emit a snuffling, hissing roar and come trotting toward him with its three sharp spikes lowered and its little eyes red.

There were many small dinosaurs, light and fleet of foot,

that were not so unconcerned with his passage. Some of them were big enough to make him feel distinctly uneasy, and he fired his first shot in self-defense when a creature the size of an ostrich leaned forward and came streaking at him with obviously malicious intent. He blew its head off at twenty paces, and had to duck the body that came clawing and scampering after him. It blundered on in a straight line, and when it finally collapsed he cooked and ate it over a fire of dead grass. It tasted like iguana, he said, and added that iguana tasted a lot like chicken.

Finally, he found a stream running down from the hills and took to its bed for greater safety. It was dry, but in the baked mud were the tracks of things that he hadn't seen and didn't want to see. He guessed, from my description, that they had been made by Tyrannosaurus or something equally big and dangerous.

Incidentally, I have forgotten the most important thing of all. Remember that Donovan's dominating idea was to prove to me, and to the world, that he had been in the Cretaceous and hobnobbed with its flora and fauna. He was a physicist by inclination, and had the physicist's flair for ingenious proofs. Before leaving, he loaded a lead cube with three quartz quills of pure radium chloride that he had been using in a previous experiment, and locked the whole thing up in a steel box. He had money to burn, and besides, he expected to get them back.

The first thing he did when he stepped out of the Egg on that fateful second trip was to dig a deep hole in the packed sand of the beach, well above high tide, and bury the box. He had seen the fossil tracks and ripple marks in the sandstone near his house, and guessed rightly enough that they dated from some time near the age to which he had penetrated. If I, or someone equally trustworthy, were to dig that box up one time coil later, he would not only have produced some very pretty proof that he had traveled in time—his name and the date were inside the cube—but an analysis of the radium, and an estimate of how much of it had turned into lead, would show how many years had elapsed since he buried it. In one fell swoop he would prove his claim, and give the world two very fundamental bits of scientific information: an exact date for the Cretaceous period, and the "distance" between successive coils in the spiral of time.

The stream bed finally petered out in a gully choked with boulders. The terrain was utterly arid and desolate, and he began to think that he had better turn back. There was nothing living to be seen, except for some small mammals like brown mice that got into his pack the first night and ate the bread he was carrying. He pegged a rock at them, but they vanished among the boulders, and an elephant gun was no good for anything their size. He wished he had a mousetrap. Mice were something that he could take back in his pocket.

The morning of the second day some birds flew by overhead. They were different from the one he killed later—more like sea gulls—and he got the idea that beyond the hills, in the direction they were flying, there would be either more wooded lowland or an arm of the sea. As it turned out, he was right.

The hills were the summit of a ridge like the spine of Italy, jutting south into the Cretaceous sea. The sea had been higher once, covering the sandy waste where the Triceratops herds now browsed, and there was a long line of eroded limestone cliffs, full of the black holes of wave-worn caves. From their base he looked back over the desert plain with its fringe of jungle along the shore of the sea. Something was swimming in schools, far out toward the horizon—something as big as whales, he thought—but he had forgotten to bring glasses and he could not tell what they were. He set about finding a way to climb the escarpment.

Right there was where he made his first big mistake. He might have known that what goes up has to come down again on the other side. The smart thing to do would have been to follow the line of the cliffs until he got into the other valley, or whatever lay beyond. Instead, he slung his gun around his neck and climbed.

The summit of the cliffs was a plateau, hollowed out by centuries of erosion into a basin full of gaudy spires of rock with the green stain of vegetation around their bases. There was evidently water and there might be animals that he could photograph or kill. Anything he found up here, he decided, would be pretty small.

He had forgotten the caves. They were high-arched, wave-eaten tunnels that extended far back into the cliffs, and from the lay of the land it was probable that they opened on the inside as well. Besides, whatever had lived on the plateau when it was at sea level had presumably been raised with it and might still be in residence. Whether it had wandered in from outside, or belonged there, it might be hungry—very hungry. It was.

There was a hiss that raised the short hair all along his spine. The mice that he had shied rocks at had heard such hisses and passed the fear of them down to their descendants, who eventually became his remote ancestors. And they had cause for fear! The thing that lurched out of the rocky maze, while it didn't top him by more than six feet and had teeth that were only eight inches long, was big enough to swallow him in three quick gulps, gun and all.

He ran. He ran like a rabbit. He doubled into crannies that the thing couldn't cram into and scrambled up spires of crumbling rock that a monkey would have found difficult, but it knew short cuts and it was downwind from him, and it thundered along behind with very few yards to spare. Suddenly he popped out of a long, winding corridor onto a bare ledge with a sheer drop to a steaming, stinking morass alive with things like crocodiles, only bigger. At the cliff's edge the thing was waiting for him.

One leap and it was between him and the crevice. He backed toward the cliff, raising his rifle slowly. It sat watching him for a moment, then raised its massive tail, teetered forward on its huge hind legs, and came running at him with its tiny foreclaws pumping like a sprinter's fists.

He threw up the gun and fired. The bullet plowed into its

throat and a jet of smoking blood sprayed him as its groping claws knocked the rifle from his grasp. Its hideous jaws closed on his upflung left arm, grinding the bones until he screamed. It jerked him up, dangling by his broken arm, ten feet in the air; then the idea of death hit it and it rolled over and lay twitching on the blood-soaked rock. Its jaws sagged open, and with what strength he had left Donovan dragged himself out of range of its jerking claws. He pulled himself up with his back against a rock and stared into the face of a second monster!

This was the one that had trailed him. The thing that had actually tasted him was a competitor. It came striding out of the shadowy gorge, the sun playing on its bronzed armor, and stopped to sniff at the thing Donovan had killed. It rolled the huge carcass over and tore out the belly, then straightened up with great gouts of bloody flesh dribbling from its jaws, and looked Donovan in the eye. Inch by inch, he tried to wedge himself into the crack between the boulders against which he lay. Then it stepped over its deceased relative and towered above him. Its grinning mask swooped down and its foul breath was in his face.

Then it was gone!

It wasn't a dream. There were the rocks—there was the carcass of the other beast—but it was gone! Vanished! In its place a wisp of bluish vapor was dissipating slowly in the sunlight. Vapor—and a voice! A woman's voice, in an unknown tongue.

She stood at the edge of the rocks. She was as tall as he, with very white skin and very black hair, dressed in shining metal cloth that was wound around her like bandage, leaving her arms and one white leg free. She was made like a woman and she spoke like a woman, in a voice that thrilled him in spite of the sickening pain in his arm. She had a little black cylinder in her hand, with a narrowed muzzle and a grip for her fingers, and she was pointing it at him. She spoke again, imperiously, questioning him. He grinned, tried to drag himself to his feet, and passed out cold.

It was two days before he came to. He figured that out later. It was night. He was in a tent somewhere near the sea, for he could hear it pounding on hard-packed sands. Above its roar there were other noises of the night; mutterings and rumblings of great reptiles, very far away, and now and then a hissing scream of rage. They sounded unreal. He seemed to be floating in a silvery mist, with the pain in his wounded arm throb, throb, throbbing to the rhythm of the sea.

Then he saw that the light was moonlight, and the silver the sheen of the woman's garment. She sat at his feet, in the opening of the tent, with the moonlight falling on her hair. It was coiled like a coronet about her head, and he remembered thinking that she must be a queen in some magic land, like the ones in fairy tales.

Someone moved, and he saw that there were others—men—crouching behind a breastwork of stone. They had cylinders like the one the woman had carried, and other weapons on tripods like parabolic microphones—great, polished reflectors of energy. The wall seemed more for concealment than protection, for he remembered the blasting power of the little cylinder and knew that no mere heap of rock could withstand it long. Unless, of course, they were fighting some foe who lacked their science. A foe native to this Cretaceous age—hairy, savage men with stones and clubs.

Realization struck him. There were no men in the Cretaceous. The only mammals were the mouselike marsupials that had robbed his pack. Then—who was the woman and how had she come here? Who were the men who guarded her? Were they—could they be—travelers in time like himself?

He sat up with a jerk that made his head swim. There was a shimmering, flowing movement in the moonlight and a small, soft hand was pressed over his mouth, an arm was about his shoulders, easing him back among the cushions. He called out and one of the men rose and came into the tent. He was tall, nearly seven feet, with silvery white hair and a

queer-shaped skull. He stared expressionlessly down at Donovan, questioning the woman in that same strange tongue.
She answered him, and Donovan felt with a thrill that she
seemed worried. The other shrugged—that is, he made a
queer, quick gesture with his hands that passed for a shrug—
and turned away. Before Donovan knew what was happening, the woman gathered him up in her arms like a babe and
started for the door of the tent.

Terry Donovan is over six feet tall and weighs two
hundred pounds. He stiffened like a naughty child. It caught
her offguard and they went down with a thud, the woman underneath. It knocked the wind out of her, and Donovan's arm
began to throb furiously, but he scrambled to his feet, and
with his good hand helped her to rise. They stood eyeing
each other like sparring cats, and then Terry laughed.

It was a hearty Irish guffaw that broke the tension, but it
brought hell down on them. Something spanged on the barricade and went whining over their heads. Something else
came arching and went through the moonlight and fell at their
feet—a metal ball the size of his head, whirring like a clock
about to strike.

Donovan moved like greased lightning. He scooped the
thing up with his good hand and lobbed it high and wide in
the direction from which it came, then grabbed the woman
and ducked. It burst in midair with a blast of white flame that
would have licked them off the face of the earth in a twin-
kling—and there was no sound, no explosion such as a normal bomb should make! There was no bark of rifles off there
in the darkness, though slugs were thudding into the barricade and screaming overhead with unpleasant regularity. The
tent was in ribbons, and seeing no reason why it should make
a better target than need be, he kicked the pole out from
under it and brought it down in a billowing heap.

That made a difference, and he saw why. The material of
the tent was evanescent, hard to see. It did something to the
light that fell on it, distorted it, acting as a camouflage. But
where bullets had torn its fabric a line of glowing green
sparks shone in the night.

The enemy had lost their target, but they had the range. A bullet whined evilly past Donovan's ear as he dropped behind the shelter of the wall. His groping hand found a familiar shape—his rifle. The cartridge belt was with it. He tucked the butt between his knees and made sure that it was loaded, then rose cautiously and peeped over the barricade.

Hot lead sprayed his cheek as a bullet pinged on the stone beside him. There was a cry from the woman. She had dropped to her knees beside the tent, and he could see that the ricochet had cut her arm. The sight of blood on her white skin sent a burning fury surging through him. He lunged awkwardly to his feet, resting the rifle on top of the wall, and peered into the darkness.

Five hundred yards away was the jungle, a wall of utter blackness out of which those silent missiles came. Nothing was visible against its shadows—or was that a lighter spot that slipped from tree to tree at the very edge of the moonlight? Donovan's cheek nestled against the stock of his gun and his eyes strained to catch that flicker of gray in the blackness. It came—the gun roared—and out of the night rang a scream of pain. A hit!

Twice before sunup he fired at fleeting shadows, without result. Beside him, the oldest of the four men—the one he had seen first—was dressing the woman's wound. It was only a scratch, but Donovan reasoned that in this age of virulent life forms, it was wise to take every precaution. There might be germs that no one had even heard of lurking everywhere. The others were about his own age, or seemed to be, with the same queer heads and white hair as their companion's. They seemed utterly disinterested in him and what he was doing.

As the first rays of the sun began to brighten the sky behind them, Donovan took stock of the situation. Their little fortress was perched on a point of rock overlooking the sea, with the plateau behind it. Salt marshes ran inland as far as he could see, edged with heavy jungle. And in No Man's Land between the two was the queerest ship he had ever seen.

It was of metal, cigar-shaped, with the gaping mouths of

rocket jets fore and after and a row of staring portholes. It was as big as a large ocean vessel and it answered his question about these men whose cause he was championing. They had come from space—from another world!

Bodies were strewn in the open space between the ship and the barricade. One lay huddled against a huge boulder, a young fellow, barely out of his teens as we would gauge it. Donovan's gaze wandered away, then flashed back. The man had moved!

Donovan turned eagerly to the others. They stared at him, blank-faced. He seized the nearest man by the shoulder and pointed. A cold light came into the other's eyes, and Donovan saw his companions edging toward him, their hands on the stubby cylinders of their weapons. He swore. Damn dummies! He flung the rifle down at the woman's sandaled feet and leaped to the top of the wall. As he stood there he was a perfect target, but no shot came. Then he was among the scattered rocks, zigzagging toward the wounded man. A moment later he slid safely into the niche behind the boulder, and lifted the other into a sitting position against his knee. He had been creased—an ugly furrow plowed along his scalp— but he seemed otherwise intact.

Donovan got his good shoulder under the man's armpit and lifted him bodily. From the hill behind the barricade a shot screamed past his head. Before he could drop to safety a second slug whacked into the body of the man in his arms, and the youth's slim form slumped in death.

Donovan laid him gently down in the shelter of the boulder. He wondered whether this would be the beginning of the end. Under fire from both sides, the little fortress could not hold out for long. A puff of vapor on the hillside told him why the fire was not being returned. The damned cylinders had no range. That was why the enemy was using bullets— air guns, or whatever the things were. All the more reason why he should save his skin while the saving was good. He ducked behind the rock, then straightened up and streaked for the shelter of the trees.

Bullets sang around him and glanced whistling from the rocks. One whipped the sleeve that hung loose at his side and another grooved the leather of his high-top boots. All came from behind—from the hill above the camp—and as he gained the safety of the forest he turned and saw the foe for the first time.

They were deployed in a long line across the top of the ridge behind the camp. They had weapons like fat-barreled rifles, with some bulky contraption at the breach. As he watched they rose and came stalking down the hillside, firing as they came.

They were black, but without the heavy features of a Negro. Their hair was as yellow as corn, and they wore shorts and tunics of copper-colored material. Donovan saw that they were maneuvering toward a spur from which they could fire down into the little fortress and pick off its defenders one by one. With the men at the barricade gone, they would be coming after him. If he started now, he might make his way through the jungle to a point where he could cut back across the hills and reach the Egg. He had a fifty-fifty chance of making it. Only—there was the woman. It was murder to leave her, and suicide to stay.

Fate answered for him. From the barricade he heard the roar of his rifle and saw one of the blacks spin and fall in a heap. The others stood startled, then raced for cover. Before they reached it, two more were down, and Donovan saw the woman's sleek black head thrust above the top of the rocky wall with the rifle butt tucked in the hollow of her shoulder.

That settled it. No one with her gumption was going to say that Terry Donovan had run out on her. Cautiously, he stuck his head out of the undergrowth and looked to left and right. A hundred feet from him one of the blacks lay half in and half out of the forest. One of the outlandish-looking rifles was beside him. Donovan pulled his head back and began to pry his way through the thick undergrowth.

The Donovan luck is famous. The gun was intact, and with it was a belt case crammed with little metal cubes that had the look of ammunition. He poked the heavy barrel into the air and pushed the button that was set in the butt. There was a crackling whisper, barely audible, and a slug went tearing through the fronds above him. He tried again, and an empty cube popped out into his palm. He examined it carefully. There was a sliding cover that had to be removed before the mechanism of the gun could get at the bullets it contained. He slipped in one of the loaded cubes and tried again. A second shot went whistling into space. Then, tucking the gun under his arm, he set out on a flanking trip of his own.

He knew the range of the weapon he was carrying, if not its nature, and he knew how to use it. He knew that if he could swing far around to the east, along the sea, he might come up on the ridge behind the blacks and catch them by surprise. Then if the gang in the fort would lend a hand, the war was as good as over.

It was easier said than done. A man with one mangled arm strapped to his side, and a twenty-pound rifle in his good hand, is not the world's best mountaineer. He worked his way through the jungle into the lee of the dunes that lay between the cliffs and the beach, then ran like blue blazes until he was out of sight of the whole fracas, cut back inland, took his lip in his teeth, and began to climb.

There were places where he balanced on spires the size and sharpness of a needle, or so he said. There were places where he prayed hard and trod on thin air. Somehow he made it and stuck his head out from behind a crimson crag to look down on a very scene.

The ten remaining blacks were holed up on the crest of the ridge. They were within range of the camp, but they didn't dare get up and shoot because of whoever was using the rifle. That "whoever"—the woman, as Donovan had suspected— was out of sight and stalking them from the north just as he was doing from the south. The fighting blood of his Irish ancestors sizzled in his veins. He slid the misshapen muzzle of his weapon out over the top of the rock and settled its butt in the crook of his good arm. He swiveled it around until it

pointed in the direction of two of the blacks who were shel-
tering under the same shallow ledge. Then he jammed down
the button and held on.

The thing worked like a machine gun and kicked like one.
Before it lashed itself out of his grip one of the foemen was
dead, two were flopping about like fish out of water, and the
rest were in full flight. As they sprang to their feet the
woman blazed away at them with the elephant gun. Then the
men from the barricade were swarming over the rock wall,
cylinders in hand, and mowing the survivors down in a suc-
cession of tiny puffs of blue smoke. In a moment it was over.

Donovan made his way slowly down the hillside. The
woman was coming to meet him. She was younger than he
had thought—a lot younger—but her youth did not soften
her. He thought that she might still be a better man than he, if
it came to a test. She greeted him in her soft tongue, and held
out the rifle. He took it, and as he touched the cold metal
a terrific jolt of static electricity knocked him from his feet.

He scrambled up ruefully. The woman had not fallen, but
her eyes blazed with fury. Then she saw that he had not acted
intentionally, and smiled. Donovan saw now why the blacks
wore metal suits. Their weapons built up a static charge with
each shot, and unless the gunner was well grounded it would
accumulate until it jumped to the nearest conductor. His
rubber-soled shoes had insulated him, and the charge built up
on him until he touched the barrel of the rifle, whereupon it
grounded through the steel and the woman's silvery gown.

They went down the hillside together. Donovan had given
the woman the gun he had salvaged, and she was examining
it carefully. She called out to the men, who stood waiting for
them, and they began to search the bodies of the blacks for
ammunition. Half an hour later they were standing on the
beach in the shadow of the great rocket. The men had carried
their equipment from the camp and stowed it away, while
Donovan and the woman stood outside bossing the job. That
is, she bossed while he watched. Then he recalled who and
where he was. Helping these people out in their little feud

was one thing, but going off with them, Heaven knew where, was another. He reached down and took the woman's hand.

"I've got to be going," he said.

Of course, she didn't understand a word he said. She frowned and asked some question in her own tongue. He grinned. He was no better at languages than she. He pointed to himself, then up the beach to the east where the Egg should be. He saluted cheerfully and started to walk away. She cried out sharply and in an instant all four men were on him.

He brought up the rifle barrel in a one-handed swing that dropped the first man in his tracks. The gun went spinning out of his hand, but before the others could reach him he had vaulted the man's body and caught the woman to him in a savage, one-arm hug that made her gasp for breath. The men stopped, their ray guns drawn. One second more and he would have been a haze of exploded atoms, but none of them dared fire with the woman in the way. Over the top of her sleek head he stared into their cold, hard eyes. Human they might be, but there was blessed little of the milk of human kindness in the way they looked at him.

"Drop those guns," he ordered, "or I'll break her damned neck!" None of them moved. "You heard me!" he barked. "Drop 'em!"

They understood his tone. Three tapering cylinders thudded on the sand. He thrust the woman forward with the full weight of his body and trod them into the sand.

"Get back," he commanded. "Go on. Scram!"

They went. Releasing the woman, he leaped back and snatched up the weapon she had dropped. He poked its muzzle at her slender waist and fitted his fingers cozily about the stock. He jerked his head back, away from the ship.

"You're coming with me," he said.

She stared inscrutably at him for a moment, then, without a word, walked past him and set off up the beach. Donovan followed her. A moment later the dunes had hidden the ship and the three men who stood beside it.

Then began a journey every step of which was a puzzle. The girl—for she was really little more—made no attempt to escape. After the first mile Donovan thrust the ray gun into his belt and caught up with her. Hours passed, and still they were slogging wearily along under the escarpment. In spite of the almost miraculous speed with which it was healing, the strain and activity of the past few hours had started his arm throbbing like a toothache. It made him grumpy, and he had fallen behind when a drumming roar made him look up.

It was the rocket ship. It was flying high, but as he looked it swooped down on them with incredible speed. A thousand feet above it leveled off and a shaft of violet light stabbed down, missing the girl by a scant ten feet. Where it hit the sand was a molten pool, and she was running for her life, zigzagging like a frightened rabbit, streaking for the shelter of the cliffs. With a shout, Donovan raced after her.

A mile ahead the ship zoomed and came roaring back at him. A black hole opened in the face of the cliff. The girl vanished in its shadows, and as the thunder of the rocket sounded unbearably loud in his ears, Donovan dived after her. The ray slashed across the rock above his head and droplets of molten magma seared his back. The girl was crouching against the wall of the cave. When she saw him she plunged into the blackness beyond.

He had had enough of hide and seek. He wanted a show-down and he wanted it now. With a shout, he leaped after the girl's receding figure and caught her by the shoulder, spinning her around.

Instantly he felt like an utter fool. He could say nothing that she could understand. The whole damned affair was beyond understanding. He had strong-armed her into coming with him—and her own men had tried to burn her down. Her—not him. Somehow, by something he had done, he had put her in danger of her life from the only people in the entire universe who had anything in common with her. He couldn't leave her alone in a wilderness full of hungry dinosaurs, with a gang of gunmen on her trail, and he couldn't take her with him. The Egg would barely hold one. He was on a spot, and there was nothing he could do about it.

There was the sound of footsteps on the gravel behind them. In the dim light he saw the girl's eyes go wide. He wheeled. Two men were silhouetted against the mouth of the cave. One of them held a ray gun. He raised it slowly.

Donovan's shoulder flung the girl against the wall. His hand flicked past his waist and held the gun. Twice it blazed and the men were gone in a puff of sparkling smoke. But in that instant, before they were swept out of existence, their guns had exploded in a misdirected burst of energy that brought the roof crashing down in a thundering avalanche, sealing the cave from wall to wall.

The shock flung Donovan to the ground. His wounded arm smashed brutally into the wall and a wave of agony left him white and faint. The echoes of that stupendous crash died away slowly in the black recesses of the cave. Then there was utter silence.

Something stirred beside him. A small, soft hand touched his face, found his shoulder, his hand. The girl's voice murmured, pleading. There was something she wanted— something he must do. He got painfully to his feet and awaited her next move. She gently detached the ray gun from his fingers, and before he knew it he was being hustled through utter darkness into the depths of the cave.

He did a lot of thinking on that journey through blackness. He put two and two together and got five or six different answers. Some of them hung together to make sense out of nightmare.

First, the girl herself. The rocket, and Donovan's faith in a science that he was proving fallible, told him that she must have come from another planet. Her unusual strength might mean that she was from some larger planet, or even some star. At any rate, she was human and she was somebody of importance.

Donovan mulled over that for a while. Two races, from the same or different planets, were thirsting for each other's blood. It might be politics that egged them on, or it might be racial trouble or religion. Nothing else would account for the fury with which they were exterminating each other. The girl had apparently taken refuge with her bodyguard on this empty planet. Possession of her was important. She might be a deposed queen or princess—and the blacks were on her trail. They found her and laid siege—whereupon Terry Donovan of 1937 A.D. came barging into the picture.

That was where the complications began. The girl, reconnoitering, had saved him from the dinosaur which was eating him. Any one would have done as much. She lugged him back to camp—Donovan flushed at the thought of the undignified appearance he must have made—and they patched him up with their miraculous green ointment. Then the scrap began, and he did his part to bring them out on top. Did it damn well, if any one was asking. Donovan didn't belong to their gang and didn't want to, so when they started for home he did likewise. Only it didn't work out that way.

She had ordered her men to jump him. She wanted to hang on to him, whether for romantic reasons, which was doubtful, or because she needed another fighting man. They didn't get very far with their attempt to gang up on him. That was where the worst of the trouble began.

Grabbing her as he had had been a mistake. Somehow that act of touching her—of doing physical violence to her person—made a difference. It was as though she were a goddess who lost divinity through his violence, or a priestess who was contaminated by his touch. She recognized that fact. She knew then that she would have short shrift at the hands of her own men if she stayed with them. So she came along. Strangely enough, the men did not follow for some time. It was not until they returned to the rocket, until they received orders from whoever was in that rocket, that they tried to kill her.

Whoever was in the rocket! The thought opened new possibilities. A priest, enforcing the taboos of his god. A politician, playing party policy. A traitor, serving the interests of the blacks. None of these did much to explain the girl's own attitude, nor the reason why this assumed potentate, if he was in the rocket during the battle, had done nothing to bring one side or the other to victory. It didn't explain why hours had passed before the pursuit began. And nothing told him what he was going to do with her when they reached the Egg. If they ever did.

The cave floor had been rising for some time when Donovan saw a gleam of light ahead. At once the girl's pace quickened, and she dropped his arm. How, he wondered, had she been able to traverse that pitch-black labyrinth so surely and quickly? Could she see in the dark, or judge her way with some strange sixth sense? It added one more puzzle to the mysteries surrounding her.

He could have danced for joy when they came out into the light. They had passed under the ridge and come out at the foot of the cliffs which he had climbed hours before. The whole landscape was familiar: the gullies in the barren plain, the fringe of swamp and jungle, and the reefs over which the oily sea was breaking. There, a few miles to the north, the Egg was hidden. There was safety—home—for one.

She seemed to know what he was thinking. She laid a reassuring hand on his arm and smiled up at him. This was his party from now on. Then she saw the pain in his eyes. His arm had taken more punishment than most men could have stood and stayed alive. Her nimble fingers peeled away the dressing and gently probed the wound to test the position of the broken bones. Evidently everything was to her liking, for she smiled reassuringly and opened a pouch at her waist, from which she took a little jar of bright-green ointment and smeared it liberally on the wound. It burned like fire, then a sensuous sort of glow crept through his arm and side, deadening the pain. She wadded the dirty bandages into a ball and threw them away. Then, before Donovan knew what was happening, she had ripped a length of the metallic-looking fabric from her skirt and was binding the arm tightly to his side.

Stepping back, she regarded him with satisfaction, then

turned her attention to the gun she had taken from him. A lip of the firing button and an empty cartridge cube popped out into her palm. She looked at him and he at her. It was all the weapon they had, and it was empty. Donovan shrugged. Nothing much mattered anyway. With an answering grimace she sent it spinning away among the rocks. Side by side, they set off toward the coast and the Egg.

It was the sky that Donovan feared now. Dinosaurs they could outwit or outrun. He thought he could even fight one of the little ones, with her to cheer him on. But heat rays shot at them from the sky, with no cover within miles, was something else again. Strangely enough, the girl seemed to be enjoying herself. Her voice was a joy to hear, even if it didn't make sense, and Donovan thought that he got the drift of her comments on some of the ungainly monstrosities that blemished the Cretaceous landscape.

Donovan had no desire to be in the jungle at night, so they took their time. He had matches, which she examined with curiosity, and they slept, back to back, beside a fire of grass and twigs in the lee of a big boulder. There was nothing to eat, but it didn't seem to matter. A sort of silent partnership had been arrived at, and Donovan, at least, was basking in its friendly atmosphere.

Every road has its ending. Noon found them standing beside the leaden hulk of the Egg, face to face with reality. One of them, and only one, could make the journey back. The Egg would not hold two, nor was there power enough in its accumulators to carry more than one back through the barrier between time coils. If the girl were to go, she would find herself alone in a world unutterably remote from her own, friendless and unable to understand or to make herself understood. If Donovan returned, he must leave her here alone in the Cretaceous jungle, with no food, no means of protection from man or beast, and no knowledge of what might be happening sixty million years later which would seal her fate for good.

There was only one answer. Her hand went to his arm and pushed him gently toward the open door of the Egg. He, and he alone, could get the help which they must have and return to find her. In six hours at the outside the Egg should be ready to make its return trip. In that six hours Donovan could find me, or some other friend, and enlist my aid!

Fortune played into his hands. There was a patter of footsteps among the fallen fronds, and a small dinosaur appeared, the body of a bird in its jaws. With a whoop, Donovan sprang at it. It dropped the bird and disappeared. The creature was not dead, but Donovan wrung its scrawny neck. Here was proof that must convince me of the truth of his story—that would bring me to their aid!

He stepped into the machine. As the door swung shut, he saw the girl raise her hand in farewell. When it opened again, he stepped out on the concrete floor of his own laboratory, sixty million years later.

His first thought was for the generators that would recharge the batteries of the Egg. Then, from the house and the laboratory, he collected the things that he would need: guns, food, water, clothing. Finally, he set out to fetch me.

He sat there, his broken arm strapped to his side with that queer metallic cloth, the torn flesh painted with some aromatic green ointment. A revolver in its holster lay on the desk at his elbow; a rifle leaned against the heap of duffel on the floor of the Egg. What did it all mean? Was it part of some incredibly elaborate hoax, planned for some inconceivable purpose? Or—fantastic as it seemed—was it truth?

"I'm leaving in ten minutes," he said. "The batteries are charged."

"What can I do?" I asked. "I'm no mechanic—no physicist."

"I'll send her back in the Egg," he told me. "I'll show you how to charge it—it's perfectly simple—and when it's ready you will send it back, empty, for me. If there is any delay, make her comfortable until I come."

I noted carefully everything he did, every setting of every

piece of apparatus, just as he showed them to me. Then, just four hours after he threw that incredible bird down at my feet, I watched the leaden door of the Egg swing shut. The hum of the generators rose to an ugly whine. A black veil seemed to envelop the huge machine—a network of emptiness which ran together and coalesced into a hole into which I gazed for interminable distances. Then it was gone. The room was empty. I touched the switch that stopped the generators.

The Egg did not return—not on that day, nor the next, nor even while I waited there. Finally, I came away. I have told his story—my story before—but they laugh as I did. Only there is one thing that no one knows.

This year there were new funds for excavation. I am still senior paleontologist at the museum, and in spite of the veiled smiles that are beginning to follow me, I was chosen to continue my work of previous seasons. I knew from the beginning what I would do. The executors of Donovan's estate gave me permission to trace the line of the ancient Cretaceous beach that ran across his property. I had a word picture of that other world as he had seen it, and a penciled sketch, scrawled on the back of an envelope as he talked. I knew where he had buried the cube of radium. And it might be that this beach of fossil sands, preserved almost since the beginning of time, was the same one in which Terry Donovan had scooped a hole and buried a leaden cube, sealed in a steel box.

I have not found the box. If it is there, it is buried under tons of rock that will require months of labor and thousands of dollars to remove. We have uncovered a section of the beach in whose petrified sands every mark made in that ancient day is as sharp and clear as though it were made yesterday: the ripples of the receding tide—the tracks of sea worms crawling in the shallow water—the trails of the small reptiles that fed on the flotsam and jetsam of the water's edge.

Two lines of footprints come down across the wet sands of that Cretaceous beach, side by side. Together they cross the forty-foot slab of sandstone which I have uncovered, and vanish where the rising tide has filled them. They are prints of a small, queerly made sandal and a rubber-soled hiking boot—of a man and a girl.

A third line of tracks crosses the Cretaceous sands and overlies those others—huge, splayed, three-toed, like the prints of some gigantic bird. Sixty million years ago, mighty Tyrannosaurus and his smaller cousins made such tracks. The print of one great paw covers both the girl's footprints as she stands for a moment, motionless, beside the man. They, too, vanish at the water's edge.

That is all, but for one thing: an inch or two beyond the point where the tracks vanish, where the lapping waters have smoothed the sand, there is a strange mark. The grains of sand are fused, melted together in a kind of funnel of green-ish glass that reminds me of the fulgurites that one often finds where lightning has struck iron-bearing sand, or where some high-voltage cable has grounded. It is smoother and more regular than any fulgurite that I have ever seen.

Two years ago I saw Terry Donovan step into the leaden Egg that stood in its cradle on the floor of his laboratory, and vanish with it into nothingness. He has not returned. The tracks which I have described, imprinted in the sands of a Cretaceous beach, are very plain, but workmen are the only people besides myself who have seen them. They see no re-semblance to human footprints in the blurred hollows in the stone. They know, for I have told them again and again dur-ing the years that I have worked with them, that there were no human beings on the earth sixty million years ago. Science says—and is not science always right?—that only the great dinosaurs of the Cretaceous age left their fossil foot-prints in the sands of time.

PALEONTOLOGY: AN EXPERIMENTAL SCIENCE

Robert R. Olsen

And one last look at the ferocious Cretaceous dinosaur Tyrannosaurus—but not, however, through the medium of a time machine. This sly and subtle story gives us a dinosaur in the San Diego Zoo—and surrounding territory. Robert R. Olsen is a geologist, born in Chicago, currently living in Kansas after a long sojourn in the Southwest. "Paleontology: An Experimental Science," a delicious parody of the standard scientific paper, was his first story; he is also the author of the odd, haunting novella of the far future, Metal, *published recently in the anthology series* New Dimensions.

"Computer reconstruction of fossil organisms" by L. R. Smizer (speaker), C. D. Halloran, P. McBride, H. C. Smith, and P. C. Eberhart, Geological Society of America Abstracts with Programs (Cordilleran Section), 1979, p. 14.

ADVANCES IN COMPUTER TECHNOLOGY have recently made possible the reconstruction of fossil organisms from the organic material found in certain fossils, at least on a theoretical basis. Methods of tissue culture from single DNA molecules have recently been placed on a routine basis, but actual reproduction of fossil organisms depends on the preservation of fragments of the DNA chain as fossil material in rocks. The destructive nature of most fossilization processes suggests that only fossils of late Tertiary age can be replicated using this technique.

In cases where abundant but fragmentary material is present in fossil form, the substance is separated from the host rock and then subjected to microanalysis to determine what parts of the DNA chain are present. Analyses of the structure of the fragments are fed into a computer which attempts to match fragments of the chain in order to obtain a composite model of the DNA, which governs the form and development of the organism. New DNA can then be synthesized, either by the difficult process of building the molecule up from simpler amino acids, or, in the ideal case, by rejoining the fragments of DNA into one complete molecule. Though the latter process has recently been performed in the laboratory, it appears that those parts of the chain where the fragments were fused is always a weak spot in the structure, and susceptible to breakage in the presence of certain chemicals.

Preliminary experiments have been carried out on several species of Pleistocene land-snails and one Pliocene ginkgo. Though some of these experiments are still in the early stages of test-tube culture, two snails appear to have developed normally, as far as can be determined; and the ginkgo, recently transferred to a soil medium, shows normal growth.

"Fossils of *Tyrannosaurus nevadensis* and other saurians, Hell's Flat, Nevada" by C. C. Morrow, Geological Society of America Abstracts with Programs (Cordilleran Section), 1979, p. 19.

Excellent preservation of saurian fossils has long been known in western Utah and easternmost Nevada, and recently a most remarkable case of preservation has been discovered. In a nearly inaccessible part of the northern Shadow Peak Mountains, Upper Cretaceous rocks are exposed in a small canyon which overlooks the area known locally as Hell's Flat. The rocks, a series of continental sandstones and shales about thirty-five feet thick, are flat-lying and rest upon a surface carved in the Middle Cambrian Bonanza King Formation. Overlying the fossiliferous Cretaceous strata are resistant Late Tertiary volcanic and volcanistic rocks, which form the higher parts of the Shadow Peak Mountains.

The Cretaceous rocks are thought to represent a river channel cut into the older material, and consist of reddish to pale yellow, medium to fine-grained sandstones and gray shales. The material is almost unconsolidated, which accounts in part for the remarkable state of preservation of the fossils.

The fossil material consists of assorted bones and skin fragments, mostly of Tyrannosaurus nevadensis, though there are also three species of Triceratops, and an unidentified form similar to Trachodon but smaller and lighter in build. All fossils are the products of perfect preservation and no chemical replacement or deletion of material has occurred. The extreme aridity of the area, among other factors, has apparently caused this remarkable phenomenon; for when a skin fragment was wetted and left overnight, a strong organic odor indicative of decay was noted the next morning. The skin material is exceptionally coarse and tough, and a gray-green color.

Several pounds of this remarkable material were collected. It should prove to be of wide interest in the study of the biochemistry of fossil organisms and the geochemistry of fossilization, subjects which have not until now received the attention they deserve, due to the lack of suitable material for experiment. This lack has now been remedied to an extent.

"Computer reconstruction of fossil DNA of *Tyrannosaurus nevadensis*" by L. R. Smizer (speaker), C. D. Halloran, P. McBride, H. C. Smith, and P. C. Eberhart, Geological Society of American Abstracts with Programs (Cordilleran Section), 1985, p. 21.

Computer reconstruction of the DNA structure of the Hell's Flat fossil material has now progressed to the point where some preliminary deductions can be made as to the biochemistry of the subject organism, T. nevadensis, and the chemistry of the fossil material.

Although T. nevadensis–derived material was the most abundant fraction of fossil matter, abundant organic constituents from the other saurian remains posed a difficult problem in the early stages of preparation. However, little DNA remained from the other fossil forms, and a pure sample of T. nev.–derived DNA was eventually isolated by molecular probe. No complete DNA molecules were found, the largest fragment containing roughly 45 percent of the total genetic information as subsequently deduced. Other major fragments, some in slightly damaged form, contained 30, 28, 17, 12, and 8 percent of the total information necessary to reconstruct the living organism. Thus, an excess of 40 percent exists in the information as received by the computer. Analysis revealed that though this surplus of information was not as great as might be desired, all the necessary information was indeed present on the fragments.

Following computer correlation and modeling of the major DNA molecule, experimentation commenced on the actual construction and culture of the molecule. Using techniques described in a previous paper (1983), the fragmentary DNA molecules were cleaned and joined together microsurgically, the molecule being implanted in the specially prepared nucleus of the egg cell of a cayman from which the host's DNA had been removed.

Chemically induced replication of the original DNA molecule has now been attained, and the embryo placed in a life-support system. Growth is quite rapid, and the birth-analog event is scheduled for August 1986, corresponding to a gestation period of 11 months.

"Ontogeny and development of an artificial specimen of *Tyrannosaurus nevadensis*," by C. D. Halloran (speaker), P. McBride, H. C. Smith, and P. C. Eberhart, Geological Society of America Abstracts with Programs (Cordilleran Section), 1987, p. 13.

The artificially created embryo of Tyrannosaurus nevadensis, which has been the subject of previous reports, was inserted in a life-support growth medium on June 12, 1985, in an attempt to cause the development of a mature individual of the species. The work was performed at the Craig University Paleontology Laboratory in Hastings, California.

Though the environment of growth of course differed markedly from that which the organism would experience in its natural state, growth was rapid and proceeded normally throughout the embryonic stage. Oxygen demand increased markedly (47 percent) in the sixth month but was successfully met due to careful supervision of the environment. By the end of the seventh month, the embryo was roughly five inches long and weighed nine ounces. At this time, definite signs of electrical activity in the brain were noted, and the birth-analog event was considered to be imminent.

The young animal, a male, was removed from the life-support system on July 7th, and placed in a terrarium stocked with insects and small reptiles of various kinds. At this time the animal was eight inches long and weighed 13 ounces. Respiratory function was somewhat sluggish for the first 7 hours but then attained a condition judged to be normal for this species. The animal was from the first a vigorous and aggressive predator, and devoured two small lizards during the first day of active life.

Seven weeks later, the specimen, now the size of a large dog, succeeded in breaking through the wire-mesh wall of the terrarium and briefly roamed at large in the Paleontology Laboratory. Several other laboratory specimens, as well as two German shepherd dogs, were lost at this time. Unfortunately also, the struggle to recapture the animal resulted in the tragic loss of Dr. Smizer, who was first to discover the creature's hiding place.

In conclusion, despite some difficulty, significant data are now being obtained from the specimen, which has been removed from the Paleontology Laboratory to more secure quarters at the Elephant Corral of the San Diego Zoo. Data already collected indicate the necessity of revising current views on the intelligence and aggressiveness of the theropods, as well as their level of activity.

"Behavioral anomalies of *Tyrannosaurus nevadensis,* as deduced from the Smizer specimen," by C. D. Halloran (speaker), H. C. Smith, and P. C. Eberhart, Geological Society of America Abstracts with Programs (Cordilleran Section), 1988, p. 8.

An ongoing program of study at the Paleontological Laboratory of Craig University has been concerned with the production of an artificial specimen of Tyrannosaurus nevadensis. Following successful production of a young specimen of the species by repair of fragmental fossil DNA, the animal was placed in the Elephant Corral of the San Diego Zoo after its strength proved to be too great for conventional laboratory care.

The San Diego facilities, modified to include two double-strength steel barriers ten feet apart, proved entirely adequate for the task of containing the Tyrannosaurus during its youth and early adulthood, providing that adequate repair and rebuilding of the inner cage was performed weekly. With maturity, the reddish-brown mottled scale pattern of the animal's youth is being gradually replaced by a greenish-brown cast that undoubtedly had some camouflage function during Cretaceous times. Molting was accomplished once monthly during the period of maximum growth, and was accompanied by unusual patterns of behavior. Instead of the usual reptilian pattern of lethargy and passivity during the molting period, the Smizer tyrannosaurus became unusually vicious and hyperactive. It was undoubtedly due to this phenomenon, plus an oversight in the maintenance of the inner cage, that the animal was able to attain the space between the inner and outer cages on December 8, resulting in the tragic death of Dr. McBride. It was reliably reported that Dr. McBride was standing at least four feet from the outer cage when the animal seized him with a foreleg and dragged him into the cage to be consumed. Since the reach of the animal's foreleg when fully extended at this stage of development was only five feet six inches, it would appear that the forelegs are more useful to the creature in food gathering than was previously thought.

The great muscular development of the hind legs of the tyrannosaurus also has a significant adaptive advantage in this particular creature. It has been frequently observed that upon securing living prey, the animal will stamp and crush the prey with its feet, thus presumably rendering the food more pliant. It is thought that this behavior is related to the habit of swallowing the food in one piece as would a more modern reptile. Since the forelegs are of little use in this procedure, the rear legs have assumed the role of food-preparing devices.

"Results of computer reconstruction of DNA of the Smizer tyrannosaurus" by C. D. Halloran (speaker), H. C. Smith, and P. C. Eberhart, Geological Society of America Abstracts with Programs (Cordilleran Section), 1989, p. 27.

Since the Smizer specimen of Tyrannosaurus nevadensis has now reached physical maturity (although continued growth, in the manner of all reptiles, is expected), it is appropriate to examine how closely the artificially reconstituted DNA, pieced together from fragments of fossil DNA from Nevada, approximates the known genetic structure of the tyrannosaurus as previously deduced. Although certain anomalies have been observed which possibly are due to faulty reconstruction, the procedure seems to have been in large part successful, and promises to make possible further reconstitutions in the future.

Anomalies in the specimen may be divided into two classes: physical/developmental anomalies, and behavioral anomalies.

Although the Smizer specimen is now as large as the largest known fossil Tyrannosaurus of any species, the junior author feels that it has not attained full maturity; if this is so, it follows that through a defect in the DNA reconstruction, the size of this specimen is greater than it should be. This theory must wait for support with time and further growth of the specimen. The rapid growth of the animal both before and after the birth-analog event has caused some authorities to object to the speed of maturation. However, it should be remembered that since the specimen has been given sufficient or even excess food throughout its life, rapid development may be more a result of opportunity than genetic anomaly. Though the animal exhibits behavioral aberrations as discussed in a previous paper, it is unknown whether this behavior was natural to the Cretaceous Tyrannosaurus nevadensis or not. Other aspects of behavior must be, as above, dependent on opportunity—as, for example, the Smizer tyrannosaurus' habit of sharpening its teeth on building concrete.

In conclusion, with the possible exception of anomalous size, the Smizer tyrannosaurus is a completely normal specimen of its type and suggests the great gains to be derived from further research into the reconstruction of fossil organisms from DNA fragments.

"Predatory habits of Tyrannosaurus nevadensis smizer" by H. C. Smith, Geological Society of America Abstracts with Programs (Cordilleran Section), 1989, p. 21.

Because Tyrannosaurus nevadensis smizer is a vigorous predator, and because of the creature's unusual size, great problems were encountered relating to the procurement of sufficient food to keep the animal both nourished and satisfied. Due to the lack of herbivorous dinosaurs of sufficient size to provide satisfactory prey for the tyrannosaurus (a lack which may soon be remedied—see Smith, in preparation, Geol. Soc. Amer. Bull.), smaller animals must be used. Normal behavior for the theropods is thought to have been for the creature to sleep for a matter of days after eating to repletion, after which the old kill would be revisited. However, with the artificial specimen, only small animals such as cattle and oxen were available for consumption. This resulted in a diminution of the resting periods of the creature, hence to increased activity, and therefore presumably to an increased demand for food.

Although the escape of the Smizer tyrannosaurus in March of this year, involving as it did the regrettable deaths of Dr. Halloran and Dr. Eberhart, was a serious setback to the project, it did involve unparalleled opportunity to observe the habits of the creature in a more natural setting. Fortunately, the creature proved to be very much afraid of automobiles, and while it is perhaps strange that it managed to escape from the San Diego area in view of this, the shyness on the part of the animal kept the loss of human life to a minimum.

Because of its unusual size, the dinosaur was observed by many people as it journeyed north toward Lake Elsinore. Having grown considerably by this time, the animal was forced to stop frequently for food, where it showed a definite preference for Hereford cattle. As many observers remarked, its behavior in rounding up the cattle predatory to crushing several of them with its hind legs was quite remarkable in view of the often postulated low degree of intelligence of the saurians.

Although the creature is still at large, capture is expected at any time. Since the creature has recently shown a diminishing fear of automobiles, the Lake Elsinore region has recently been evacuated, and the situation is viewed as stable. Herds of cattle are driven into the area weekly to keep the specimen from roaming too far in its search for food.

"Death and postmortem examination of Tyrannosaurus nevadensis smizer" by H. C. Smith, Geological Society of America Abstracts with Programs (Cordilleran Section), 1990, p. 17.

Although the creature was naturally of inestimable scientific value, care of the reconstructed Tyrannosaurus nevadensis proved to be a formidable problem, particularly after its escape in March 1989. After the creature had moved north to the vicinity of Lake Elsinore, the onset of cool weather in October 1989 caused definite signs of restlessness in the animal. Finally, on November 4th, in a cold rain, the creature began to move south rapidly. It was at this point that the civil authorities requested (People of California vs. Smith) that the creature be put to death. Although conscious of the immense amount of data yet unacquired, the author endeavored to comply.

Since traditional methods of attack had failed, causing many needless tragedies, it was felt that the only means of subduing the beast was to use weaknesses in its own reconstituted genetic structure against it. Since it was known that slight flaws existed in the structure of the DNA, the creature was injected with K-ryocyanin at close range by bazooka. Although this treatment would have no immediate effect, it would prevent the replication of new body cells by breaking down the structure of DNA.

However, before the animal succumbed, it nearly succeeded in reaching the Mexican border, ultimately collapsing in downtown San Diego. At this time, the creature was reliably estimated to be five stories tall (as demonstrated by the absence of fatalities or damage above the sixth floor of the Union Building). This translates to an overall length of roughly 100 feet. This measurement was confirmed when shortly afterwards the creature fell dead in the street, where it could be measured. Death was caused by cellular deterioration brought on by the injection, and occurred one week and two days after injection.

In the future it is to be recommended that more caution be used in the selection of subjects for artificial regeneration, although the process itself must be considered totally successful. In particular, the procedure will be of great value in research into the behavior of extinct animals. Preferred specimens of predators should be more intelligent, and hence more tractable, than the great reptiles. For example, there is some controversy concerning the feeding habits of the early cave bears, with some writers maintaining that they were strictly carnivorous, as opposed to the omnivorous modern bears. The Paleontology Laboratory is currently caring for an embryo of Arctotherium californicum, commonly known as the giant cave bear, developed from fossil material found at Rancho La Brea; after the animal is born this fall, answers to this and many other questions will undoubtedly be found.

THE DOCTOR

Ted Thomas

The long era of the dinosaurs came to its end. The great beasts died out, and the relatively few species of reptiles that survived—crocodiles, turtles, lizards—settled into minor niches of existence. Now the world was dominated by smaller, quicker, hairer creatures–mammals, ancestors of today's elephants and tigers and horses and camels and giraffes. And, almost certainly in Africa some five or ten million years ago, one kind of mammal learned to walk about on its hind legs, and to use its front limbs for grasping things and then for making things, and the creature called man arrived on the scene.

This tight, harsh little story by Ted Thomas, a writer and patent attorney from Pennsylvania, is set deep in prehistory but long after the time of man's early evolution. The truly primeval human forms, those small apelike beings called australopithecines that have been discovered in so many parts of Africa, are already gone; the people of Thomas' story, half a million years ago, belong to no particular race of prehistoric man, but they are obviously fairly well advanced toward our physical form, and have developed the rudiments of a culture, including the use of fire. And what would it be like to be thrust among them suddenly, with your twentieth-century intelligence and your twentieth-century technical skills? Would you become a king? An oracle? A sorcerer? What would it be like?

WHEN GANT FIRST OPENED his eyes he thought for an instant he was back in his home in Pennsylvania. He sat up suddenly and looked wildly around in the dark of the cave, and then he remembered where he was. The noise he made frightened his wife and his son, Dun, and they rolled to their feet, crouched, ready to leap. Gant grunted reassuringly at them and climbed off the moss-packed platform he had built for a bed. The barest glimmerings of dawn filtered into the cave, and the remnants of the fire glowed at the mouth. Gant went to the fire and put some chips on it and blew on them. It had been a long time since he had had such a vivid memory of his old life half a million years away. He looked at the wall of the cave, at the place where he kept his calendar, painfully scratched into the rock. It had been ten years ago today when he had stepped into that molybdenum-steel cylinder in the Bancroft Building at Pennsylvania State University. What was it he had said? "Sure, I'll try it. You ought to have a medical doctor in it on the first trial run. You physicists could not learn anything about the physiological effects of time travel. Besides, this will make history, and I want to be in on it."

Gant stepped over the fire and listened carefully at the mouth of the cave, near the log barrier. Outside he heard the sound of rustling brush and heavy breathing, and he knew he could not leave now. He drank some water from a gourd and ate some dried bison with his wife and son. They all ate quietly.

Dawn came, and he stepped to the mouth of the cave and listened. The great animal had left. He waved to his wife and Dun, dragged aside the barrier, and went out.

He went along the face of the cliff, staying away from the heavy underbrush at its foot. He would go into it when he returned, and he would look for food.

In the marsh that lay beyond the underbrush was one of the many monuments to his failures. In the rocks and tree stumps there, he had tried to grow penicillium molds on the sweet juices of some of the berries that abounded in the region. He had crushed the berries and placed the juices in a hundred different kinds of receptacles. For three years he had tried to raise the green mold, but all he ever produced was a slimy gray mass that quickly rotted when the sun struck it.

He hefted the heavy stone axe in his right hand. As he approached the cave he was looking for, he grunted loudly and then went in. The people inside held their weapons in their hands, and he was glad he had called ahead. He ignored them and went to a back corner to see the little girl.

She sat on the bare stone, leaning against the rock with her mouth open, staring dully at him as he came up to her, her eyes black against the thick blonde hair that grew on her face. Gant whirled at the others and snarled at them, and snatched a bearhide from the bed of the man and carried it to the girl. He wrapped her in it and then felt the part of her forehead where there was no hair. It was burning hot, must be about 105 degrees, possibly a little more. He put her down on the rock and thumped her chest and heard the solid, hard sound of filled lungs. It was full-blown pneumonia, no longer any doubt. She gasped for breath, and there was no breath. Gant picked her up again and held her. He sat with her for over an hour, changing her position frequently in his arms, trying to make her comfortable as she gasped. He held a handful of wet leaves to her forehead to try to cool her burning face, but it did not seem to help. She went into convulsions at the end.

He laid the body on a rock ledge and pulled the mother over to see it. The mother bent and touched the girl gently on the face and then straightened and looked at Gant helplessly. He picked up the body and walked out of the cave and down into the woods. It took several hours to dig a hole deep enough with a stick.

He hunted on the way back to the caves, and he killed a short, heavy-bodied animal that hung upside down from the lower branches of a tree. It emitted a foul odor as he killed it, but it would make a good meal. He found a large rock outcropping with a tiny spring coming out from under it. A mass of newly sprouted shoots grew in the soggy ground. He

picked them all, and headed back to his cave. His wife and
Dun were there and their faces brightened when they saw
what he brought. His wife immediately laid out the animal
and skinned it with a fragment of sharp, shiny rock. Dun
watched her intently, leaning over while it cooked to smell
the fragrant smoke. Gant looked at the short, thick, hairy
woman tending the cooking, and he looked at the boy. He
could easily see himself in the thin-limbed boy. Both his wife
and his son had the heavy brows and the jutting jaw of the
cave people. But Dun's body was lean and his eyes were blue
and sparkling, and he often sat close to Gant and tried to go
with him when he went out of the cave. And once, when the
lightning blazed and the thunder roared. Gant had seen the
boy standing at the mouth of the cave staring at the sky in
puzzlement, not fear, and Gant had put a hand on his
shoulder and tried to find the words that told of electrical
discharges and the roar of air rushing into a void, but there
were no words.

The meat was done and the shoots were softened, and the
three of them squatted at the fire and reached for the food.
Outside the cave they heard the sound of movement in the
gravel, and Gant leaped for his club while his wife and Dun
retreated to the rear of the cave. Two men appeared, one sup-
porting the other, both empty-handed. Gant waited until he
could see that one of them was injured; he could not place his
right foot on the ground. Then Gant came forward and helped
the injured man to a sitting position at the mouth of the cave.
He leaned over to inspect the foot. The region just above the
ankle was discolored and badly swollen, and the foot was at a
slight angle to the rest of the leg. Both the fibula and the tibia
seemed to be broken, and Gant stood up and looked around
for splints. The man would probably die; there was no one to
take care of him during the weeks needed for his leg to heal,
no one to hunt for him and give him food and put up with his
almost complete inactivity.

Gant found two chips from logs and two short branches

and some strips from a cured hide. He knelt in front of the man and carefully held his hands near the swollen leg so the man could see he was going to touch it.

The man's great muscles were knotted in pain and his face was gray beneath the hair. Gant waved the second man around to one side where he could keep an eye on him, and then he took the broken leg and began to apply tension. The injured man stood it for a moment and then roared in pain and instinctively lashed out with his good leg. Gant ducked the kick, but he could not duck the blow from the second man. It hit him on the side of the head and knocked him out of the mouth of the cave. He rolled to his feet and came back in. The second man stood protectively in front of the injured man, but Gant pushed him aside and knelt down again. The foot was straight, so Gant placed the chips and branches on the leg and bound them in place with the leather thongs. Weak and helpless, the injured man did not resist. Gant stood up and showed the second man how to carry the injured man. He helped them on their way.

When they left, Gant returned to his food. It was cold, but he was content. For the first time they had come to him. They were learning. He hurt his teeth on the hard meat and he gagged on the spongy shoots, but he squatted in his cave and he smiled. There had been a time long ago when he had thought that these people would be grateful to him for his work, that he would become known by some such name as The Healer. Yet here he was, years later, happy that at last one of them had come to him with an injury. Yet Gant knew them too well by now to be misled. These people did not have even the concept of medical treatment, and the day would probably come when one of them would kill him as he worked.

He sighed, picked up his club, and went out of the cave. A mile away was a man with a long gash in the calf of his left leg. Gant had cleaned it and packed it with moss and tied it tight with a hide strip. It was time to check the wound, so he walked the mile carefully, on the lookout for the large creatures that roamed the forests. The man was chipping rock in front of his cave, and he nodded his head and waved and showed his teeth in a friendly gesture when he saw Gant. Gant showed his teeth in turn and looked at the leg. He saw that the man had removed the moss and bandage, and had rubbed the great wound with dung. Gant bent to inspect the wound and immediately smelled the foul smell of corruption. Near the top of the wound, just beneath the knee, was a mass of black, wet tissue. Gangrene. Gant straightened and looked around at some of the others near the cave. He went to them and tried to make them understand what he wanted to do, but they did not pay much attention. Gant returned and looked down on the wounded man, noting that his movements were still quick and coordinated, and that he was as powerfully built as the rest of them. Gant shook his head; he could not perform the amputation unaided, and there was no help to be had. He tried again to show them that the man would die unless they helped him, but it was no use. He left.

He walked along the foot of the cliffs, looking in on the caves. In one he found a woman with a swollen jaw, in pain. She let him look in her mouth, and he saw a rotted molar. He sat down with her and with gestures tried to explain that it would be painful at first if he removed the tooth, but that it would soon be better. The woman seemed to understand. Gant took up a fresh branch and scraped a rounded point on one end. He picked up a rock twice the size of his fist, and placed the woman in a sitting position with her head resting on his thigh. He placed the end of the stick low on the gum to make sure he got the root. Carefully he raised the rock, knowing he would have but one try. He smashed the rock down and felt the tooth give way and saw the blood spout from her mouth. She screamed and leaped to her feet and turned on Gant, but he jumped away. Then something struck him from behind and he found himself pinned to the ground with two men sitting on him. They growled at him and one picked up a rock and the stick and smashed a front tooth from Gant's mouth. Then they threw him out of the cave. He rolled down through the gravel and came up short against a bush. He leaped to his feet and charged back into the cave. One of the men swung a club at him, but he ducked and slammed the rock against the side of the man's head. The other ran. Gant went over to the woman, picking as he went a half-handful of moss from the wall of the cave. He stood in front of her and packed some of the moss in the wound in his front jaw, and leaned over to show her the bleeding had stopped. He held out the moss to her, and she quickly took some and put it in the proper place in her jaw. She nodded to him and patted his arm and rubbed the blood out of the hair on her chin. He left the cave, without looking at the unconscious man.

Some day they would kill him. His jaw throbbed as he walked along the gravel shelf and headed for home. There would be no more stops today, and so he threaded his way along the foot of the cliff. He heard sounds of activity in several of the caves, and in one of the largest of them he heard excited voices yelling. He stopped, but his jaw hurt too much to go in. The noise increased and Gant thought they might be carving up a large kill. He was always on the lookout for meat, so he changed his mind and went in. Inside was a boy about the age of Dun, lying on his back, gasping for air. His face had a bluish tinge, and at each intake of air his muscles tensed and his back arched with the effort to breathe. Gant pushed to his side and forced his mouth open. The throat and uvula were greatly swollen, the air passage almost shut. He quickly examined the boy, but there was no sign of injury or disease. Gant was puzzled, but then he concluded the boy must have chewed or eaten a substance to which he was sensitive. He looked at the throat again. The swelling was continuing. The boy's jutting jaws made mouth-to-mouth resuscitation impossible. A tracheotomy was indicated. He went over to the fire and smashed one piece of flint chopping stone on another, and quickly picked over the pieces. He chose a short, sharp fragment and stooped over the boy. He touched the point of the fragment against the skin just beneath the larynx, squeezed his thumb and forefinger on the fragment to measure a distance a little over half an inch from the point, and then thrust down and into the boy's throat until his thumb and forefinger just touched the skin. Behind him he heard a struggle, and he looked up in time to see several people restrain a woman with an axe. He watched to see that they kept her out of the cave and away from him before he turned back to the boy. By gently turning the piece of flint he made an opening in the windpipe. He turned the boy on his side to prevent the tiny trickle of blood from running into the opening. The result was dramatic. The boy's struggles stopped, and the rush of air around the piece of flint sounded loud in the still of the cave. The boy lay back and relaxed and breathed deeply, and even the people in the cave could tell he was now much better. They gathered around and watched silently, and Gant could see the interest in their faces. The boy's mother had not come back.

For half an hour Gant sat holding the flint in the necessary position. The boy stirred restlessly a time or two, but Gant quieted him. The people drifted back to their activities in the cave, and Gant sat and tended his patient. He leaned over the boy. He could hear the air beginning to pass through his throat once again. In another fifteen minutes the boy's throat was open enough, and Gant withdrew the flint in one swift movement. The boy began to sit up, but Gant held him down and pressed the wound closed. It stayed closed, and Gant got up. No one paid any attention when he left.

He went along the gravel shelf, ignoring the sounds of life that came out of the caves as he went by. He rounded a boulder and saw his own cave ahead.

The log barrier was displaced and he could hear snarls and grunts as he ran into the semidarkness inside. Two bodies writhed on the floor of the cave. He ran closer and saw that his wife and another woman were struggling there, raking each other's skin with thick, sharp nails, groping for each other's jugular vein with long, yellow teeth. Gant drove his heel into the side of the woman's body, just above the kidney. The air exploded from her lungs and she went limp. He twisted a hand in her hair and yanked her limp body away from his wife's teeth and ran for the entrance of the cave dragging her after him. Outside, he threw the limp body down the slope. He turned and caught his wife as she came charging out. She fought him, trying to get to the woman down the slope, and it was only because she was no longer trying to kill that he was able to force her back into the cave.

Inside, she quickly stopped fighting him. She went and knelt over something lying at the foot of his bed. He rubbed his sore jaw and went over to see what it was. He stared down in the dim light of the cave. It was Dun, and he was dead. His head had been crushed. Gant cried out and leaned against the wall. He knelt and hugged Dun's warm body to him, pushing his wife aside. He pressed his face into the boy's neck and thought of the years that he had planned to spend in teaching Dun the healing arts. He felt a heavy pat on his shoulder and looked up. His wife was there, awkwardly patting him on the shoulder, trying to comfort him. Then he remembered the woman who had killed his son.

He ran out of the cave and looked down the slope. She was not there, but he caught a flash of movement down the gravel shelf and he could see her staggering toward her cave. He began to run after her, but stopped. His anger was gone, and he felt no emotion save a terrible emptiness. He turned and went back into the cave for Dun's body. In the forest he slowly dug a deep hole. He felt numb as he dug, but when it was done and he had rolled a large stone on top of the grave, he kneeled down near it, held his face in his hands and cried. Afterward, he followed the stream bed to a flat table of solid rock. At the edge of the rock table, where the wall of rock began to rise to the cliffs above, half hidden in the shrub pine, was a mass of twisted metal wreckage. He looked down on it and thought again of that day ten years ago. Here, on the site of Pennsylvania State University, at College Park, Pennsylvania, was where he started and where he ended. But a difference of half a million years lay between the start and the end.

Once tears had come to his eyes when he looked at the wreckage, but no longer. There was work to do here and he was the only one who could do it. He nodded and turned to climb to his cave. There were cold meat and shoots there, and a wife, and perhaps there could be another son. And this day, for the first time, an injured man had come to see him.

THE LINK
Cleve Cartmill

The nineteenth century saw the discovery of hundreds of sites of prehistoric human occupation all over Europe. The bones, the tools, the carvings, even the mural paintings of ancient mankind came to light from France and England to Russia. It became apparent that over the past hundred thousand years two human species of markedly different physical form had occupied Europe simultaneously. One, known as the Neanderthal folk after the German valley of Neander where their fossil bones first were found, had sloping foreheads, massive brow ridges, thick bones, weak chins. The other, generally known as the Cro-Magnon people after the first discovery site in France, were tall, slender people rather like ourselves in general physical appearance. It was easy to leap to the conclusion that the stocky, shuffling, brutish-looking Neanderthals were an early and obsolete form of humanity who eventually evolved into those graceful and elegant people who were our own ancestors.

More recent research has destroyed this simple notion. It now seems fairly certain that the Neanderthals and the Cro-Magnons represent two independent lines of human evolution, descended from some common ancestor of perhaps half a million years ago. In separate ways they developed almost side by side, and it is wrong to think of the Neanderthals as more primitive, more apelike, more brutish. Indeed, the special bodily traits of the Neanderthals may have made them more fit than the others to endure the punishing climate of Europe in the glacial periods of the past hundred thousand years. Nor were the physical differences between the two human stocks apparently as extreme as they seemed to the first students of the fossil record, though they were considerable enough to warrant drawing the distinction between them. What is certain is that as the last ice age began to end, some 25,000 years ago, the Neanderthal stock disappeared. Conquered by the Cro-Magnon type, or simply absorbed by marriage into the other gene pool? We may never know; the vanishing of the Neanderthals is one of the great anthropological mysteries.

Although we know that most of the conventional notions about the relationship between these two prehistoric human peoples are faulty, the myth of the struggle between them remains a vital and vigorous part of fiction. Here the late Cleve Cartmill, a journalist from southern California who was a well-known science-fiction writer a generation ago, gives us, in a story written in 1942, a look at the classic theme of the first of the modern type of human being emerging into a world of Neanderthals.

LOK KNEW THAT HE WAS DIFFERENT from his brothers after the incident with the big black and yellow cat.

It stood in the trail and looked at him. True, it drew back its lips, exposing long, yellow tusks, but it did not growl insults, it did not attack.

After a time, the cat said, "I could eat you."

Lok returned the steady, yellow gaze.

The cat asked, "Why don't you run into the trees like the others? What are you doing here?

"I am seeing pictures," Lok replied.

The cat arched its back and snarled with suspicion. "What is that?"

"Why . . . why," Lok faltered, "things."

The cat edged back a pace.

"Things," Lok continued. "My brothers have tried to kill me. I am alone. I am going . . . going—" He broke off, puzzled, and stared with vacant, dark eyes at the cat.

"You have no hair," the cat said, moving forward again.

"I have, I have!" Lok cried desperately, and shook long, black locks over his face. "Look!"

"That!" the cat sneered. "It is not like the others."

The others. Lok sensed a power within himself when he thought of the others, a power that did not quite come into focus. It swelled up into his chest, however, and he straightened so that his knuckles were not on the ground.

"I am Lok," he said with dignity. "Therefore, step aside. I would pass."

He marched deliberately toward the cat. It crouched back on its haunches, spitting between fangs, but it gave way. Its eyes were wide and yellow, no longer instruments of sight now that it was suddenly afraid. Roaring incoherent blasphemies, it backed down the narrow path as Lok advanced. With one last cry of rage, it leaped into the wall of vines to one side, and Lok passed on, his low and leathery brow creased in thought.

He forgot the cat on the instant, but this new power held him erect as he moved away from the country of his tribe.

His inner perception strove to grasp what had happened to him, and, as he marched along the trail, he sifted the symphony of the jungle with subconscious attention. He noted the quiet wrought by the roars of the curve-toothed jungle king. He felt the sleepy rhythm of the hot afternoon begin to flow again; somewhere a red and green bird shouted harsh and senseless cries; succulent beetles buzzed stupidly in trees; off to the right a troupe of his little brown cousins swung by fingers and tails and chattered of drinking nuts; moving toward him on the trail swelled grunts of the white tusks.

This latter sound snapped him back to a realization of danger. He wanted no quarrel with a tribe of these quick, dark prima donnas, with their tiny, sharp hoofs and short, slashing tusks. Even the jungle king himself would tackle no more than one at a time. Lok broke through the green trail wall and went hand over hand up a thick vine, to wait for the white tusks to pass.

They trotted into sight, twenty yards away, four full-grown males and three females. The leader, an old boar, with tiny, red eyes, grunted tactical instructions in case of attack at the next trail curve.

Lok felt an ancient fury, and from the safety of a high limb he jumped up and down and screamed imprecations at the bristled band.

"Cowards!" he yelled, flinging handfuls of twigs and leaves at them. "Weaklings! Fish food! If you come up here, I will fight you all!"

At his first cry, the males had wheeled and stood shoulder to shoulder facing his tree, looking up at him with steady, gleaming eyes. The females huddled behind this ivory-pointed rampart, waiting without sound or motion.

The old leader grunted his contempt for Lok and his race.

"Come down," he invited. "Fool!"

Lok ceased his age-old antics, and regarded his actions with a dull sense of wonder. True, he had always done this; it was a part of life to insult other inhabitants of his world from a place of safety. He had done this with his brothers, and with his mother while he was still small enough to sit in her hand.

Yet this new part of himself which controlled his new sense of power sneered at such conduct. Lok felt at first like hanging his head; then he felt the need to assert himself.

He climbed down the vine, without fear. He marched toward the white tusks who now held their armored muzzles low to the ground in attack position.

"Wait!" the leader grunted to his companions. "This one has a strange smell."

Advancing steadily, Lok said, "Step aside, I would pass. I am Lok. I am master."

When he was within three paces, the white tusks acted.

"Go!" grunted the leader to the huddled females. "Remember his smell!"

The leader and the three younger boars backed away as Lok advanced. When they had retreated twenty paces in this fashion, they broke and wheeled at a signal from the old one, and pattered after the vanished females.

Lok stood motionless for some time, gazing vacantly but

steadily at the bend of trail around which the white tusks had fled. Beside the last image of their curling tails and bobbing hindquarters now formed the picture of the furious, but frightened, cat.

For the first time in his twelve years of life, Lok used past experience to form a theory. It was vague and confused, but he felt that he could re-enter the tribe and rule in place of the Old One. He was Lok. He was master.

He departed from the trail and climbed to a remembered treetop pathway which would lead him to his tribe. As he leaped and swung from swaying limb to limb a troublesome feeling grew within his head. He felt that a matter of importance should be considered, but its form and shape escaped his powers of concentration.

His passage did not disturb the life of the sultry green forest. Gaudy birds flitted through the gloom, and hunting beasts made fleeting shadows at times below him. The sun dropped, stars flared overhead, and Lok found a sleeping crotch for the night.

Sleep evaded him. Not because of night cries of questioning white owls, or of brief threshings in the nearby pool of a gurgling stream, or of directionless roars of the big cats. He was accustomed to this pattern of sound.

The disturbance was deep within himself, a troubling problem knocking at the door of memory. It was a new sensation, this groping backward. Heretofore he had been satisfied if there was fruit, if rotten logs yielded fat, white grubs. He had been content when fed and sheltered.

Consideration of shelter brought the problem nearer to recognition and, as he concentrated, it burst into form. The problem was one of the passage of seasons. Since he had left the tribe, followed by foaming threats of his brothers and the Old One, the rains had come twice. His lack of a protective furry coat had driven him into caves, where he had shivered through the long, damp months.

Well did he know now what had made him uneasy. The tribe might not know him, after this long space of separation.

An event took place, and during the time it affected them they considered it. Once it was over, it was as though it had never existed. Thus it had been for him, too, until now.

Lok's head began to ache, but he clung stubbornly to the pictures that formed in his thoughts. He saw himself forced to subdue the strongest of the tribe before he could take his rightful place at their head.

He was Lok. He was master. But he was not as strong as some, and in a fight where strength alone would determine the outcome he might be subdued and killed.

Restless, wide awake, he shook his head angrily and climbed to the highest level in search of a place where he might sleep. He moved from one tree to another, grumbling to himself. He crossed the stream near the drinking pool which gleamed in full brilliance under the shining eye of night.

He was instantly thirsty, and dropped lower. As he did so, his watchful eyes caught movement at one edge of the pool, and the arm of a ripple moved lazily across the bright surface. A long snout lurked there. Though he was large and unafraid, Lok wished to avoid a brush with those long, fanged jaws or the flashing armored tail. He half turned to go upstream to a place of safety, but was arrested by a sound on the trail. He caught the delicate scent of a spotted jumper, and presently saw a trio, mother and two small twins, advancing to the pool in dainty leaps. The mother's long, leaf-shaped ears were rigid, twitching toward every rustle in the night. She held her shapely head high, testing the air with suspicious nostrils, and the end of every pace found her poised for instant flight. The little ones, crowding her heels, duplicated her every motion.

Lok eyed the tableau with excitement, knowing what was coming. He could see the faint outline of the long snout motionless in the shallows near the path. A meal was in preparation.

The mother led her twins to the edge of the pool and stood watch while they dipped trusting muzzles in the water.

Lok saw blurred motion as the long snout's tail whipped one of the little twins into the pool and powerful jaws dragged it under. With a cry of terror the mother and the remaining twin flashed into the darkness, the sound of their racing hoofs smothered by the threshing in the pool.

The turbulent surface darkened, and Lok cried out once from suppressed emotion. Presently he returned to his sleeping crotch, his thirst forgotten in consideration of what he had seen.

The long snout, Lok knew, was no match for spotted jumpers on land. Although the long snout could move for a short distance with great speed, the spotted jumper could simply vanish while one looked at it. Yet the long snout had caught, killed and eaten one of the small spotted jumpers.

Another factor, in addition to simple speed or strength, had made this possible, and Lok beat against his head with a closed hand trying to call it to mind. The long snout had waited like one of the big cats above a trail—

Lok felt the solution begin to form and fixed wide, empty eyes to the dark while he made pictures inside his head.

He had seen a cat crouched on a limb in an all-day vigil, waiting without motion until its chosen prey trotted along the trail below. Then a flashing arc, a slashing blow, and the cat had slain an inhabitant sometimes more than twice its own size and speed.

He had seen also a fear striker, many times as long as Lok was tall, coiled in hunger beside a trail for a whole day or night until the proper-sized victim passed. Then a flashing strike, whipping coils, a crushing of bones, and the fear striker held the limp body of one he could not possibly have caught by speed alone.

Yet the lying-in-wait alone was not the answer to the problem of his conquering the tribe, Lok felt. It was not his way to crouch near a rotten log until the Old One, for example, came to tear it apart for grubs and then fling himself on the hungry one. No, not that, but still the essence of what he sought was there.

Each denizen of the world in his own fashion delivered a death blow to his prey. With the long snout's tail—

Lok cried out in the night as he found the answer. "I am master!" he shouted. "I am Lok!"

Ignoring the sleepy protest of a bird in the neighboring tree, he slipped to the ground and coursed through the brush seeking his weapon, a short, stout limb.

When he found it, he stood in the darkness swinging it in vicious arcs, filled with an inner excitement. Pictures formed again in his mind.

When two males of his tribe fought, they shouted preliminary insults until rage was at a sufficient pitch for loose-armed, bare-fanged combat. How devastating, Lok thought, to step in during the insult stage and surprise his opponent with a death blow.

As soon as vivid dawn brought raucous, screaming wakefulness to the jungle, Lok continued toward the land of his tribe. He found sustained travel in the trees impossible while hampered with his weapon, and dropped to the jungle floor, slashing vines aside with the club when the going was thick.

Once he climbed a tree for long fruit to satisfy his hunger, and once he drank from a stream, searching somewhat eagerly for a long snout on whom he might try his new weapon.

He came at midday to the edge of a wide, treeless plain covered with waist-high yellow grass. Lok hesitated to cross it on foot, for out there, lurking near the herds of the striped feeders, one sometimes saw big heads.

These were yellow, catlike killers, more powerful than the jungle cats, more feared than any. They were not only powerful, they were vile and ruthless when in bad temper.

Yet if he did not cross the plain he would be forced into the trees for a long circuit and must abandon his weapon.

That decided him. He was fond of this heavy, knobbed length of wood. It seemed to give him an additional arm, and it doubled his courage. He set out through the yellow grass, circling a grazing tribe of striped feeders in the hope that he might pass unchallenged.

Presently he struck a path wriggling in his general direction, and it was on this path, in the center of the plain where there was no shelter, that he met a huge, golden-eyed big head.

It came upon him face to face, trotting as noiselessly as Lok, a heavy-maned, full-grown male. The two froze in their tracks, and the big head gave a roar of surprise. Lok drew back his weapon, holding it near one end with both hands.

"I will kill you," Lok said, a slight quaver in his voice, "if you do not go away."

"What?" the big head roared in disbelief.

Lok repeated his threat in a more steady voice.

The big head crouched, swishing his tufted tail.

"You have a strange smell," he said.

Lok detected a note of uneasiness and his courage rose to reckless heights.

"You are a coward!" he cried, and jumped up and down on the sun-baked trail. "Weakling! Fish food!"

The big head hesitated a second. Then with a roar of unintelligible rage he launched himself at Lok, jaws wide and red, claws unsheathed.

Lok darted to one side and swung his club. All his strength was in the blow which caught the big head in his yellow ribs while in mid-air. The tawny beast twisted, was deflected out of the path and fell heavily in the dry grass. He was on his feet instantly and in the air again, coming at Lok almost faster than his eye could follow.

Lok felt a hopeless surprise when his blow did not kill the big head, and confidence in his weapon deflated. But he swung again, and the club thudded home on the big head's neck. The powerful body jerked again in the air and sprawled away from the path.

The big head was not so quick in resuming attack. He crouched in the grass which his fall had flattened, and roared gibberish at Lok, who held his club at the ready.

A little of Lok's confidence returned as he looked steadily into the blazing eyes, which had taken on tinge of reddish green. Yet he was afraid, for he well knew the power of those fanged, dripping jaws, and the death in each front paw.

Entirely aside from his thoughts of self-preservation, Lok was exhilarated by the scene: the sleek tan body rippling with taut muscles, the wide grassy theater of action, and the excited yaps of an approaching troupe of dead eaters gathering at a distance to dispose of the loser.

Flecks of dark sweat spotted the smooth body of the big head, and Lok felt his own body growing moist and then cool as a light breeze brushed past.

Without warning, the big head leaped a third time. Lok, caught slightly unaware, swung his club without definite aim and without the full power which he had put into his previous blows. He caught the cat just below one ear.

As the blow struck, Lok had the impression of a drinking nut being broken by striking it against a stone. It was a satisfying sensation as it ran up the club into his arms, but he attached no importance to it until he saw its result.

For the big head twisted again in the air and tumbled into the grass, dead with a crushed skull, lips skinned back from long, yellow fangs. Lok stood well away from the still body for a few moments, eyeing it with a dull sense of wonder.

His other blows had been mightier than this which terminated the battle, yet they had wrought no apparent damage. After a short time, he prodded the motionless body from a distance with his club.

"Coward!" he snarled softly. "Arise!"

When further abuse brought no reaction, Lok shouldered his club and went on his way, and the slinking dead eaters swarmed upon the corpse behind him.

He examined the plain in all directions for evidence of other big heads but saw nothing except the upraised heads and pointed ears of a herd of striped feeders who had heard the roars of battle. Lok continued cautiously toward the far jungle wall, thinking of the strange effect of a light blow on the head as compared to a heavy blow on the body of the big head. He felt no sense of accomplishment, although he was perhaps the first of his tribe to vanquish their most feared enemy. He was puzzled.

He soon dismissed the matter, however, for the more pressing problem of locating the tribe. When he reached his home country, a land of fruit and grubs near the foothills of a tall mountain range, he roamed in a wide circle. As he searched, an uneasiness grew within him, a sense of need for action.

Something was wrong, something completely dissociated from his finding the tribe. Other denizens of the forest felt it, too: birds reflected it in sharp, nervous cries, and the jungle reverberated now and then with baffled roars of big cats.

On the second night, while Lok was drowsing in the crotch of a thick, white tree, a distant growing murmur brought him awake. The murmur grew in volume to a sullen rushing roar as a wall of wind moved through the night.

On all sides was the crash of falling trees: first an ear-splitting crack as wind-strain shattered the trunk, a groaning *sw-i-i-sh* and finally an earth-shaking *boom!*

Lok shivered with discomfort in the sleeping crotch. He understood his uneasiness of the past two days—the rainy season was about to begin. Although he was fairly safe in this stout tree, he longed for the dry protection of the cave he now remembered.

A far-off mutter of rain deepended as it rushed across the treetops with the sound of a great herd of stampeded striped feeders. Lok felt a certain terror, which increased as brilliant twisting tongues lashed out of a roaring sky.

He shrank close to the tree, which now leaned at a steady angle from the push of the wind, and grew wetter and more uncomfortable as the night wore on. During the lull when the quiet center of the storm moved past, he shivered in dread of the wind which would now blow, even more fiercely, perhaps in the opposite direction.

When a leaden but dry dawn broke, Lok resumed his

search for the tribe, torn between the desire for leadership and the desire for shelter.

Fallen trees were everywhere, and though the rotten cores of many housed fat grubs, Lok took to the forest roof, where his passage was unhindered by wet, tangled vines or a myriad of tiny, poisonous many legs and whip tails that scurried about.

The sun came out later in the morning, and Lok found the tribe near midday in a steaming clearing.

Perhaps fifty in number, from huge gray-tufted males to babies clinging to their mothers, they eyed Lok with sullen suspicion as he dropped from a tree and advanced to the center of the clearing, swinging his club in one hand.

"I am Lok," he said. "I have returned to rule the tribe."

The females scuttled behind the males, who formed a wide half circle of beetle-browed suspicion.

"This hairless one has a sickening smell," one said.

"Kill him!" cried another.

Lok moved a pace nearer. "Wait!" he commanded.

They were quiet.

"I have slain a big head," Lok said, swinging the club. "I am master."

The Old One stepped out of the half circle and advanced to within ten paces.

"Fish food!" the Old One yelled. "Coward! Go before I tear out your throat!"

He bounced up and down, as was the custom of fighters, on his squat legs, and made his face as frightening as possible with wide, slavering jaws. Behind him the others emulated his example, howling and hurling threats. The clearing was in instant bedlam as the females augmented the cries and their babies clung to them in loud terror.

Into the midst of the insult and confusion, Lok stepped forward and swung his club.

Its sharp crack against the skull of the Old One cut all sound. The Old One brushed at his head with a hand as though driving away an annoying insect, and then fell like a shattered tree, his jaws and eyes still wide with anger.

Into the silence, Lok said, ''I have slain the Old One. I am master.''

They had not yet grasped the event and were quiet, save for the babies who whimpered softly.

''I have gone,'' Lok continued, gesturing, ''far out there. There is a dry place safe from the rain and wind. It is good. I will lead you. There is food.''

They stared at him with dull, uncomprehending eyes. For a long time there was no sound except for the babies and the far-off cries of birds while Lok stood in the center of the clearing with the dead Old One at his feet. Then one of the young males spoke.

''He has a smell I hate, this hairless scum.''

The hate filled them instantly, and the entire tribe once more shrieked insults and threats of death. Some of the more foolhardy males rushed forward a few steps, and Lok's club slashed out the second life.

This brought another moment of quiet, and a big, gray female moved out of the ruck.

''Go!'' she growled from foam-flecked jaws. ''I, myself, will kill you!''

''Mother!'' Lok cried. ''I am Lok!''

''Mother?'' she snarled. ''Pink filth!''

''Kill him!'' bawled half a dozen throats, and the males closed in.

Confusion and lust for death filled the air again as Lok backed away, swinging his club on the hairy beasts that crowded him with foaming mouths and screaming lungs. Each swing took its toll, and Lok remembered the lesson he had learned on the grassy plain. He struck each blow at a head, and the crushing skulls brought a tingling excitement into his arms and a wild exhilaration to his brain.

One of the larger males caught Lok by an arm and, as he bent to sink teeth home in the wrist, Lok took careful aim and shattered his head like a ripe fruit. The sound of its cracking cut sharply into the incoherent roars of the attackers.

''I am master!'' Lok screamed, thinking of the split skulls. ''I am Lok!''

And he swung again, and again.

When he was near the jungle edge, Lok's arms were tiring. The last three males he hit rose shakily to elbows and knees. Lok turned and fled. There were too many.

None followed. They returned to the still forms which marked the trail of battle, and Lok watched them try to shake life back into the dead for a time. Presently they tired of this, and the largest male called them into the forest. They trooped away, chattering lightly of drinking nuts, leaving the wounded to follow as best they might.

Lok's brooding eyes followed until they were hidden from sight and the sound of their chatter had faded. He looked at his club, spattered with blood, and at the dozen dead which littered the clearing floor. A greater sense of power and superiority than he had felt before now flooded his being, but this was also tempered with a feeling of desolation.

For he was alone again. He who had returned to his own was driven forth once more.

When the first dead eater slunk cautiously into the clearing, Lok turned to go.

He had gone but a short distance from the clearing toward the far country of the caves when he heard a moaning off to one side.

He sprang aloft and sat quietly for time, listening. The moans were repeated, and Lok moved nearer.

A female of his tribe was pinned lightly under a tree. Lok dropped to the ground and approached. She was unconscious, but after he had prodded her a few times with his club she opened her eyes and cried out with terror.

"I am Lok," he said.

She groaned again and tried to push the tree off her body.

Lok squatted on his haunches to watch. She strained at the tree in an agony of effort, trying to free her legs, but it was beyond her strength. Presently Lok tired of watching and turned away.

"Help me!" she cried again in the words and voice of a baby to its mother.

Lok stood over her again and poked her with his club, shaking his head in bewilderment. She looked up at him with wide, dark, pain-ridden eyes which took in his smooth, hairless body.

"I am hurt," she whimpered.

Lok crouched again as she renewed her efforts to push away the tree. His brows wrinkled in concentration as he tried to focus his thought. He poked his club at her.

"You are alone, too," he said.

She grasped the club with both hands and pulled. Lok, in surprise, turned it loose, and she cried out in anger and pain.

The picture of her desire burst into his mind and he leaped to his feet, dancing with excitement.

"I am Lok," he chattered. "I slew the Old One."

He grasped his end of the club, leaned back on his heels and tugged. She clung to it desperately, and presently she slid out from under the tree.

Lok stood over her as she rolled and kicked her skinned legs, crying aloud in anguish. Now and then he poked her experimentally. Presently she tried to rise.

Lok sat on his heels and looked at her for a long time. She returned his gaze steadily.

"I am Lok," he said finally. "I am master."

"Yes," she answered. "Yes."

Without understanding the deep calm which had taken possession of him, Lok slung her over his shoulder and began the long journey to the place of caves. As he trotted along the twisting trail, he swung his club now and then against a thick vine, feeling keen satisfaction at the sharp crack of the blows.

"I have killed a big head," he said proudly to the female, who clung to him tenderly. "I have killed a big head and"— he hesitated, searching his brain for a term to describe the dead he had strewn over the clearing— "and other animals," he concluded.

THE DAY IS DONE

Lester del Rey

The other great theme of Neanderthal vs. Cro-Magnon is the close of the story—the new people triumphant, the ancient Neanderthals routed and on their way to extinction. It has rarely been handled better than in this poignant 1939 story by the veteran writer and editor Lester del Rey.

HWOOGH SCRATCHED the hair on his stomach and watched the sun climb up over the hill. He beat listlessly on his chest and yelled at it timidly, then grumbled and stopped. In his youth, he had roared and stumped around to help the god up, but now it wasn't worth the effort. Nothing was. He found a fine flake of sweaty salt under his hair, licked it off his fingers, and turned over to sleep again.

But sleep wouldn't come. On the other side of the hill there was a hue and cry, and somebody was beating a drum in a throbbing chant. The old Neanderthaler grunted and held his hands over his ears, but the Sun-Warmer's chant couldn't be silenced. More ideas of the Talkers.

In his day, it had been a lovely world, full of hairy grumbling people; people a man could understand. There had been game on all sides, and the caves about had been filled with the smoke of cooking fires. He had played with the few young that were born—though each year fewer children had come into the tribe—and had grown to young manhood with the pride of achievement. But that was before the Talkers had made this valley one of their hunting grounds.

Old tradition, half told, half understood, spoke of the land in the days of old, when only his people roamed over the broad tundra. They had filled the caves and gone out in packs too large for any animal to withstand. And the animals swarmed into the land, driven south by the Fourth Glaciation. Then the great cold had come again, and times had been hard. Many of his people had died.

But many had lived, and with the coming of the warmer, drier climate again, they had begun to expand before the Talkers arrived. After that—Hwoogh stirred uneasily—for no good reason he could see, the Talkers took more and more of the land, and his people retreated and diminished before them. Hwoogh's father had made it understood that their little band in the valley were all that were left, and that this was the only place on the great flat earth where Talkers seldom came.

Hwoogh had been twenty when he first saw them, great long-legged men, swift of foot and eye, stalking along as if they owned the earth, with their incessant mouth noises. In the summer that year, they pitched their skin-and-wattle tents at the back of the hill, away from the caves, and made magic to their gods. There was magic on their weapons, and the beasts fell their prey. Hwoogh's people had settled back, watching fearfully, hating numbly, finally resorting to begging and stealing. Once a young buck had killed the child of a Talker, and been flayed and sent out to die for it. Thereafter, there had been a truce between Cro-Magnon and Neanderthaler.

Now the last of Hwoogh's people were gone, save only himself, leaving no children. Seven years it had been since Hwoogh's brother had curled up in the cave and sent his breath forth on the long journey to his ancestors. He had always been dispirited and weak of will, but he had been the only friend left to Hwoogh.

The old man tossed about and wished that Keyoda would return. Maybe she would bring food from the Talkers. There was no use hunting now, when the Talkers had already been up and killed all the easy game. Better that a man should sleep all the time, for sleep was the only satisfying thing left in the topsy-turvy world; even the drink the tall Cro-Magnons made from mashed roots left a headache the next day.

He twisted and turned in his bed of leaves at the edge of the cave, grunting surlily. A fly buzzed over his head provocatively, and he lunged at it. Surprise lighted his features as his fingers closed on the insect, and he swallowed it with a momentary flash of pleasure. It wasn't as good as the grubs in the forest, but it made a tasty appetizer.

The sleep god had left, and no amount of lying still and snoring would lure him back. Hwoogh gave up and squatted down on his huanches. He had been meaning to make a new head for his crude spear for weeks, and he rummaged around in the cave for materials. But the idea grew farther away the closer he approached work, and he let his eyes roam idly over the little creek below him and the fleecy clouds in the sky. It was a warm spring, and the sun made idleness pleasant.

The sun god was growing stronger again, chasing the old fog and mist away. For years, he had worshiped the sun god as his, and now it seemed to grow strong again only for the Talkers. While the god was weak, Hwoogh's people had been mighty; now that its long sickness was over, the Cro-Magnons spread out over the country like the fleas on his belly.

Hwoogh could not understand it. Perhaps the god was mad at him, since gods are utterly unpredictable. He grunted, wishing again for his brother, who had understood such things better.

Keyoda crept around the boulder in front of the cave, interrupting his brooding. She brought scraps of food from the tent village and the half-chewed leg of a horse, which Hwoogh seized on and ripped at with his strong teeth. Evidently the Talkers had made a big kill the day before, for they were lavish with their gifts. He grunted at Keyoda, who sat under the cave entrance in the sun, rubbing her back.

Keyoda was as hideous as most of the Talkers were to Hwoogh, with her long dangling legs and short arms, and the ungainly straightness of her carriage. Hwoogh remembered the young girls of his own day with a sigh; they had been beautiful, short and squat, with forward-jutting necks and nice low foreheads. How the flat-faced Cro-Magnon women could get mates had been a puzzle to Hwoogh, but they seemed to succeed.

Keyoda had failed, however, and in her he felt justified in his judgment. There were times when he felt almost in sympathy with her, and in his own way he was fond of her. As a child, she had been injured, her back made useless for the work of a mate. Kicked around by the others of her tribe, she had gradually drifted away from them, and when she stumbled on Hwoogh, his hospitality had been welcome to her. The Talkers were nomads who followed the herds north in the summer, south in the winter, coming and going with the seasons, but Keyoda stayed with Hwoogh in his cave and did the few desultory tasks that were necessary. Even such a half-man as the Neanderthaler was preferable to the scornful pity of her own people, and Hwoogh was not unkind.

"Hwunkh?" asked Hwoogh. With his stomach partly filled, he felt more kindly toward the world.

"Oh, they come out and let me pick up their scraps—me, who was once a chief's daughter!—same as they always do." Her voice had been shrewish, but the weariness of failure and age had taken the edge from it. " 'Poor, poor Keyoda,' thinks they, 'let her have what she wants, just so it don't mean nothin' we like.' Here." She handed him a roughly made spear, flaked on both sides of the point, but with only a rudimentary barb, unevenly made. "One of 'em give me this—it ain't the like of what they'd use, I guess, but it's good as you could make. One of the kids is practicing."

Hwoogh examined it; good, he admitted, very good, and the point was fixed nicely in the shaft. Even the boys, with their long limber thumbs that could twist any which way, made better weapons than he; yet once he had been famous among his small tribe for the nicety of his flint work.

Making a horse gesture, he got slowly to his feet. The shape of his jaw and the attachment of his tongue, together with a poorly developed left frontal lobe of his brain, made speech rudimentary, and he supplemented his glottals and labials with motions that Keyoda understood well enough. She shrugged and waved him out, gnawing on one of the bones.

Hwoogh wandered about without much spirit, conscious that he was growing old. And vaguely, he knew that age should not have fallen upon him for many snows; it was not the number of seasons, but something else, something that he could feel but not understand. He struck out for the hunting fields, hoping that he might find some game for himself that would require little effort to kill. The scornful gifts of the Talkers had become bitter in his mouth.

But the sun god climbed up to the top of the blue cave without Hwoogh's stumbling on anything. He swung about to return, and ran into a party of Cro-Magnons returning with the carcass of a reindeer strapped to a pole on their shoulders. They stopped to yell at him.

"No use, Hairy One!" they boasted, their voices light and gay. "We caught all the game this way. Turn back to your cave and sleep."

Hwoogh dropped his shoulders and veered away, his spear dragging limply on the ground. One of the party trotted over to him lightly. Sometimes Legoda, the tribal magic man and artist, seemed almost friendly, and this was one of the times.

"It was my kill, Hairy One," he said tolerantly. "Last night I drew strong reindeer magic, and the beast fell with my first throw. Come to my tent and I'll save a leg for you. Keyoda taught me a new song that she got from her father, and I would repay her."

Legs, ribs, bones! Hwoogh was tired of the outer meat. His body demanded the finer food of the entrails and liver. Already his skin was itching with a rash, and he felt that he must have the succulent inner parts to make him well; always, before, that had cured him. He grunted, between appreciation and annoyance, and turned off. Legoda pulled him back.

"Nay, stay, Hairy One. Sometimes you bring good fortune

to me, as when I found the bright ocher for my drawing. There is meat enough in the camp for all. Why hunt today?'' As Hwoogh still hesitated, he grew more insistent, not from kindness, but more from a wish to have his own way. ''The wolves are running near today, and one is not enough against them. We carve the reindeer at the camp as soon as it comes from the poles. I'll give you first choice of the meat!''

Hwoogh grunted a surly acquiescence and waddled after the party. The dole of the Talkers had become gall to him, but liver was liver—if Legoda kept his bargain. They were chanting a rough marching song, trotting easily under the load of the reindeer, and he lumbered along behind, breathing hard at the pace they set.

As they neared the village of the nomads, its rough skin tents and burning fires threw out a pungent odor that irritated Hwoogh's nostrils. The smell of the long-limbed Cro-Magnons was bad enough without the dirty smell of a camp and the stink of their dung-fed fires. He preferred the accustomed moldy stench of his own musty cave.

Youths came swarming out at them, yelling with disgust at being left behind on this easy hunt. Catching sight of the Ne-anderthaler, they set up a howl of glee and charged at him, throwing sticks and rocks and jumping at him with play fury. Hwoogh shivered and crouched over, menacing them with his spear, and giving voice to throaty growls. Legoda laughed.

''In truth, O Hairy Chokanga, your voice should drive them from you. But see, they fear it not. Kuck, you two-legged pests! Out and away! Kuck, I say!'' They leaped back at his voice and dropped behind, still yelling. Hwoogh eyed them warily, but so long as it suited the pleasure of Legoda, he was safe from their pranks.

Legoda was in a good mood, laughing and joking, tossing his quips at the women until his young wife came out and silenced it. She sprang at the reindeer with her flint knife, and the other women joined her.

"Heyo," called Legoda. "First choice goes to Chokanga, the Hairy One. By my word, it is his."

"Oh, fool!" There was scorn in her voice and in the look she gave Hwoogh. "Since when do we feed the beasts of the caves and the fish of the river? Art mad, Legoda. Let him hunt for himself."

Legoda tweaked her back with the point of his spear, grinning. "Aye, I knew thou'dst cry at that. But then, we owe his kind some say—this was his hunting ground when we were but pups, straggling into this far land. What harm to give to an old man?" He swung to Hwoogh and gestured. "See, Chokanga, my word is good. Take what you want, but see that it is not more than your belly and that of Keyoda can hold this night."

Hwoogh darted in and came out with the liver and the fine sweet fat from the entrails. With a shrill cry of rage, Legoda's mate sprang for him, but the magic man pushed her back.

"Nay, he did right! Only a fool would choose the haunch when the heart of the meat was at hand. By the gods of my father, and I expected to eat of that myself! O Hairy One, you steal the meat from my mouth, and I like you for it. Go, before Heya gets free."

Tomorrow, Hwoogh knew, Legoda might set the brats on him for this day's act, but tomorrow was in another cave of the sun. He drew his legs under him and scuttled off to the left and around the hill, while the shrill yells of Heya and the lazy good humor of Legoda followed. A piece of liver dangled loose, and Hwoogh sucked on it as he went. Keyoda would be pleased, since she usually had to do the begging for both of them.

And a little of Hwoogh's self-respect returned. Hadn't he outsmarted Legoda and escaped with the choicest meat? And had Keyoda ever done as well when she went to the village of the Talkers? Ayeee, they had a thing yet to learn from the cunning brain of old Hwoogh!

Of course the Talkers were crazy; only fools would act as Legoda had done. But that was none of his business. He patted the liver and fat fondly and grinned with a slight return of good humor. Hwoogh was not one to look a gift horse in the mouth.

The fire had shrunk to a red bed of coals when he reached the cave, and Keyoda was curled up on his bed, snoring loudly, her face flushed. Hwoogh smelled her breath, and his suspicions were confirmed. Somehow, she had drunk of the devil brew of the Talkers, and her sleep was dulled with its stupor. He prodded her with his toe, and she sat up bleary-eyed.

"Oh, so you're back. Ayeee, and with liver and fat! But that never came from your spear throw; you been to the village and stole it. Oh, but you'll catch it!" She grabbed at the meat greedily and stirred up the fire, spitting the liver over it.

Hwoogh explained as best he could, and she got the drift of it. "So? Eh, that Legoda, what a prankster he is, and my own nephew, too." She tore the liver away, half raw, and they fell to eagerly, while she chuckled and cursed by turns. Hwoogh touched her nose and wrinkled his face up.

"Well so what if I did?" Liquor had sharpened her tongue. "That no-good son of the chief come here, after me to be telling him stories. And to make my old tongue free, he brings me the root brew. Ah, what stories I'm telling—and some of 'em true, too!" She gestured toward a crude pot. "I reckon he steals it, but what's that to us? Help yourself, Hairy One. It ain't ever' day we're getting the brew."

Hwoogh remembered the headaches of former experiments, but he smelled it curiously and the lure of the magic water caught at him. It was the very essence of youth, the fire that brought life to his legs and memories to his mind. He held it up to his mouth, gasping as the beery liquid ran down his throat. Keyoda caught it before he could finish and drained the last quart.

"Ah, it strengthens my back and puts the blood a-running hot through me again." She swayed on her feet and sputtered out the fragments of an old skin-scraping song. "Now, there you go—can't you never learn not to drink it all to once? That way, it don't last as long, and you're out before you get to feeling good."

Hwoogh staggered as the brew took hold of him, and his knees bent even farther under him. The bed came up in his face, his head was full of bees buzzing merrily, and the cave spun around him. He roared at the cave, while Keyoda laughed.

"Heh! To hear you a-yelling, a body might think you was the only Chokanga left on earth. But you ain't—no, you ain't!"

"Hwunkh?" That struck home. To the best of Hwoogh's knowledge, there were no others of his kind left on earth. He grabbed at her and missed, but she fell and rolled against him, her breath against his face.

"So? Well, it's the truth. The kid up and told me. Legoda found three of 'em, just like you, he says, up the land to the east, three springs ago. You'll have to ask him—I dunno nothing about it." She rolled over against him, grunting half-formed words, and he tried to think of this new information. But the brew was too strong for his head, and he was soon snoring beside her.

Keyoda was gone to the village when he awoke, and the sun was a spear length high on the horizon. He rummaged around for a piece of the liver, but the flavor was not as good as it had been, and his stomach protested lustily at going to work again. He leaned back until his head got control of itself, then swung down to the creek to quench a thirst devil that had seized on him in the night.

But there was something he should do, something he half remembered from last night. Hadn't Keyoda said something about others of his people? Yes, three of them, and Legoda knew. Hwoogh hesitated, remembering that he had bested

Legoda the day before; the young man might resent it today. But he was filled with an overwhelming curiosity, and there was a strange yearning in his heart. Legoda must tell him.

Reluctantly, he went back to the cave and fished around in a hole that was a secret even from Keyoda. He drew out his treasures, fingering them reverently, and selecting the best. There were bright shells and colored pebbles, a roughly drilled necklace that had belonged to his father, a sign of completed manhood, bits of this and that with which he had intended to make himself ornaments. But the quest for knowledge was stronger than the pride of possession; he dumped them out into his fist and struck out for the village.

Keyoda was talking with the women, whining the stock formula that she had developed, and Hwoogh skirted around the camp, looking for the young artist. Finally he spotted the Talker out behind the camp, making odd motions with two sticks. He drew near cautiously, and Legoda heard him coming.

"Come near, Chokanga, and see my new magic." The young man's voice was filled with pride, and there was no threat to it. Hwoogh sighed with relief, but sidled up slowly. "Come nearer, don't fear me. Do you think I'm sorry of the gift I made? Nay, that was my own stupidity. See."

He held out the sticks and Hwoogh fingered them carefully. One was long and springy, tied end to end with a leather thong, and the other was a little spear with a tuft of feather on the blunt end. He grunted a question.

"A magic spear, Hairy One, that flies from the hand with wings, and kills beyond the reach of other spears."

Hwoogh snorted. The spear was too tiny to kill more than rodents, and the big stick had not even a point. But he watched as the young man placed the sharp stick to the tied one, and drew back on it. There was a sharp twang, and the little spear sailed out and away, burying its point in the soft bark of a tree more than two spear throws away. Hwoogh was impressed.

"Aye, Chokanga, a new magic that I learned in the south

last year. There are many there who use it, and with it they can throw the point farther and better than a full-sized spear. One man may kill as much as three!''

Hwoogh grumbled; already they killed all the good game, and yet they must find new magic to increase their power. He held out his hand curiously, and Legoda gave him the long stick and another spear, showing him how it was held. Again there was a twang, and the leather thong struck at his wrist, but the weapon sailed off erratically, missing the tree by yards. Hwoogh handed it back glumly—such magic was not for his kind. His thumbs made the handling of it even more difficult.

Now, while the magic man was pleased with his superiority, was a good time to show the treasure. Hwoogh spread it out on the bare earth and gestured at Legoda, who looked down thoughtfully.

''Yes,'' the Talker conceded. ''Some of it is good, and some would make nice trinkets for the women. What is it you want—more meat, or one of the new weapons? Your belly was filled yesterday; and with my beer, which was stolen, I think, though for that I blame you not. The boy has been punished already. And this weapon is not for you.''

Hwoogh snorted, wriggled and fought for expression, while the young man stared. Little by little, his wants were made known, partly by signs, partly by the questions of the Cro-Magnon. Legoda laughed.

''So, there is a call of the kind in you, Old Man?'' He pushed the treasure back to Hwoogh, except one gleaming bauble. ''I would not cheat you, Chokanga, but this I take for the love I bear you, as a sign of our friendship.'' His grin was mocking as he stuck the valuable in a flap of his clout.

Hwoogh squatted down on his heels, and Legoda sat on a rock as he began. ''There is but little to tell you, Hairy One. Three years ago I did run onto a family of your kind—a male and his mate, with one child. They ran from us, but we were near their cave, and they had to return. We harmed them not, and sometimes gave them food, letting them accompany us on the chase. But they were thin and scrawny, too lazy to hunt. When we returned next year, they were dead, and so far as I know, you are the last of your kind.''

He scratched his head thoughtfully. "Your people die too easily, Chokanga; no sooner do we find them and try to help them than they cease hunting and become beggars. And then they lose interest in life, sicken and die. I think your gods must be killed off by our stronger ones.''

Hwoogh grunted a half assent, and Legoda gathered up his bow and arrows, turning back toward camp. But there was a strange look on the Neanderthaler's face that did not escape the young man's eyes. Recognizing the misery in Hwoogh's expression, he laid a hand on the old man's shoulder and spoke more kindly.

"That is why I would see to your well-being, Hairy One. When you are gone, there will be no more, and my children will laugh at me and say I lie when I spin the tale of your race at the feast fire. Each time that I kill, you shall not lack for food.''

He swung down the single street toward the tent of his family, and Hwoogh turned slowly back toward his cave. The assurance of food should have cheered him, but it only added to his gloom. Dully, he realized that Legoda treated him as a small child, or as one whom the sun god had touched with madness.

Hwoogh heard the cries and laughter of children as he rounded the hill, and for a minute he hesitated before going on. But the sense of property was well developed in him, and he leaped forward grimly. They had no business near his cave.

They were of all ages and sizes, shouting and chasing each other about in a crazy disorder. Having been forbidden to come on Hwoogh's side of the hill, and having broken the rule in a bunch, they were making the most of their revolt. Hwoogh's fire was scattered down the side of the hill into the creek, and they were busily sorting through the small store of his skins and weapons.

Hwoogh let out a savage yell and ran forward, his spear held out in jabbing position. Hearing him, they turned and jumped back from the cave entrance, clustering up into a tight group. "Go on away, Ugly Face," one yelled. "Go scare the wolves! Ugly Face, Ugly Face, waaaah!"

He dashed in among them, brandishing his spear, but they darted back on their nimble legs, slipping easily from in front of him. One of the older boys thrust out a leg and caught him, tripping him down on the rocky ground. Another dashed in madly and caught his spear away, hitting him roughly with it. From the time of the first primate, the innate cruelty of thoughtlessness had changed little in children.

Hwoogh let out a whooping bellow, scrambled up clumsily and was in among them. But they slipped nimbly out of his clutching hands. The little girls were dancing around glee-fully, chanting, "Ugly Face ain't got no mother, Ugly Face ain't got no wife, waaaah on Ugly Face!" Frantically he caught at one of the boys, swung him about savagely, and tossed him on the ground, where the youth lay white and silent. Hwoogh felt a momentary glow of elation at his strength. Then somebody threw a rock.

The old Neanderthaler was tied down crudely when he swam back to consciousness, and three of the boys sat on his chest, beating the ground with their heels in time to a victory chant. There was a dull ache in his head, and bruises were swelling on his arms and chest where they had handled him roughly. He growled savagely, heaving up, and tumbled them off, but the cords were too strong for him. As surely as if grown men had done it, he was captured.

For years they had been his enemies, ever since they had found that Hwoogh-baiting was one of the pleasant occupations that might relieve the tedium of camp life. Now that the old feud was about finished, they went at the business of sub-duing him with method and ingenuity.

While the girls rubbed his face with soft mud from the creek, the boys ransacked the cave and tore at his clothes. The rough bag in which he had put his valuables came away in their hands, and they paused to distribute this new wealth. Hwoogh howled madly.

But a measure of sanity was returning to them, now that the first fury of the fight was over, and Kechaka, the chief's eldest son, stared at Hwoogh doubtfully. "If the elders hear of this," he muttered unhappily, "there will be trouble. They'd not like our bothering Ugly Face."

Another grinned, "Why tell them? He isn't a man, anyway, but an animal; see the hair on his body! Toss old Ugly Face in the river, clean up his cave, and hide these treasures. Who's to know?"

There were half-hearted protests, but the thought of the beating waiting for them added weight to the idea. Kechaka nodded finally and set them to straightening up the mess they had made. With broken branches, they eliminated the marks of their feet, leaving only the trail to the creek.

Hwoogh tossed and pitched in their arms as four of them picked him up; the bindings loosened somewhat, but not enough to free him. With some satisfaction, he noted that the boy he had caught was still retching and moaning, but that was no help to his present position. They waded relentlessly into the water, laid him on it belly down, and gave him a strong push that sent him gliding out through the rushing stream. Foaming and gasping, he fought the current, struggling against his bonds. His lungs ached for air, and the current buffeted him about; blackness was creeping up on his mind.

With a last desperate effort he tore loose the bonds and pushed up madly for the surface, gulping in air greedily. Water was unpleasant to him, but he could swim, and he struck out for the bank. The children were disappearing down the trail and were out of sight as he climbed from the water, bemoaning his lost fire that would have warmed him. He lumbered back to his cave and sank soddenly on the bed.

He, who had been a mighty warrior, bested by a snarling pack of Cro-Magnon brats! He clenched his fists savagely and growled, but there was nothing he could do. Nothing!

The futility of his own effort struck down on him like a burning knife. Hwoogh was an old man, and the tears that ran from his eyes were the bitter, aching tears that only age can shed.

Keyoda returned late, cursing when she found the fire gone, but her voice softened as she spied him huddled in his bed, staring dully at the wall of the cave. Her old eyes spotted the few footprints the boys had missed, and she swore with a vigor that was almost youthful before she turned back to Hwoogh.

"Come, Hairy One, get out of that cold, wet fur!" Her hands were gentle on the straps, but Hwoogh shook her aside. "You'll be sick, lying there on them few leaves, all wet like that. Get off the fur, and I'll go back to the village for fire. Them kids! Wait'll I tell Legoda!"

Seeing there was nothing he would let her do for him, she turned away down the trail. Hwoogh sat up to change his furs, then lay back. What was the use? He grumbled a little when Keyoda returned with fire, but refused the delicacies she had wheedled at the village, and tumbled over into a fitful sleep.

The sun was long up when he awoke to find Legoda and Keyoda fussing over him. There was an unhappy feeling in his head, and he coughed. Legoda patted his back. "Rest, Hairy One. You have the sickness devil that burns the throat and runs at the nose, but that a man can overcome. Ayeee, how the boys were whipped! I, personally, attended to that, and this morning not one is less sore than you. Before they bother you again, the moon will eat up the sun."

Keyoda pushed a stew of boiled liver and kidneys at him, but he shoved it away. Though the ache in his head had gone down, a dull weight seemed to rest on his stomach, and he could not eat. It felt as though all the boys he had fought were sitting on his chest and choking him.

Legoda drew out a small painted drum and made heavy magic for his recovery, dancing before the old man and shaking the magic gourd that drove out all sickness devils. But this was a stronger devil. Finally the young man stopped and left for the village, while Keyoda perched on a stone to watch over the sick man. Hwoogh's mind was heavy and numb, and his heart was leaden in his breast. She fanned the flies away, covering his eyes with a bit of skin, singing him some song that the mothers lulled their children with.

He slept again, stirring about in a nightmare of Talker mockery, with a fever flushing his face. But when Legoda came back at night, the magic man swore he should be well in three days. "Let him sleep and feed him. The devil will leave him soon. See, there is scarce a mark where the stone hit."

Keyoda fed him, as best she could, forcing the food that she begged at the village down his throat. She lugged water from the creek as often as he cried for it, and bathed his head and chest when he slept. But the three days came and went, and still he was not well. The fever was little higher, and the cold little worse, than he had gone through many times before. But he did not throw it off as he should have done.

Legoda came again, bringing his magic and food, but they were of little help. As the day drew to a close, he shook his head and spoke low words to Keyoda. Hwoogh came out of a half stupor and listened dully.

"He tires of life, Keyoda, my father's sister." The young man shrugged. "See, he lies there not fighting. When a man will not try to live, he cannot."

"Ayyeah!" Her voice shrilled dolefully. "What man will not live if he can? Thou art foolish, Legoda."

"Nay. His people tire easily of life, O Keyoda. Why, I know not. But it takes little to make them die." Seeing that Hwoogh had heard, he drew closer to the Neanderthaler. "O Chokanga, put away your troubles and take another bite out of life. It can still be good, if you choose. I have taken your gift as a sign of friendship, and I would keep my word. Come to my fire, and hunt no more; I will tend you as I would my father."

Hwoogh grunted. Follow the camps, eat from Legoda's hunting, be paraded as a freak and a half-man! Legoda was kind, sudden and warm in his sympathy, but the others were scornful. And if Hwoogh should die, who was to mourn him? Keyoda would go back to her people, Legoda would forget him, and not one Chokanga would be there to show them the ritual for burial.

Hwoogh's old friends had come back to him in his dreams, visiting him and showing the hunting grounds of his youth. He had heard the grunts and grumblings of the girls of his race, and they were awaiting him. That world was still empty of the Talkers, where a man could do great things and make his own kills, without hearing the laughter of the Cro-Magnons. Hwoogh sighed softly. He was tired, too tired to care what happened.

The sun sank low, and the clouds were painted a harsh red. Keyoda was wailing somewhere, far off, and Legoda beat on his drum and muttered his magic. But life was empty, barren of pride.

Ths sun dropped from sight, and Hwoogh sighed again, sending his last breath out to join the ghosts of his people.

THE GNARLY MAN
L. Sprague de Camp

The Neanderthals, it is generally supposed, died out at least fifteen or twenty thousand years ago, perhaps earlier. There are, so far as we know, no pockets of embattled survivors hidden snugly in some remote corner of the Alps or the Pyrenees. But what if one of those prehistoric men had, in fact, somehow survived into our own day? It isn't very likely—but it's a lovely notion, and L. Sprague de Camp makes the most of it in this playful and charming story.

DR. MATILDA SADDLER first saw the gnarly man on the evening of June 14th, 1956, at Coney Island. The spring meeting of the Eastern Section of the American Anthropological Association had broken up, and Dr. Saddler had had dinner with two of her professional colleagues, Blue of Columbia and Jeffcott of Yale. She mentioned that she had never visited Coney and meant to go there that evening. She urged Blue and Jeffcott to come along, but they begged off.

Watching Dr. Saddler's retreating back, Blue of Columbia crackled: "The Wild Woman from Wichita. Wonder if she's hunting another husband?" He was a thin man with a small gray beard and a who-the-hell-are-you-sir expression.

"How many has she had?" asked Jeffcott of Yale.

"Three to date. Don't know why anthropologists lead the most disorderly private lives of any scientists. Must be that they study the customs and morals of all these different peoples, and ask themselves, 'If the Eskimos can do it, why can't we?' I'm old enough to be safe, thank God."

"I'm not afraid of her," said Jeffcott. He was in his early

forties and looked like a farmer uneasy in store-bought clothes. "I'm so very thoroughly married."

"Yeah? Ought to have been at Stanford a few years ago, when she was there. It wasn't safe to walk across the campus, with Tuthill chasing all the females and Saddler all the males."

Dr. Saddler had to fight her way off the subway train, as the adolescents who infest the platform of the B.M.T.'s Stillwell Avenue Station are probably the worst-mannered people on earth, possibly excepting the Dobu Islanders of the western Pacific. She didn't much mind. She was a tall, strongly built woman in her late thirties, who had been kept in trim by the outdoor rigors of her profession. Besides, some of the inane remarks in Swift's paper on occulturation among the Arapaho Indians had gotten her fighting blood up.

Walking down Surf Avenue toward Brighton Beach, she looked at the concessions without trying them, preferring to watch the human types that did and the other human types that took their money. She did try a shooting gallery, but found knocking tin owls off their perch with a .22 too easy to be much fun. Long-range work with an army rifle was her idea of shooting.

The concession next to the shooting gallery would have been called a sideshow if there had been a main show for it to be a sideshow to. The usual lurid banner proclaimed the uniqueness of the two-headed calf, the bearded woman, Arachne the spider-girl, and other marvels. The pièce de resistance was Ungo-Bungo, the ferocious ape-man, captured in the Congo at a cost of twenty-seven lives. The picture showed an enormous Ungo-Bungo squeezing a hapless Negro in each hand, while others sought to throw a net over him.

Although Dr. Saddler knew perfectly well that the ferocious ape-man would turn out to be an ordinary Caucasian with false hair on his chest, a streak of whimsicality impelled her to go in. Perhaps, she thought, she could have some fun with her colleagues about it.

The spieler went through his leather-lunged harangue. Dr.

Saddler guessed from his expression that his feet hurt. The tattooed lady didn't interest her, as her decorations obviously had no cultural significance, as they have among the Polynesians. As for the ancient Mayan, Dr. Saddler thought it in questionable taste to exhibit a poor microcephalic idiot that way. Professor Yogi's legerdemain and fire-eating weren't bad.

A curtain hung in front of Ungo-Bungo's cage. At the appropriate moment there were growls and the sound of a length of chain being slapped against a metal plate. The spieler wound up on a high note: ". . . ladies and gentlemen, the one and only Ungo-Bungo!" The curtain dropped.

The ape-man was squatting at the back of his cage. He dropped his chain, got up, and shuffled forward. He grasped two of the bars and shook them. They were appropriately loose and rattled alarmingly. Ungo-Bungo snarled at the patrons, showing his even yellow teeth.

Dr. Saddler stared hard. This was something new in the ape-man line. Ungo-Bungo was about five feet three, but very massive, with enormous hunched shoulders. Above and below his blue swimming trunks, thick grizzled hair covered him from crown to ankle. His short stout-muscled arms ended in big hands with thick gnarled fingers. His neck projected slightly forward, so that from the front he seemed to have but little neck at all.

His face— Well, thought Dr. Saddler, she knew all the living races of men, and all the types of freaks brought about by glandular maladjustment, and none of them had a face like that. It was deeply lined. The forehead between the short scalp hair and the brows on the huge supraorbital ridges receded sharply. The nose, though wide, was not apelike; it was a shortened version of the thick hooked Armenoid or "Jewish" nose. The face ended in a long upper lip and a retreating chin. And the yellowish skin apparently belonged to Ungo-Bungo.

The curtain was whisked up again.

Dr. Saddler went out with the others, but paid another

dime, and soon was back inside. She paid no attention to the spieler, but got a good position in front of Ungo-Bungo's cage before the rest of the crowd arrived.

Ungo-Bungo repeated his performance with mechanical precision. Dr. Saddler noticed that he limped a little as he came forward to rattle the bars, and that the skin under his mat of hair bore several big whitish scars. The last joint of his left ring finger was missing. She noted certain things about the proportions of his shin and thigh, of his forearm and upper arm, and his big splay feet.

Dr. Saddler paid a third dime. An idea was knocking at her mind somewhere, trying to get in; either she was crazy or physical anthropology was haywire or—something. But she knew that if she did the sensible thing, which was to go home, the idea would plague her from now on.

After the third performance she spoke to the spieler. "I think your Mr. Ungo-Bungo used to be a friend of mine. Could you arrange for me to see him after he finishes?"

The spieler checked his sarcasm. His questioner was so obviously not a—not the sort of dame who asks to see guys after they finish.

"Oh, him," he said. "Calls himself Gaffney—Clarence Aloysius Gaffney. That the guy you want?"

"Why, yes."

"Guess you can." He looked at his watch. "He's got four more turns to do before we close. I'll have to ask the boss." He popped through a curtain and called, "Hey, Morrie!" Then he was back. "It's okay. Morrie says you can wait in his office. Foist door to the right."

Morrie was stout, bald, and hospitable. "Sure sure," he said, waving his cigar. "Glad to be of soivice, Miss Saddler. Chust a min while I talk to Gaffney's manager." He stuck his head out. "Hey, Pappas! Lady wants to talk to your ape-man later. I meant lady. Okay." He returned to orate on the difficulties besetting the freak business. "You take this Gaffney, now. He's the best damn ape-man in the business; all that hair really grows outa him. And the poor guy really has a face like that. But do people believe it? No! I hear 'em going out, saying about how the hair is pasted on, and the whole thing is a fake. It's mortifying." He cocked his head listening. "That rumble wasn't no rolly-coaster; it's gonna rain. Hope it's over by tomorrow. You wouldn't believe the way a rain can knock ya receipts off. If you drew a coive, it would be like this." He drew his finger horizontally through space, jerking it down sharply to indicate the effect of rain. "But as I said, people don't appreciate what you try to do for 'em. It's not just the money; I think of myself as an ottist. A creative ottist. A show like this got to have balance and proportion, like any other ott——"

It must have been an hour later when a slow, deep voice at the door said, "Did somebody want to see me?"

The gnarly man was in the doorway. In street clothes, with the collar of his raincoat turned up and his hat brim pulled down, he looked more or less human, though the coat fitted his great sloping shoulders badly. He had a thick knobby walking stick with a leather loop near the top end. A small dark man fidgeted behind him.

"Yeah," said Morrie, interrupting his lecture. "Clarence, this is Miss Saddler. Miss Saddler, this is our Mister Gaffney, one of our outstanding creative ottists."

"Pleased to meetcha," said the gnarly man. "This is my manager, Mr. Pappas."

Dr. Saddler explained, and said she'd like to talk to Mr. Gaffney if she might. She was tactful; you had to be to pry into the private affairs of Naga headhunters, for instance. The gnarly man said he'd be glad to have a cup of coffee with Miss Saddler; there was a place around the corner that they could reach without getting wet.

As they started out, Pappas followed, fidgeting more and more. The gnarly man said, "Oh, go home to bed, John. Don't worry about me." He grinned at Dr. Saddler. The effect would have been unnerving to anyone but an anthropologist. "Every time he sees me talking to anybody, he thinks it's some other manager trying to steal me.'' He spoke General American, with a suggestion of Irish brogue in the lowering of the vowels in words like ''man'' and ''talk.'' ''I made the lawyer who drew up our contract fix it so it can be ended on short notice.''

Pappas departed, still looking suspicious. The rain had practically ceased. The gnarly man stepped along smartly despite his limp. A woman passed with a fox terrier on a leash. The dog sniffed in the direction of the gnarly man, and then to all appearances went crazy, yelping and slavering. The gnarly man shifted his grip on the massive stick and said quietly, ''Better hang on to him, ma'am.'' The woman departed hastily. ''They just don't like me,'' commented Gaffney. ''Dogs, that is.''

They found a table and ordered their coffee. When the gnarly man took off his raincoat, Dr. Saddler became aware of a strong smell of cheap perfume. He got out a pipe with a big knobby bowl. It suited him, just as the walking stick did. Dr. Saddler noticed that the deep-sunk eyes under the beetling arches were light hazel.

''Well?'' he said in his rumbling drawl.

She began her questions.

''My parents were Irish,'' he answered. ''But I was born in South Boston—let's see—forty-six years ago. I can get you a copy of my birth certificate. Clarence Aloysius Gaffney, May second, 1910.'' He seemed to get some secret amusement out of that statement.

''Were either of your parents of your somewhat unusual physical type?''

He paused before answering. He always did, it seemed. ''Uh-huh. Both of 'em. Glands, I suppose.''

''Were they both born in Ireland?''

''Yep. County Sligo.'' Again that mysterious twinkle.

She paused. ''Mr. Gaffney, you wouldn't mind having some photographs and measurements made, would you? You could use the photographs in your business.''

"Maybe." He took a sip. "Ouch! Gazooks, that's hot!"

"What?"

"I said the coffee's hot."

"I mean, before that."

The gnarly man looked a little embarrassed. "Oh, you mean the 'gazooks'? Well, I—uh—once knew a man who used to say that."

"Mr. Gaffney, I'm a scientist, and I'm not trying to get anything out of you for my own sake. You can be frank with me."

There was something remote and impersonal in his stare that gave her a slight spinal chill. "Meaning that I haven't been so far?"

"Yes. When I saw you I decided that there was something extraordinary in your background. I still think there is— Now, if you think I'm crazy, say so and we'll drop the subject. But I want to get to the bottom of this."

He took his time about answering. "That would depend." There was another pause. Then he said, "With your connections, do you know any really first-class surgeons?"

"But—yes, I know Dunbar."

"The guy who wears a purple gown when he operates? The guy who wrote a book on God, Man, and the Universe?"

"Yes. He's a good man, in spite of his theatrical mannerisms. Why? What would you want of him?"

"Not what you're thinking. I'm satisfied with my—uh—unusual physical type. But I have some old injuries—broken bones that didn't knit properly—that I want fixed up. He'd have to be a good man, though. I have a couple of thousand in the savings bank, but I know the sort of fees those guys charge. If you could make the necessary arrangements—"

"Why, yes, I'm sure I could. In fact I could guarantee it. Then I was right? And you'll—" She hesitated.

"Come clean? Uh-huh. But remember, I can still prove I'm Clarence Aloysius if I have to."

"Who are you, then?"

Again there was a long pause. Then the gnarly man said, "Might as well tell you. As soon as you repeat any of it, you'll have put your professional reputation in my hands, remember.

"First off, I wasn't born in Massachusetts. I was born on the upper Rhine, near Mommenheim, and as nearly as I can figure out, about the year fifty thousand B.C."

Dr. Saddler wondered whether she'd stumbled on the biggest thing in anthropology or whether this bizarre man was making Baron Münchausen look like a piker.

He seemed to guess her thoughts. "I can't prove that, of course. But so long as you arrange about that operation, I don't care whether you believe me or not."

"But—but—how?"

"I think the lightning did it. We were out trying to drive some bison into a pit. Well, this big thunderstorm came up, and the bison bolted in the wrong direction. So we gave up and tried to find shelter. And the next thing I knew I was lying on the ground with the rain running over me, and the rest of the clan standing around wailing about what had they done to get the storm-god sore at them, so he made a bull's-eye on one of their best hunters. They'd never said that about me before. It's funny how you're never appreciated while you're alive.

"But I was alive, all right. My nerves were pretty well shot for a few weeks, but otherwise I was all right except for some burns on the soles of my feet. I don't know just what happened, except I was reading a couple of years ago that scientists had located the machinery that controls the replacement of tissue in the medulla oblongata. I think maybe the lightning did something to my medulla to speed it up. Anyway I never got any older after that. Physically, that is. And except for those broken bones I told you about. I was thirty-three at the time, more or less. We didn't keep track of ages. I look older now, because the lines in your face are bound to get sort of set after a few thousand years, and because our hair was always gray at the ends. But I can still tie an ordinary Homo sapiens in a knot if I want to.''

"Then you're—you mean to say you're—you're trying to tell me you're—''

"A Neanderthal man? Homo neanderthalensis? That's right.''

Matilda Saddler's hotel room was a bit crowded, with the gnarly man, the frosty Blue, the rustic Jeffcott, Dr. Saddler herself, and Harold McGannon the historian. This McGannon was a small man, very neat and pink-skinned. He looked more like a New York Central director than a professor. Just now his expression was one of fascination. Dr. Saddler looked full of pride; Professor Jeffcott looked interested but puzzled; Dr. Blue looked bored. (He hadn't wanted to come in the first place.) The gnarly man, stretched out in the most comfortable chair and puffing his overgrown pipe, seemed to be enjoying himself.

McGannon was asking a question. "Well, Mr.—Gaffney? I suppose that's your name as much as any.''

"You might say so,'' said the gnarly man. "My original name was something like Shining Hawk. But I've gone under hundreds of names since then. If you register in a hotel as 'Shining Hawk' it's apt to attract attention. And I try to avoid that.''

"Why?'' asked McGannon.

The gnarly man looked at his audience as one might look at willfully stupid children. "I don't like trouble. The best way to keep out of trouble is not to attract attention. That's why I have to pull up stakes and move every ten or fifteen years. People might get curious as to why I never got any older.''

"Pathological liar,'' murmured Blue. The words were barely audible, but the gnarly man heard them.

"You're entitled to your opinion, Dr. Blue,'' he said affably. "Dr. Saddler's doing me a favor, so in return I'm letting you all shoot questions at me. And I'm answering. I don't give a damn whether you believe me or not."

McGannon hastily threw in another question. "How is it that you have a birth certificate, as you say you have?"

"Oh, I knew a man named Clarence Gaffney once. He got killed by an automobile, and I took his name."

"Was there any reason for picking this Irish background?"

"Are you Irish, Dr. McGannon?"

"Not enough to matter."

"Okay. I didn't want to hurt any feelings. It's my best bet. There are real Irishmen with upper lips like mine."

Dr. Saddler broke in. "I meant to ask you, Clarence." She put a lot of warmth into his name. "There's an argument as to whether your people interbred with mine, when mine over-ran Europe at the end of the Mousterian. It's been thought that the 'old black breed' of the west coast of Ireland might have a little Neanderthal blood."

He grinned slightly. "Well—yes and not. There never was any back in the Stone Age, as far as I know. But these long-lipped Irish are my fault."

"How?"

"Believe it or not, but in the last fifty centuries there have been some women of your species that didn't find me too repulsive. Usually there were no offspring. But in the six-teenth century I went to Ireland to live. They were burning too many people for witchcraft in the rest of Europe to suit me at that time. And there was a woman. The result this time was a flock of hybrids—cute little devils they were. So the 'old black breed' are my descendants."

"What did happen to your people?" asked McGannon. "Were they killed off?"

The gnarly man shrugged. "Some of them. We weren't at all warlike. But then the tall ones, as we called them, weren't either. Some of the tribes of the tall ones looked on us as le-gitimate prey, but most of them let us severely alone. I guess they were almost as scared of us as we were of them. Sav-ages as primitive as that are really pretty peaceable people.

You have to work so hard and there are so few of you, that there's no object in fighting wars. That comes later, when you get agriculture and livestock, so you have something worth stealing.

"I remember that a hundred years after the tall ones had come, there were still Neanderthalers living in my part of the country. But they died out. I think it was that they lost their ambition. The tall ones were pretty crude, but they were so far ahead of us that our things and our customs seemed silly. Finally we just sat around and lived on what scraps we could beg from the tall ones' camps. You might say we died of an inferiority complex."

"What happened to you?" asked McGannon.

"Oh, I was a god among my own people by then, and naturally I represented them in dealings with the tall ones. I got to know the tall ones pretty well, and they were willing to put up with me after all my own clan were dead. Then in a couple of hundred years they'd forgotten all about my people, and took me for a hunchback or something. I got to be pretty good at flintworking, so I could earn my keep. When metal came in I went into that, and finally into blacksmithing. If you put all the horseshoes I've made in a pile, they'd—well, you'd have a damn big pile of horseshoes anyway."

"Did you limp at that time?" asked McGannon.

"Uh-huh. I busted my leg back in the Neolithic. Fell out of a tree, and had to set it myself, because there wasn't anybody around. Why?"

"Vulcan," said McGannon softly.

"Vulcan?" repeated the gnarly man. "Wasn't he a Greek god or something?"

"Yes. He was the lame blacksmith of the gods."

"You mean you think that maybe somebody got the idea from me? That's an interesting idea. Little late to check up on it, though."

Blue leaned forward, and said crisply, "Mr. Gaffney, no

real Neanderthal man could talk as entertainingly as you do. That's shown by the poor development of the frontal lobes of the brain and the attachments of the tongue muscles."

The gnarly man shrugged again. "You can believe what you like. My own clan considered me pretty smart, and then you're bound to learn something in fifty thousand years."

Dr. Saddler said, "Tell them about your teeth, Clarence."

The gnarly man grinned. "They're false, of course. My own lasted a long time, but they still wore out somewhere back in the Paleolithic. I grew a third set, and they wore out too. So I had to invent soup."

"You what?" It was the usually taciturn Jeffcott.

"I had to invent soup, to keep alive. You know, the bark-dish-and-hot-stones method. My gums got pretty tough after a while, but they still weren't much good for chewing hard stuff. So after a few thousand years I got pretty sick of soup and mushy foods generally. And when metal came in I began experimenting with false teeth. I finally made some pretty good ones. Amber teeth in copper plates. You might say I invented them too. I tried often to sell them, but they never really caught on until around 1750 A.D. I was living in Paris then, and I built up quite a little business before I moved on." He pulled the handkerchief out of his breast pocket to wipe his forehead; Blue made a face as the wave of perfume reached him.

"Well, Mr. Caveman," snapped Blue sarcastically, "how do you like our machine age?"

The gnarly man ignored the tone of the question. "It's not bad. Lots of interesting things happen. The main trouble is the shirts."

"Shirts?"

"Uh-huh. Just try to buy a shirt with a twenty neck and twenty-nine sleeve. I have to order 'em special. It's almost as bad with hats and shoes. I wear an eight and a half, and a thirteen shoe." He looked at his watch. "I've got to get back to Coney to work."

McGannon jumped up. "Where can I get in touch with you again, Mr. Gaffney? There's lots of things I'd like to ask you."

The gnarly man told him. "I'm free mornings. My working hours are two to midnight on weekdays, with a couple of hours off for dinner. Union rules, you know."

"You mean there's a union for you show people?"

"Sure. Only they call it a guild. They think they're artists, you know."

Blue and Jeffcott watched the gnarly man and the historian walking slowly toward the subway together. Blue said, "Poor old Mac! I always thought he had sense. Looks like he's swallowed this Gaffney's ravings hook, line, and sinker."

"I'm not so sure," said Jeffcott, frowning. "There's something funny about the business."

"What?" barked Blue. "Don't tell me that you believe this story of being alive fifty thousand years? A caveman who uses perfume? Good God!"

"N-no," said Jeffcott. "Not the fifty-thousand part. But I don't think it's a simple case of paranoia or plain lying either. And the perfume's quite logical, if he was telling the truth."

"Huh?"

"Body odor. Saddler told us how dogs hate him. He'd have a smell different from ours. We're so used to ours that we don't even know we have one, unless somebody goes without a bath for a couple of months. But we might notice his if he didn't disguise it."

Blue snorted. "You'll be believing him yourself in a minute. It's an obvious glandular case, and he's made up this story to fit. All that talk about not caring whether we believe him or not is just bluff. Come on, let's get some lunch. Say, did you see the way Saddler looked at him every time she said 'Clarence'? Wonder what she thinks she's going to do with him?"

Jeffcott thought. "I can guess. And if he is telling the truth, I think there's something in Deuteronomy against it."

The great surgeon made a point of looking like a great surgeon, to pince-nez and Vandyke. He waved the X-ray negatives at the gnarly man, pointing out this and that.

"We'd better take the leg first," he said. "Suppose we do that next Tuesday. When you've recovered from that we can tackle the shoulder."

The gnarly man agreed, and shuffled out of the little private hospital to where McGannon awaited him in his car. The gnarly man described the tentative schedule of operations, and mentioned that he had made arrangements to quit his job at the last minute. "Those two are the main things," he said. "I'd like to try professional wrestling again some day, and I can't unless I get this shoulder fixed so I can raise my left arm over my head."

"What happened to it?" asked McGannon.

The gnarly man closed his eyes, thinking. "Let me see. I get things mixed up sometimes. People do when they're only fifty years old, so you can imagine what it's like for me.

"In 42 B.C. I was living with the Bituriges in Gaul. You remember that Caesar shut up Werkinghetorich—Vercingetorix to you—in Alesia, and the confederacy raised an army of relief under Caswallon."

"Caswallon?"

The gnarly man laughed shortly. "I meant Wercaswallon. Caswallon was a Briton, wasn't he? I'm always getting those two mixed up.

"Anyhow, I got drafted. That's all you can call it; I didn't want to go. It wasn't exactly my war. But they wanted me because I could pull twice as heavy a bow as anybody else.

"When the final attack on Caesar's ring of fortifications came, they sent me forward with some other archers to provide a covering fire for their infantry. At least that was the plan. Actually I never saw such a hopeless muddle in my life. And before I even got within bow-shot, I fell into one of the Romans' covered pits. I didn't land on the point of the stake, but I fetched up against the side of it and busted my shoulder. There wasn't any help, because the Gauls were too busy running away from Caesar's German cavalry to bother about wounded men.''

The author of *God, Man, and the Universe* gazed after his departing patient. He spoke to his head assistant. "I looked over those X-rays pretty closely. That skeleton never belonged to a human being.

"Hmm. Hmm," said Dunbar. "That's right, he wouldn't be human, would he? Hmm. You know, if anything happened to him—"

The assistant grinned understandingly. "Of course there's the S.P.C.A."

"We needn't worry about them. Hmm." He thought, you've been slipping: nothing big in the papers for a year. But if you published a complete anatomical description of a Neanderthal man—or if you found out why his medulla functions the way it does—hmm—of course it would have to be managed properly—"

"Let's have lunch at the Natural History Museum," said McGannon. "Some of the people there ought to know you."

"Okay," drawled the gnarly man. "Only I've still got to get back to Coney afterward. This is my last day. Tomorrow Pappas and I are going up to see our lawyer about ending our contract. It's a dirty trick on poor old John, but I warned him at the start that this might happen."

"I suppose we can come up to interview you while you're—ah—convalescing? Fine. Have you ever been to the Museum, by the way?"

"Sure," said the gnarly man. "I get around."

"What did you—ah—think of their stuff in the Hall of the Age of Man?"

"Pretty good. There's a little mistake in one of those big

wall paintings. The second horn on the woolly rhinoceros ought to slant forward more. I thought about writing them a letter. But you know how it is. They say 'Were you there?' and I say 'Uh-huh' and they say 'Another nut.' ''

"How about the pictures and busts of Paleolithic men?"

"Pretty good. But they have some funny ideas. They always show us with skins wrapped around our middles. In summer we didn't wear skins, and in winter we hung them around our shoulders where they'd do some good.

"And then they show those tall ones that you call Cro-Magnon men clean shaven. As I remember, they all had whiskers. What would they shave with?"

"I think," said McGannon, "that they leave the beards off the busts to—ah—show the shape of the chins. With the beards they'd all look too much alike."

"Is that the reason? They might say so on the labels." The gnarly man rubbed his own chin, such as it was. "I wish beards would come back into style. I look much more human with a beard. I got along fine in the sixteenth century when everybody had whiskers.

"That's one of the ways I remember when things happened, by the haircuts and whiskers that people had. I remember when a wagon I was driving in Milan lost a wheel and spilled flour bags from hell to breakfast. That must have been in the sixteenth century, before I went to Ireland, because I remember that most of the men in the crowd that collected had beards. Now—wait a minute—maybe that was the fourteenth. There were a lot of beards then too."

"Why, why didn't you keep a diary?" asked McGannon with a groan of exasperation.

The gnarly man shrugged characteristically. "And pack around six trunks full of paper every time I move? No, thanks."

"I—ah—don't suppose you could give me the real story of Richard the Third and the princes in the Tower?"

"Why should I? I was just a poor blacksmith or farmer or something most of the time. I didn't go around with the big shots. I gave up all my ideas of ambition a long time before that. I had to, being so different from other people. As far as I can remember, the only real king I ever got a good look at was Charlemagne, when he made a speech in Paris one day. He was just a big tall man with Santa Claus whiskers and a squeaky voice.''

Next morning McGannon and the gnarly man had a session with Svedberg at the Museum, after which McGannon drove Gaffney around to the lawyer's office, on the third floor of a seedy old office building in the West Fifties. James Robinette looked something like a movie actor and something like a chipmunk. He glanced at his watch and said to McGannon: "This won't take long. If you'd like to stick around I'd be glad to have lunch with you." The fact was that he was feeling just a trifle queasy about being left with this damn queer client, this circus freak or whatever he was, with his barrel body and his funny slow drawl.

When the business had been completed, and the gnarly man had gone off with his manager to wind up his affairs at Coney, Robinette said, ''Whew! I thought he was a halfwit, from his looks. But there was nothing halfwitted about the way he went over those clauses. You'd have thought the damn contract was for building a subway system. What is he, anyhow?''

McGannon told him what he knew.

The lawyer's eyebrows went up. ''Do you believe his yarn?''

''I do. So does Saddler. So does Svedberg up at the Museum. They're both topnotchers in their respective fields. Saddler and I have interviewed him, and Svedberg's examined him physically. But it's just opinion. Fred Blue still swears it's a hoax or a case of some sort of dementia. Neither of us can prove anything.''

''Why not?''

''Well—ah—how are you going to prove that he was or was not alive a hundred years ago? Take one case: Clarence says he ran a sawmill in Fairbanks, Alaska, in 1906 and '07, under the name of Michael Shawn. How are you going to find out whether there was a sawmill operator in Fairbanks at that time? And if you did stumble on a record of a Michael Shawn, how would you know whether he and Clarence were the same? There's not a chance in a thousand that there'd be a photograph or a detailed description you could check with. And you'd have an awful time trying to find anybody who remembered him at this late date.

"Then, Svedberg poked around Clarence's face, and said that no human being ever had a pair of zygomatic arches like that. But when I told Blue that, he offered to produce photographs of a human skull that did. I know what'll happen: Blue will say that the arches are practically the same, and Svedberg will say that they're obviously different. So there we'll be."

Robinette mused, "He does seem damned intelligent for an ape-man."

"He's not an ape-man really. The Neanderthal race was a separate branch of the human stock; they were more primitive in some ways and more advanced in others than we are. Clarence may be slow, but he usually grinds out the right answer. I imagine that he was—ah—brilliant, for one of his kind, to begin with. And he's had the benefit of so much experience. He knows us; he sees through us and our motives." The little pink man puckered up his forehead. "I do hope nothing happens to him. He's carrying around a lot of priceless information in that big head of his. Simply priceless. Not much about war and politics; he kept clear of those as a matter of self-preservation. But little things, about how people lived and how they thought thousands of years ago. He gets his periods mixed up sometimes, but he gets them straightened out if you give him time.

"I'll have to get hold of Pell, the linguist. Clarence knows dozens of ancient languages, such as Gothic and Gaulish. I was able to check him on some of them, like vulgar Latin; that was one of the things that convinced me. And there are archeologists and psychologists. . . .

"If only something doesn't happen to scare him off. We'd never find him. I don't know. Between a man-crazy female scientist and a publicity-mad surgeon—I wonder how it'll work out."

The gnarly man innocently entered the waiting room of Dunbar's hospital. He as usual spotted the most comfortable chair and settled luxuriously into it.

Dunbar stood before him. His keen eyes gleamed with anticipation behind their pince-nez. "There'll be a wait of about half an hour, Mr. Gaffney," he said. "We're all tied up now, you know. I'll send Mahler in; he'll see that you have anything you want." Dunbar's eyes ran lovingly over the gnarly man's stumpy frame. What fascinating secrets mightn't he discover once he got inside it?

Mahler appeared, a healthy-looking youngster. Was there anything Mr. Gaffney would like? The gnarly man paused as usual to let his massive mental machinery grind. A vagrant impulse moved him to ask to see the instruments that were to be used on him.

Mahler had his orders, but this seemed a harmless enough request. He went and returned with a tray full of gleaming steel. "You see," he said, "there are called scalpels."

Presently the gnarly man asked, "What's this?" He picked up a peculiar-looking instrument.

"Oh, that's the boss's own invention. For getting at the midbrain."

"Midbrain? What's that doing here?"

"Why, that's for getting at your—that must be there by mistake—"

Little lines tightened around the queer hazel eyes. "Yeah?" He remembered the look Dunbar had given him, and Dunbar's general reputation. "Say, could I use your phone a minute?"

"Why—I suppose—what do you want to phone for?"

"I want to call my lawyer. Any objections?"

"No, of course not. But there isn't any phone here."

"What do you call that?" The gnarly man rose and walked toward the instrument in plain sight on a table. But Mahler was there before him, standing in front of it.

"This one doesn't work. It's being fixed."

"Can't I try it?"

"No, not till it's fixed. It doesn't work, I tell you."

The gnarly man studied the young physician for a few seconds. "Okay, then I'll find one that does." He started for the door.

"Hey, you can't go out now!" cried Mahler.

"Can't I? Just watch me!"

"Hey!" It was a full-throated yell. Like magic more men in white coats appeared. Behind them was the great surgeon. "Be reasonable, Mr. Gaffney," he said. "There's no reason why you should go out now, you know. We'll be ready for you in a little while."

"Any reason why I shouldn't?" The gnarly man's big face swung on his thick neck, and his hazel eyes swiveled. All the exits were blocked. "I'm going."

"Grab him!" said Dunbar.

The white coats moved. The gnarly man got his hand on the back of a chair. The chair whirled, and became a dissolving blur as the men closed on him. Pieces of chair flew about the room, to fall with the dry sharp pink of short lengths of wood. When the gnarly man stopped swinging, having only a short piece of the chair back left in each fist, one assistant was out cold. Another leaned whitely against the wall and nursed a broken arm.

"Go on!" shouted Dunbar when he could make himself heard. The white wave closed over the gnarly man, then broke. The gnarly man was on his feet, and held young Mahler by the ankles. He spread his feet and swung the shrieking Mahler like a club, clearing the way to the door. He turned, whirled Mahler around his head like a hammer thrower, and let the now mercifully unconscious body fly. His assailants went down in a yammering tangle.

One was still up. Under Dunbar's urging he sprang after

the gnarly man. The latter had gotten his stick out of the umbrella stand in the vestibule. The knobby upper end went whoosh past the assistant's nose. The assistant jumped back and fell over one of the casualties. The front door slammed, and there was a deep roar of "Taxi!"

"Come on!" shrieked Dunbar. "Get the ambulance out!"

James Robinette sat in his ofice on the third floor of a seedy old office building in the West Fifties, thinking the thoughts that lawyers do in moments of relaxation.

He wondered about that damn queer client, that circus freak or whatever he was, who had been in a couple of days before with his manager. A barrel-bodied man who looked like a halfwit and talked in a funny slow drawl. Though there had been nothing halfwitted about the acute way he had gone over those clauses. You'd think the damn contract had been for building a subway system.

There was a pounding of large feet in the corridor, a startled protest from Miss Spevak in the outer office, and the strange customer was before Robinette's desk, breathing hard.

"I'm Gaffney," he growled between gasps. "Remember me? I think they followed me down here. They'll be up any minute. I want your help."

"They? Who's they?" Robinette winced at the impact of that damned perfume.

The gnarly man launched into his misfortunes. He was going well when there were more protests from Miss Spevak, and Dr. Dunbar and four assistants burst into the office.

"He's ours," said Dunbar, his glasses agleam.

"He's an ape-man," said the assistant with the black eye.

"He's a dangerous lunatic," said the assistant with the cut lip.

"We've come to take him away," said the assistant with the torn pants.

The gnarly man spread his feet and gripped his stick like a baseball bat.

Robinette opened a desk drawer and got out a large pistol. "One move toward him and I'll use this. The use of extreme

violence is justified to prevent commission of a felony, to
wit, kidnapping."

The five men backed up a little. Dunbar said, "This isn't
kidnapping. You can only kidnap a person, you know. He
isn't a human being, and I can prove it."

The assistant with the black eye snickered. "If he wants
protection, he better see a game warden instead of a lawyer."

"Maybe that's what you think," said Robinette. "You
aren't a lawyer. According to the law he's human. Even cor-
porations, idiots, and unborn children are legally persons,
and he's a damn sight more human than they are."

"Then he's a dangerous lunatic," said Dunbar.

"Yeah? Where's your commitment order? The only persons who can apply for one are (a) close relatives and (b)
public officials charged with the maintenance of order.
You're neither."

Dunbar continued stubbornly. "He ran amuck in my hospital and nearly killed a couple of my men, you know. I
guess that gives us some rights."

"Sure," said Robinette. "You can step down to the
nearest station and swear out a warrant." He turned to the
gnarly man. "Shall we slap a civil suit on 'em, Gaffney?"

"I'm all right," said the individual, his speech returning to
its normal slowness. "I just want to make sure these guys
don't pester me anymore."

"Okay. Now listen, Dunbar. One hostile move out of you
and we'll have a warrant out for you for false arrest, assault
and battery, attempted kidnapping, criminal conspiracy, and
disorderly conduct. We'll throw the book at you. And there'll
be a suit for damages for sundry torts, to wit, assault, depri-
vation of civil rights, placing in jeopardy of life and limb,
menace, and a few more I may think of later."

"You'll never make that stick," snarled Dunbar. "We
have all the witnesses."

"Yeah? And wouldn't the great Evan Dunbar look sweet
defending such actions? Some of the ladies who gush over
your books might suspect that maybe you weren't such a

damn knight in shining armor. We can make a prize monkey of you, and you know it.''

"You're destroying the possibility of a great scientific discovery, you know, Robinette.''

"To hell with that. My duty is to protect my client. Now beat it, all of you, before I call a cop.'' His left hand moved suggestively to the telephone.

Dunbar grasped at a last straw. "Hmm. Have you got a permit for that gun?''

"Damn right. Want to see it?''

Dunbar sighed. "Never mind. You would have.'' His greatest opportunity for fame was slipping out of his fingers. He drooped toward the door.

The gnarly man spoke up. "If you don't mind, Dr. Dunbar. I left my hat at your place. I wish you'd send it to Mr. Robinette here. I have a hard time getting hats to fit me.''

Dunbar looked at him silently and left with his cohorts.

The gnarly man was giving the lawyer further details when the telephone rang. Robinette answered: "Yes . . . Saddler? Yes, he's here. . . . Your Dr. Dunbar was going to murder him so he could dissect him. . . . Okay.'' He turned to the gnarly man. "Your friend Dr. Saddler is looking for you. She's on her way up here.''

"Herakles!'' said Gaffney. "I'm going.''

"Don't you want to see her? She was phoning from around the corner. If you go out now you'll run into her. How did she know where to call?''

"I gave her your number. I suppose she called the hospital and my boarding house, and tried you as a last resort. This door goes into the hall, doesn't it? Well, when she comes in the regular door I'm going out this one. And I don't want you saying where I've gone. Nice to have known you, Mr. Robinette.''

"Why? What's the matter? You're not going to run out now, are you? Dunbar's harmless, and you've got friends. I'm your friend.''

"You're durn tootin' I'm gonna run out. There's too much

trouble. I've kept alive all these centuries by staying away from trouble. I let down my guard with Dr. Saddler, and went to the surgeon she recommended. First he plots to take me apart to see what makes me tick. If that brain instrument hadn't made me suspicious I'd have been on my way to the alcohol jars by now. Then there's a fight, and it's just pure luck I didn't kill a couple of those interns or whatever they are and get sent up for manslaughter. Now Matilda's after me with a more than friendly interest. I know what it means when a woman looks at you that way and calls you 'dear.' I wouldn't mind if she weren't a prominent person of the kind that's always in some sort of garboil. That would mean more trouble sooner or later. You don't suppose I like trouble, do you?''

"But look here, Gaffney, you're getting steamed up over a lot of damn—"

"Ssst!" The gnarly man took his stick and tiptoed over to the private entrance. As Dr. Saddler's clear voice sounded in the outer office, he sneaked out. He was closing the door behind him when the scientist entered the inner office.

Matilda Saddler was a quick thinker. Robinette hardly had time to open his mouth when she flung herself at and through the private door with a cry of "Clarence!"

Robinette heard the clatter of feet on the stairs. Neither the pursued nor the pursuer had waited for the creaky elevator. Looking out the window he saw Gaffney leap into a taxi. Matilda Saddler sprinted after the cab, calling, "Clarence! Come back.'' But the traffic was light and the chase correspondingly hopeless.

They did hear from the gnarly man once more. Three months later Robinette got a letter whose envelope contained, to his vast astonishment, ten ten-dollar bills. The single sheet was typed even to the signature.

Dear Mr. Robinette:
  I do not know what your regular fees are, but I hope that the enclosed will cover your services to me of last July.

Since leaving New York I have had several jobs. I pushed a hack (as we say) in Chicago, and I tried out as pitcher on a bush-league baseball team. Once I made my living by knocking over rabbits and things with stones, and I can still throw fairly well. Nor am I bad at swinging a club like a baseball bat. But my lameness makes me too slow for a baseball career.

I now have a job whose nature I cannot disclose because I do not wish to be traced. You need pay no attention to the postmark; I am not living in Kansas City, but had a friend post this letter there.

Ambition would be foolish for one in my peculiar position. I am satisfied with a job that furnishes me with the essentials and allows me to go to an occasional movie, and a few friends with whom I can drink beer and talk.

I was sorry to leave New York without saying good-bye to Dr. Harold McGannon, who treated me very nicely. I wish you would explain to him why I had to leave as I did. You can get in touch with him through Columbia University.

If Dunbar sent you my hat as I requested, please mail it to me, General Delivery, Kansas City, Mo. My friend will pick it up. There is not a hat store in this town where I live that can fit me.

With best wishes, I remain,

Yours sincerely,

Shining Hawk
alias Clarence Aloysius Gaffney

BRAVE NEW WORD

J. Francis McComas

We have reached the time when prehistory is shading into history, when we are concerned no longer with the physical evolution of humanity but with the development of culture. And in this warm and eloquent story we see the process of technological growth at work, the conflicts and interactions that brought mankind from the era of crude stone hatchets to that of modern scientific wizardry.

J. Francis McComas is the author of only half a dozen or so science-fiction stories, but he was an influential editor in the field, co-founder with Anthony Boucher of The Magazine of Fantasy & Science Fiction *and co-editor with Raymond Healy of the finest of all science-fiction anthologies,* Adventures in Time and Space *(1946).*

THE TRAVELERS TO THE HOT COUNTRY arrived today, carrying many things, so tonight there will be dancing and all the hearts of The People will be good. As ever, when the travelers return, I remember how the thing began with Sleepy Hawk, that greater doer of deeds, that laughter, that maker of words.

Most of The People think the matter had its beginning later; but I, whose oldest father had the story from the mouth of Sleepy Hawk himself, think otherwise. The true beginning was when Long Ax, that angry man, had his new ax handle break in his hand the very first time he swung the weapon. Long Ax had chosen the wood with care and knowledge, made it straight with his knife and then, in the chosen way, fixed it to the great stone ax his oldest father had given him.

Then, at the very first trial swing at one of the big trees that grew by the river where The People were camped, the handle had splintered, the great stone head had bounced from the tree to the river water, and Long Ax, a splinter driven into his thumb, danced about, shouting with pain and anger.

Since all this was a very bad sign, the rest of the young men looked very solemn. All, that is, except Sleepy Hawk, who fell on his back and laughed. He laughed so loud and so long that the other four thought he might never stop, but choke himself to death there by the river.

"Why do you laugh?" cried Long Ax. "Now I must make another handle! We can't start until I do!"

"Yes," asked Hungry Dog, who was fat and liked to sit in Long Ax's shadow, "why do you laugh?"

Sleepy Hawk stopped choking himself and said, "I'm sorry. But you looked so—so—" He looked in his head for a word, could not find one and said, "so—laugh-making! One moment you were swinging your great ax, the next moment you were dancing about, a little boy with a splinter in your hand! And the fine new handle for your ax was nothing but wood for the fire!"

At Sleepy Hawk's words, even Mountain Bear, the quiet man, laughed softly deep in his throat.

The face of Long Ax colored the angry red and he said, "How would you like to stay here and laugh while the others follow *me* on our hunt?"

Sleepy Hawk sat up then and looked at the other. His face did look something like that of a hawk that sleeps, with his sharp curved nose and his half-closed eyes. But it was the face of a hawk just waiting to wake and pounce.

"How would you like to try to make me?" he said very softly.

Long Ax was still red with anger but he looked away from Sleepy Hawk, toward the river.

"You have a knife and I have nothing," he growled.

With a move so fast it could barely be seen Sleepy Hawk

jumped to his feet, took the knife from his belt and tossed it away.

"Now, I have no knife."

"Enough!" cried Mountain Bear, who was a quiet man but strong like his name animal. "Save your blows for our enemies! Long Ax, I have a stick for a spear, dry and tough. You may have it for your ax. Sleepy Hawk, take up your knife. You know we would not go on a fight or a hunt without you to lead us."

So there was peace, but later, while waiting for Long Ax to bind together haft and head of his weapon, Mountain Bear said to Sleepy Hawk, "I cannot understand you. Always you laugh. And there is nothing to smile about in life."

"Yes, there is! Each thing of life, even the worst thing, has a part of it that will make you laugh, if only you will see it."

"Ha! I suppose you laugh even when you are with a woman!"

"Sometimes. If it is the proper woman and her heart is like mine."

But, as I said, most of The People think the matter had its beginning later, there on the ledge of the mountain of the Mud Dwellers, halfway down the great cliff, when the five young men came face to face with six of the little Mud Dwellers and there was no going back for any man.

For, after much thought, the band had decided to go toward the sun and into the mountain of the Mud Dwellers, rather than to the cold mountains and the Dwellers-in-Caves. The young men of The People wanted women. Those Dwellers-in-Caves, who made such queer markings on the walls of their homes, were strong and not easy to surprise. Too, their women were fierce, not kind and pleasing like those of the Mud Dwellers.

So they made a long journey, over a strange country. First, the river had dried into a hot land. After that, they seemed to be in the time of the long sun, come before they had thought, and the skins of animals they wore were hot on their backs. Sleepy Hawk wound into a tight roll his skin of a big cat and wrapped it around his waist. After a while, the others did the same.

Sleepy Hawk looked at them, running slowly along, the water pouring off their bodies, and said, "It is cooler by the side of our river."

Even Long Ax grinned at this although his tongue was swollen in his mouth.

The heat of the long sun fell on them and what little water they found made their hearts sick and their minds weak. So the young man went a day and a night without drinking.

Then, when they felt they could run no longer, they saw before them that great mountain rising straight up from the ground to the sky which held in its heart the little caves of the little men that The People called the Mud Dwellers. They stopped and looked up at the mountain.

"Oo-ee!" cried Hungry Dog. "That will be a hard run!"

But Sleepy Hawk found a trickle of water and they drank it without having their bellies cry out against them.

So the five young men of The People climbed the mountain that day and found its top was broad and flat. They moved carefully across the ground, ducking from tree to tree. Once, they found a pile of rocks that had, in the long ago, been a Mud Dwellers' home, before the wars of The People had driven them down inside the mountain, where the little men thought that they might live more safely.

"These do not look like rocks," said Mountain Bear, stopping to look at them.

"They are not rocks," said Sleepy Hawk. "I have heard that the Mud Dwellers mix dried grass with mud, shape this into blocks and let the heat of the sun make the blocks hard. They build their caves with these hard blocks."

"That is a foolish waste of time," said Mountain Bear.

"And we waste time," said Sleepy Hawk. "We must reach the edge of their home place before dark."

So, just before the hiding of the sun, the young hunters came to where the top of the mountain suddenly ended. They crouched down and looked over the edge. There was a great cut, going deep to the heart of the mountain; and down, far down at the bottom of the cut, they could see, moving like bugs on a raw hide, a few of the Mud Dwellers.

"We'll rest here until the first morning light," Sleepy Hawk told them.

"Then climb down as far as we can?" asked Mountain Bear.

Sleepy Hawk nodded.

"Then we should watch another day, I think," said Long Ax.

Sleepy Hawk nodded again.

"We'll have to be quick," said Short Spear.

"Take women only," grunted Long Ax. "Weapons too, if there are any."

"And food!" added Hungry Dog.

"No food!" cried all the others.

"They do not eat," Cat-in-the .Mud told Hungry Dog. "Their food is taken from the ground and it is dirty."

Sleepy Hawk smiled a little at this, but said nothing.

Yet it did not work out as they planned. The five young men waked at the first light and slowly, quietly, they climbed down the steep side of the cut in the mountain. But as they crawled around a high rock to a narrow ledge, six men of the Mud Dwellers came up onto the ledge from the down trail. All stopped suddenly and stared at each other.

Then each side took a step forward, raised their weapons, then stopped again, weapons half lifted in their hands.

"Well," Long Ax growled deep in his throat, "why do we wait?"

"For the same reason they do!" Sleepy Hawk's voice was sharp.

He waved his hand and they all looked quickly about them. There was the long, narrow ledge, with the mountain

going straight up from one side and, from the other, straight
down in a heart-choking drop. And at each end of the ledge
stood a little group of men, angry, uncertain, the length of
three steps of a tall man between them.

"Who can win a fight in such a place?" asked Sleepy
Hawk.

"We can!" growled Long Ax. "They are but little men!"

"But they are six and we are five, so all is equal."

"Throw spears and after them!" cried Long Ax.

Cat-in-the-Mud and Hungry Dog raised their weapons. As
they did so, three of the Mud Dwellers lifted their arms.

"Stop!" cried Sleepy Hawk. Over his shoulder he said to
Long Ax, "I am chief here. Now look, all of you. They
throw, we throw. None can miss. If any men are left after the
throwing, they fight. Perhaps one of all here lives. Then
what? If that one is of The People, can he, wounded, alone,
ever hope to return to our river? No!"

"You are right," said Mountain Bear.

"They will call for help," warned Cat-in-the-Mud.

"Soon enough to fight then," said Sleepy Hawk. "There
is little room for more on this ground."

"True enough," said Mountain Bear.

"Now, quiet, all of you," ordered Sleepy Hawk, "and let
me think."

He watched the Mud Dwellers. They were strange little
men. Around their waists they wore belts of dried skin, but in
these belts were set little pieces of colored stone. They wore
smaller belts around their heads, to keep their long hair from
falling over their eyes, and these belts, too, had the pieces of
stone in them.

Sleepy Hawk liked these colored stones very much. But he
did not think he would get any from the Mud Dwellers, who,
though small, stood their ground as bravely as did The People, frowning, with knives and spears ready for the fight.

"Look at their spears," Sleepy Hawk said.

"They have two handles!" There was wonder in Cat-in-the-Mud's voice.

"Yes. One goes back from the hand, then joins the other which goes forward to the head of the spear."

"I don't understand," Mountain Bear said softly.

"Neither do I." Sleepy Hawk frowned. "Two handles . . . I would like a closer look at those strange spears."

"Enough of this women's chatter!" screamed Long Ax. "Let us fight like men!"

Sleepy Hawk shrugged.

"If the rest of you feel that we should get ourselves killed," he said quietly, "and leave our bones here for mud Dwellers to hang in their caves, why—let Long Ax begin the fight."

None moved.

Long Ax called out again but still no man of the other four moved and Long Ax closed his mouth tightly.

For a time there was silence on the ledge. Sleepy Hawk watched the Mud Dwellers; he had a wish to talk with them, to learn what they might be thinking. Now, like many of The People, Sleepy Hawk had a woman from the Mud Dwellers in his family, and from her had learned a few of their love words, the words that a mother says to a child that pleases her. But that was all. When The People caught a Mud Dweller woman it was her duty to learn their talk, not theirs to learn her noises.

So there was nothing he could say to them. He watched. They, too, stood as did The People, their leader a little in front of them, staring at his enemies, his men behind him, looking about nervously, their knives and strange two-handled spears ready for blood.

It seemed then to Sleepy Hawk that the two groups of men looked like two deer caught in the trap sands of a river. A deer so caught by the water hiding below the quiet-looking sands cannot step forward, nor can it move backward. So it was with the men. Their legs were caught on the rock. They dared not move either up or down. All of them, The People and Mud Dwellers, could only stand still and wait for what would happen.

And thinking of the men trapped like silly deer, Sleepy Hawk laughed aloud.

"Why do you laugh?" snarled Hungry Dog. Fright was in his voice.

Sleepy Hawk was choking again, as he always did when laughing swelled in his throat.

"This is—this is all very—" He choked and his breath flew out between his lips and he made a word.

"What was that?" cried Mountain Bear. "What did you say?"

"I said, *funny.*"

"What does *funny* mean?"

"It is a word I have made and it means laugh-making. All this—we and they standing here, of us all none daring to go a step forward or back—it is very laugh-making . . . very *funny!*"

"We have a crazy man for a chief," growled Long Ax. "Or a fool. It takes little to make a fool laugh—"

But Sleepy Hawk was not listening. He was watching the leader of the Mud Dwellers and he was so startled by what that one was doing that he gave no ear to Long Ax's words. For the Mud Dweller was smiling. At first, it was a little smile, on the mouth only, but then, as Sleepy Hawk started to laugh again, the Mud Dweller's smile shone in his eyes, he opened his mouth and laughed as loudly as Sleepy Hawk ever did.

The two of them stood and laughed with each other while their followers looked at them uneasily and Long Ax muttered words of anger that he knew Sleepy Hawk could not hear.

Then, perhaps because his heart was warmed by his laughing, or because he was a great thinker, as the later days of his life proved, Sleepy Hawk did a very strange thing. First he put his knife back in his belt, so that his left hand held nothing. Then he dropped his spear from his right hand. Mountain Bear cried out at this, but Sleepy Hawk did not listen. He stepped forward one step and raised his right hand, so that the chief of the Mud Dwellers could see that it was empty.

The Mud Dweller's smile was now on his lips only. He looked very hard at Sleepy Hawk, then he slowly nodded his head. Then he moved his hands slowly so that the two handles of his spear came apart. In one hand, he held a spear with a sharp stone head. In the other, just a simple, harmless stick with a hook at one end. He dropped these to the ground and stepped toward Sleepy Hawk, his right hand raised.

The two of them came close together. Sleepy Hawk said a Mud Dweller word that they all knew, one that a mother uses when her child makes her smile at his play. The Mud Dweller's smile became smaller; the young men saw that he did not like the use of that word between men. So Sleepy Hawk pointed at the young men of The People, then at the Mud Dwellers, making fearful frowns to show each of them angry at the other. Then he pointed to himself and laughed. He pointed to the Mud Dweller and laughed. He swept his arm around the air, pointing at both sides and laughing.

Then, slowly and clearly, Sleepy Hawk said his new word.

The chief of the Mud Dwellers nodded and said it after him.

"Fun-nee!" he said.

Sleepy Hawk held out his empty right hand and the Mud Dweller slowly reached out and touched Sleepy Hawk's hand with his.

"Very funny," answered Sleepy Hawk, grinning. Then, hoping the Mud Dweller might know the tongue of The People, he said, "I am Sleepy Hawk."

But the Mud Dweller did not understand. He said some words, in the high bird voice of the Mud Dwellers. Nor did Sleepy Hawk understand the Mud Dweller's words, so the two men just stood there, their right hands touching, smiling.

"Do any of you know any of the Mud Dwellers' words among men?" asked Sleepy Hawk.

The young men shook their heads.

"Never mind. Put down your weapons."

"Is that wise?" asked Mountain Bear.

"It is. Put them down."

So all the young men except Long Ax lowered their spears and put their knives and axes in their belts.

"Long Ax! I command you—" Sleepy Hawk began, but the chief of the Mud Dwellers turned his head and said a few words to his followers and they, slowly, took apart their two-handled spears and set them on the ground and those that had knives in their hands put these back in their belts. So Long Ax, too, let his weapon rest on the ground.

While their men stood, not at peace, but not ready for war, the two chiefs made talk with their hands; and after a while Sleepy Hawk nodded many times and turned to his followers and said, "Now we may go. With no spears in our backs. I have his promise."

"What is that worth!" cried Long Ax. "I do not turn my back on an enemy."

"Stay here, then," answered Sleepy Hawk. He himself waved at the Mud Dweller, turned and took a step back toward the upward trail.

Then he stopped, so suddenly that Mountain Bear, who was behind him, bumped into Sleepy Hawk.

"What is the matter with you?" cried Mountain Bear.

"Let us stay a little longer. I want one of those spears."

Sleepy Hawk looked again at the Mud Dweller, smiled, and very slowly, took the knife from his belt. The Mud Dweller frowned, but made no move when he saw that Sleepy Hawk held the knife by its blade and offered it to him.

"One does not give presents to an enemy," said Hungry Dog.

"This is no present. Watch and see."

The Mud Dweller took Sleepy Hawk's knife and looked at it. It was a good knife, with a blade of sharp flint and a handle made of the polished horn of old humpback. It was easy to see that the Mud Dweller wanted the knife.

Then Sleepy Hawk pointed to the little headbelt with its

polished stones. Then he pointed to himself, then to the knife, and finally, to the Mud Dweller.

The Mud Dweller reached behind his head and took off the belt. Its bright-colored stones sparkled in the sun's light. The Mud Dweller handed it to Sleepy Hawk, who fastened it around his head. The Mud Dweller weighed the knife in his hand, nodded twice, and put the knife in the belt around his waist.

"Ha!" said Mountain Bear. "I thought you wanted a spear."

"Be quiet! I shall get one."

"How?"

"You shall see."

Once more Sleepy Hawk made as if to go. And once more he stopped and turned back to the Mud Dweller. That little man watched with sharp eyes. Sleepy Hawk took his rolled-up skin of a mountain cat from around his waist, shook it out so that the Mud Dweller could see, and spread it on the ground.

The Mud Dweller felt of the skin and his fingers saw how soft it was, having been well cured by Sleepy Hawk's oldest mother. Sleepy Hawk looked up at the sun, covered his eyes and shivered. The Mud Dweller watched closely. Sleepy Hawk uncovered his eyes but still shivered. Then he reached for the skin and wrapped it around him. As soon as it covered him all over, he stopped shaking and smiled.

The chief of the Mud Dwellers nodded to show he understood that when the time of the little sun came, the skin would keep him warm and dry.

He reached toward Sleepy Hawk for the skin of the big cat.

"Careful!" Mountain Bear called softly.

Sleepy Hawk let the skin fall to the ground. The Mud Dweller reached for it again, but Sleepy Hawk raised his hand, shook his head just a little and walked over to where the two parts of the chief's spear lay on the ground. A Mud Dweller started for Sleepy Hawk, but his chief called out and the man was quiet. Sleepy Hawk picked up the two parts of the weapon but did not take them away. Instead he carried them back to the chief of the Mud Dwellers.

Sleepy Hawk made slow, careful signs. He lifted in his hand the spear that was no spear, but just a harmless stick. He shook it, held each end of it in turn, very close to his eyes, then, shaking his head, he let that stick fall to the ground. Next, Sleepy Hawk looked at the spear that was a proper spear, felt its sharp point with his thumb and nodded. After that, he picked up the other stick and held both parts out toward the Mud Dweller.

The Mud Dweller shook his head.

Sleepy Hawk stirred the cat's skin with his toe.

The Mud Dweller frowned just a little, then nodded. He moved his hand to show that Sleepy Hawk could have the two spears and reached down for the skin. But Sleepy Hawk shook his head and held out the stick part that was not a spear at all.

The Mud Dweller smiled, took both parts from Sleepy Hawk's hands. He looked around him, then moved to the rim of the ledge and stood there, looking upward.

"Now we shall see how a man throws that spear," Sleepy Hawk said softly.

"Surely he will not throw it *up* the mountain," said Mountain Bear.

But that is what the little man did. The Mud Dweller put the pieces together and raised his arm back to throw. One of the shafts went back from his hand. The queer hook at its end held the shaft of the true spear. Then the Mud Dweller threw and, as the stick in his hand made his arm twice as long as any man's, so was his throw twice as strong and the spear flew up the mountain, farther than the farthest spear ever thrown by any of The People. It landed beside the trail down which the young men had come and stood there, its point deep in the ground.

"Oo—ee!" whistled Mountain Bear.

"A stick that throws!" cried Sleepy Hawk.

"The stick throws the spear!" said Cat-in-the-Mud. He grinned sourly at Long Ax. "Their weapons are better than ours. Sleepy Hawk is a very wise chief."

And Hungry Dog nodded and moved away from Long Ax.

Then the chief of the Mud Dwellers took up Sleepy Hawk's spear and showed him how to fit it on the throwing stick. He seemed to think of something new, then, for he pointed to his own spear sticking in the ground high up the mountain. He made a sign to keep Sleepy Hawk's spear, then pointed at Sleepy Hawk and to the spear up by the trail.

"A wise man," Sleepy Hawk said to Mountain Bear. "He wants to keep my spear and I will take his as we pass by it."

"Wait!" cried Mountain Bear. "I want one of those spear throwers!"

And he unwrapped his bear's skin from where it was wound around his middle and walked over to one of the Mud Dwellers. After him came the rest of the young men of The People, even the angry Long Ax, and The People and the Mud Dwellers stood beside each other, smiling and talking, even though there was no understanding of what was said.

And all of them laughed when a little, fat Mud Dweller offered Hungry Dog some small, round brown things and made signs that Hungry Dog should eat them. Which Hungry Dog did, of course.

"Good!" he cried with his mouth full, as a man should not. "Eat them! They're good!"

"Now, Hungry Dog," said Sleepy Hawk, "give them some dried meat."

Hungry Dog looked unhappy at this but he took some dried flesh of deer and offered it to the Mud Dwellers. After chewing a little bit, they smiled and rubbed their middles to show that the dried meat was good to their insides.

Now the sun was straight up in the sky. The giving and receiving was finished and the men stood about, tired, hot, but peaceful. Sleepy Hawk made signs to the Mud Dweller chief, pointing up the mountain. That man nodded, but he looked sad. Then Sleepy Hawk looked up at the sun, waved his hand across the sky, pointed down at the ledge, held up his fingers many times. The Mud Dweller smiled.

Sleepy Hawk thought a long time, looking hard at the Mud Dweller, then he said a word. Mountain Bear, who was standing by, had never heard this word before.

Sleepy Hawk pointed to the Mud Dwellers and the young men of The People, at the skins and the weapons, and at the belts with the colored stones.

He said the word again.

The Mud Dweller said the word after Sleepy Hawk.

Sleepy Hawk and the Mud Dweller said the word together.

Then the young men of The People waved to the Mud Dwellers and started the climb back to the top of the mountain.

When they reached the flat top of the mountain and rested awhile, Sleepy Hawk laughed softly and said to Mountain Bear, "You know, I have another, better knife at home. And my cat's skin was old. I shall hunt for another one." He laughed again. "But I have never had a stick that throws spears farther than can a man's arms. And when I seek a wife, I shall give her father some of the colored stones. Even the chief of all our chiefs should then be willing to give me his oldest daughter—the beautiful one."

Mountain Bear hefted the throwing stick. "We are coming back?"

"Yes. I want more throwing sticks. I want many belts with their stones of many colors. Yes, in three hands of suns I will return to . . ."

"To what?" asked Mountain Bear. "I heard you make a word."

"Yes. I made a word to tell of giving one thing to get another. I taught it to that chief of the Mud Dwellers. So, from now on, unless some fool like Long Ax makes trouble, the Mud Dweller and I will not fight. We will *trade*."

And that is why we go peacefully to the land of Mud Dwellers and bring back many things without war. And that

is why the youngest young son of Sleepy Hawk, who is like
the old man was, is planning to go up the mountains where
the Dwellers-in-Caves are. He thinks they will trade us the
strange colors they put on the walls of their caves and other
things for our throwing sticks and skins and bright stones.

THE PEAT BOG
Poul Anderson

And in this story prehistory and history overlap, for it is set in the first century A.D., *which in some parts of the world is already thousands of years into the historic era, while in others the ancient rites and customs of the primeval days still endure. Poul Anderson, scholar and poet as well as vastly popular author of science fiction, offers a haunting and powerful view of those two worlds in collision as our closing work.*

WE TRAVELED OVERLAND from Massilia to Colonia Agrippina, where we spent the winter while Memmius studied language and gathered intelligence. He required me to join him in the first of these, and said he hoped I could be of value in the second; but I wasn't. That land weighed on me too heavily.

It was not so much that the town was small and raw, most of the streets only hog-wallows twisting between timber houses whose shapes were all wrong, the population a garrison among peasants and barbarians, like a weir staked out in a dark slow river. One expects this on a frontier. In truth, our passage through Gaul had agreeably surprised me by the extent to which civilization had flowed north out of the Narbonnese in the bare hundred or so years since divine Julius opened that sluice gate. Paved roads, orderly fields, neat little cities where one might find not just an amphitheater but men who quoted Euripides or Aristotle as naturally as would a born Greek. When I remarked on this to Memmius, the leather of his face had crinkled upward, and he drawled:

"Look closer, Philon. Those people don't even walk like you or me, let alone think the same way. And wait till we get farther north, where the bodies themselves are nothing you'll find anywhere around the Midworld Sea. Rome's spread thinner than I really care to say out loud. New territories like Britain, it's obvious enough there; but here too, here too."

As we came into German country, the alienness grew according to his prediction. In itself, that didn't trouble me. Memmius' enterprises had already taken us as far afield as Mauretania and Pontus. If anything—after I began to catch a bit of the language, which struck me as rather pleasingly resonant, not the harsh gabble it's often called—if anything, I felt less far from home here than in, say, Jerusalem. Here, the attitude did not seem to be shameless importunity and slyness cloaking a resentment which seethed in the marrow. Instead, my impression was of an odd blend of somewhat boorish affability with inward pride. "You beat us in these parts, but we won in the Teutoburg Forest, both fair and square. Now let's see if we can't get along." So their eyes appeared to say. I knew I might be reading what wasn't there into that blueness. Maybe it came from my liking the frank way they strode along, girls almost as big and handsome as boys.

And trees were ablaze with autumn, stubble fields golden, air cool: misty of mornings but star-brilliant at night, by day full of humus odors and wild goose calls. If the fare and accommodations were coarse, beer preferable to what passed locally for wine, the ride long between each pair of stopping places, why, I have never minded that. I expected to find reasonable contentment in Colonia.

What I did not foresee was, first, the confinement, the shrinking of the world to a stockade and fosse. Oh, it was not impossible to go out: even, by prearrangement, across the river, where the unconquered Chatti were milder than the reputation they have in Rome. But there was soon no point in it; I had seen everything the countryside had to offer of human variety that lay within a day's round trip. This was the more true when those days really began to shorten.

The town rated no such name. It was hardly more than a military outpost, set down by Claudius a few years ago upon what had been a marketplace for yeomen, fishers, charcoal burners, woodsrunners. Memmius felt it had great potential. However, that did us no good now. Now was a commandant, the top of the social heap, whose brain was cast iron; a hairy half-educated oaf who grunted us through our language lessons; what few books I had brought along and quickly memorized; chilly rooms, smoky fires, gloom.

Winter cast me far down. It was warmer than I had anticipated, or I should say less cold. But the dankness gnawed into the liver, even as the murk—heavy gray skies above snow and mud, until day's brief glimmer was swallowed by monstrous black—ate at my soul. O islands white against sun-dazzled lapping purple, a temple seen through olive trees as tiny and bright as a star! They danced in my head like the wisps of a dream.

Memmius seemed unaffected, the same deceptively easygoing businessman he had always shown to the world. He studied, fared about, talked, questioned, bargained, bribed, joked, insinuated, did all that a Roman of the equestrian class might do and more besides, but never in a hurry, never letting on that his purpose included anything save a commercial venture. Whether his source of information be the provincial governor passing through or a raggedy crone peddling turnips on an icy corner, an arrogant princely warrior come the whole way from Scandia to see what glory he might pick up or a lout from just across the river, a courtesan who knew everybody or a slave girl rented for a few nights from her horizon-bound rustic owner—he asked, he probled, he learned, he pondered.

I kept records of whatever he chose me to witness or to be told afterward. And, having a gift for tongues, I presently spoke better German than he did. But otherwise I was sad and useless. He tried to jolly me out of it.

One night he even called me to his bed, a thing he had not done for half a dozen years, when I turned fourteen and laughed that I was getting too angular for his taste. (Then he manumitted me and gave me regular employment. At first I mostly attended his wife; a Greek amanuensis-cum-factotum is an elegant thing for a Roman lady to have. Later he began using me for real, often confidential work. How burstingly proud I was when he explained: "We're not bound north only to see if we can open new trade. We'll also be on a mission for Caesar." And the characteristically sardonic: "Caesar's ministers, at least; Nero seems to consider other interests more urgent. . . . The fact is, Britain's near the boiling point, Gaul not as quiet as it might be, the Germans beyond the marches are moving about, and new powers are rising, seaborne, on the far side of the Cimbrian Chersonese. . . . Maybe those chiefs plan no threat to Rome's holdings, no alliances with rebels. Maybe. That's for Rome to find out, and try to influence. We've agents in Scandia and the islands. My task is to find out how things are on the peninsula; if possible, to stiffen those tribes against the easterners. . . ." He, Gnaus Valerius Memmius, asked me what I, freedman Philon, who did not even know my father's name, what I thought about this!)

But that night wasn't what we'd sometimes, earlier had. He was kindly as always, yet—a trifle too abstracted, or too competent?—or had simply too long a while passed? He still had the hawk profile, but it was grizzled and deeply furrowed. I think he sensed the same as myself, for at length he raised his leanness on an elbow, stroked my cheek, and said, smiling a bit through guttering yellow lamplight: "Philon, I believe you need a girl."

"No, not really." I huddled against him, though mainly because the room was cold. The breath puffed white from our lips.

"She'd keep you warm," he said. "And me, for that matter. In spring, when we leave, I can resell her, maybe for a profit if she's gotten pregnant."

Her name was Gerda and she was, indeed, quite appealing, a stocky blonde who was anxious to learn our wishes and, once she discovered we wouldn't mistreat her, given to singing little songs while she worked around the house. I didn't always blow out the flame and pretend she was Hephaestion to my Alexander; sometimes I enjoyed that she was Gerda, who demanded no more than I wanted to give.

Not that we often slept together. I wasn't that interested. And Memmius was: largely because she was a Longobard, captured in some clash with the Chatti and passed westward hand to hand. North of the Longobards dwell the Saxons, and north of the Saxons are the Cimbrians, among others, and it is from the Cimbrian peninsula that that horde came which almost overwhelmed Rome, a century and a half ago. The tribes there are still powerful. It's not strictly true that they asked for our friendship, when a Roman fleet visited them a while back. That report was the kind of self-serving which every delegation to the barbarians makes. They did show our men hospitality, and they are—like their rivals to the east—actively trading with us. That's all.

The trade is usually through a long chain of middlemen. We don't know enough about what's going on in those parts. Rome has had some catastrophic surprises in the past. On the other hand, granted sufficient information and connections, Rome has been able to play one foreign faction off against another. Like, say, the Cimbrians versus the Scandians. . . .

Gerda didn't greatly brighten my mood, though. Springtime did, sunlight and greenness, messages from outside, packing up and ho-ha for saddle leather under me again! Lately I've been remembering her, bulge-bellied and weeping, when Memmius handed her over to a dealer. At the time, I was too wild with my own freedom to notice.

We jogged through Belgic Gaul to Gesoriacum. I'd done considerable detail work for us, arranging that a ship and crew and trade goods be there when we arrived. The goods were perfectly genuine: silverware, glassware, fine cloth, oils; for those people who dwell between the German and Suebian Seas have a shrewd awareness of the value of their

amber, furs, hides, tallow, beeswax. "I am at least as concerned," Memmius said, "with establishing a profitable con-
nection as I am with bulwarking the legions."

Beyond the sandy isles and half-drowned marshlands of
Frisia, the peninsula thrusts northward. It is also low country,
yet not flat; hills rise steep to offer tremendous vistas across
moors where only the yellow of gorse breaks the darkling
reach of heather. The west coast, like much of the interior, is
virtually treeless. What few oaks and evergreens have laid
root in its poor soil are stunted, witchily gnarled, bent to the
east as if straining from the endless wind. It comes off the
sea, that wind, bleak and salt, roaring, streaming; clouds flee
before it, their shadows scythe over the earth, sweeps of half-
night and half-day like time in the eyes of a god. Nevertheless heaven arches so vast that—save in the frequent rains—
the clouds seem lost therein, as do the thousands of water-
fowl, storks, herons, hawks, eagles, crows, ravens, every
kind of wings aloft.
Our pilot was Eporedorix, Gaul who had been here often
before and led us to a sheltered bay where the amber buyers
customarily stop. This merchantman was too deep-bottomed
to beach like the light barbarian craft, which depend more on
oars or paddles than on sail. Captain Scaubo growled he'd
sooner lie at anchor anyway, just in case. "You're a suspicious old Lusitanian, aren't you?" I jested. He looked sour.
Memmius grinned: "That's how he got to be old, Philon."
Nobody was around when the dinghy set us ashore. We
were well in advance of the bartering season. For months the
tribesmen would be working their farms, chasing deer across
the heaths, trapping hares, catching fish and seal and the
lesser whales, to replenish larders gone hollow during the
winter. Women and children would gather oysters and, after
every storm, amber that had been cast on the beaches.
"We'll have a short wait, though," Memmius assured me.
"Word about us will move around fast." He had deliberately
come early, to get settled and begin gathering firsthand infor-

mation free of the tumult which marts and moots would create.

I stared at enormous manlessness and asked, "How will they know?"

"Oh, natives, they got instincts, like animals," Scaubo grunted.

Memmius shrugged. "It looks simpler to me," he said, "to posit that a herdboy can spy our smoke from ten miles away, and his brothers can lope thirty miles in a day to tell the neighbors." He turned. A red cloak flapped around his tunic. "Let's pitch camp. And unload the horses, especially. I want to be sure they've got their land legs when our yokels arrive."

Soon we had a snug cluster of tents. Scaubo supervised the assembling of a small shrine, and himself made the thank-offering to Neptune for safe passage. Memmius added one to Mercury, since we would be faring along roads now, though I knew he believed in no gods—merely in that dance of blind atoms which Lucretius has written of—and acted pious lest he rouse superstitious fears. This country was so daunting.

Myself, I wandered off. In chilly dusk, in a clump of grass behind a dune, I found a coltsfoot growing, the first frail flower of spring, and knelt to call without words upon Aphrodite. Memmius is wily and learned, he is doubtless right about the absurdity of the myths, very possibly most of the world arises from a play of forces and nothing else; but She is. I have felt Her too often to imagine otherwise.

I am alone—I did not speak to Her—my heart flutters like a snared swallow. I am alike full of grief and of a joy I know will come to me in the future, alike awed and terrified. I feel how tiny are the years of my life but feel too that they are infinitely deep, and none of this do I understand. Lady of All, what do You want of me?

Surf growled outside the bay. The tide was coming in, that eternal onslaught we do not know in the Midworld Sea.

I slept poorly, with many dreams.

The next day, however, opened in peace except for brief,

thunderful hailstorm. We explored the area, finding countless
traces of former encampments: fire sites, potsherds, gnawed
bones, crude carvings on boulders which might have been
done in idleness or might be sacred. Generations of feet,
hoofs, wheels had worn a trail from inland through the brush,
so broad and hard-packed it could almost be called a road.
Some of the younger sailors and I took weapons and followed
it a few miles. Near the end of our venture we came upon a
row of great mounds. Though overgrown, several of them
had in the course of ages worn down to expose the stone
chambers within.

I froze. "But I've seen dolmens like that at home!" I
cried.

"You find them everywhere along the coasts, from Caria
to here and maybe farther," said Hippodamas, who had become my friend on the sea trip, being a fellow Greek and a
bright, good-looking lad. "We saw them when we rounded
Armorica, and rows of standing stones too, stark as teeth in a
dead giant's jaw."

"Who made them?" I whispered.

"Who knows? I dug into one once. Full of skeletons."

"Tombs—" It came upon me that here was no new land.
It was ancient beyond knowing, secret beyond imagining.

Hippodamas saw me shiver and laid a comforting arm
around my waist. No fool, he was yet no brooder like me,
but lived toughly and merrily in each day as it came. We
walked thus awhile, till everybody decided to turn around.
Then we found ourselves at the tail of the line. He laid his
mouth to my ear and murmured, "You know, Philon, since
you shaved this morning, your face could be a girl's."

Beneath the wind, my cheeks heated.

"A touch too strong in the chin, maybe," he went on, a
teasing which softened to: "But those're nice lips, and
straight nose, curly black hair, fine hazel eyes. . . . How
about it?"

"Uh," I mumbled in a wave of confusion.

"We've been warned how chaste the German women

are,'' he laughed. A marvelous interplay of muscles went through his arm where it circled above my hips. ''That whore in Gesoriacum is far behind me. Hm?''

''I—I—'' It did not seem to be me that stammered, ''No, I'm sorry, Hippodamas, but—''

He let go. ''Don't tell me you've never, like a Jew.''

''No, but—''

''Ah,'' he said coldly. ''Your patron, then. Quite. I understand.'' He left me and fell into overanimated conversation with a shipmate.

But I don't understand! I wanted to cry after him. It's only . . . I don't know what it is. Here, here, She has made something ready for me. I can't imagine how I know—

Staring around: This stern strange country, oh, that must have stirred a thing to life in me, a longing for— But I am already free! A freedman, at least, under the supervision of a kindly and interesting man who . . . who will surely be visiting Greece again, next year or the year after, for a while, and will want me to come along . . . won't he?

Hippodamas, don't be angry because I have fallen into Her hands.

I was outwardly silent the rest of that day. Next noon the dwellers arrived.

We saw them from afar, but were nonetheless surprised. True, most were locals as expected, on foot, unarmored, bearing spears, axes, long cutting-action swords of soft brown iron, or mere cudgels—about thirty altogether. But at their head came half a dozen riders in helmet and ringmail.

Eporedorix bustled about directing us in how to form up. He wanted no bristling defensive ranks that, by assuming hostility, might provoke it. Rather, we took stances from which we could instantly leap to form a shield-locked square. Memmius donned his toga and advanced in proper Roman dignity. From my post I peered and peered, every thew aquiver, pulse loud in my skull and throat. Were these the terrible Cimbrians?

They averaged taller than men of the Midworld, but not inordinately so, perhaps three or four inches; and their build was more stocky than lean. While some had sun-bleached hair whiter than flax, that of others was brown, red, or black. They cropped it short, like their beards. The only really alien feature was the eyes, sea-pale in those weathered faces. They wore knee-length tunics of coarse wool, to which several added leather cloaks and linen trousers. Fabrics were dyed with woad, madder, and-dimly-berry juices. Their shoes were hairy, strapped around the foot and laced to the ankle.

Such were the walkers: men of this neighborhood, farmers, fishers, hunters, trappers, diggers of peat, who had so little worth stealing that whole lifetimes might pass without a war other than the strife against nature which had no truce. They were brave, hardy, and, I thought then, simple.

The riders, on hammer-headed shaggy dun ponies, resembled them in many ways, but were a little bigger, much straighter, their hands not misshapen from toil—an upper class. Their conical nose-guarded helmets and knee-length ring-byrnies seemed well made, and might give better protection than legionary's loricae. The clothes beneath were of good, colorful stuff. They were clean-shaven but wore their hair somewhat longer than the peasants, drawing it into a braid that hung down the left shoulder.

They halted at the edge of the strand. Memmius trod forth, right arm raised. "Greeting," he said in his German. "We come in peace, as friends, from Rome the Great."

The natives looked nonplussed. One or two snickered. The leading horseman rode from their line, dipped his lance, and, smiling, replied, "Greeting and welcome to the country of the High Jutes"—in accented but comprehensible Latin.

I could only gape. Memmius recovered fast, spoke smooth phrases, told us to lay aside our arms, and invited the barbarians to dine.

"We thank you," said their leader. Beneath his courtesy twinkled the same amusement as before. He had a fine voice, deep and melodious, rising slowly from the depths of the barrel chest. "I am Hesting, son of Beroan, king—or perhaps you'd call me duke—of High Jutland, on whose Weststrands you have landed." Springing to earth with a litheness unusual for his compact build, he clasped Memmius' hand and arm in the Roman manner.

My gaze followed him around. He was not young—past forty, I guessed—though he carried himself so well that this could only be told from the gray in his ruddy locks, furrows and crinkles in his face, unconscious masterfulness in his bearing. Crowsfeet around lightning-blue eyes, lines across broad brow, calipers from strongly curved nose to wide mobile mouth, startling dimples, bespoke years of looking across wide horizons, of thought, and of laughter. Suddenly I imagined Odysseus resembling, not idealized cold marble, but Hesting the Jute.

Through wind and surf, while cloud shadows chilled and the quick wan sun touched me, smelling salt and kelp, feeling sand hiss past my ankles, I watched the chieftain and heard him. He met Scaubo and Eporedorix with easy politeness, as if they were already old comrades. He passed among our crewmen, while heartening his followers with jokes in their own rough tongue, till both groups relaxed and started shyly to mingle.

By then I had discovered that the language here, while akin to what we had studied in Colonia, was sufficiently different that Memmius and I were lucky to hit on a speaker of Latin. We had a good foundation, of course, and ought soon to be reasonably fluent in Jutish; but Hesting could expedite matters for us no end. It made me wonder if Her will had brought him.

He explained things frankly and amicably while we showed him around our camp and ship, spread the best repast we could, made the gifts to him and his men which barbarians always expect (and Homer's heroes did). We Romans had—as usual, his eyes if not his lips seemed to chuckle— taken an overhasty view of a complex situation. (Memmius nodded, unsurprised. How accurate a picture can you compile from a few travelers' tales and, otherwise, third- or fourth-hand rumor?) The Cimbrians proper, whom Hesting called Himmeri, lived to the north of his own folk. Beyond them were the Vandals. The High Jutes ("I'd say the name comes less from boasting, though we get plenty of that, than from our holding the highest part of the country") occupied the middle of the peninsula, its major section. South of them dwelt the Heruls, Angles, and lesser folk.

These were all separate kingdoms, if that is the right word when a king is, essentially, no more than president at meetings of tribal chieftains, leader in war, and head priest. (Later I would learn what a clumsy simplification that was too, which we made at the time out of Hesting's laconic answers to questions.) But since they were of the same basic stock, they tended more and more to call themselves, collectively, Jutes.

This was the easier to do because nowadays they fought each other far less often than they did the Danes. These were another set of folk, related but distinct, currently migrating from Scandia into the islands, driving out or subjugating the inhabitants. Their swift, many-oared ships had long been raiding the eastern coast of the peninsula. Hesting expected a full-scale invasion this summer. It did not seem to perturb him.

He did not precisely chance to be in our vicinity. Every spring, after the equinoctial ceremonies at Holy Lake, the Goddess—Whom he called Nerthus while he signed his brow, lips, breast, and loins—traveled around the realm to bless it, as She did in other processions in the other kingdoms. He must accompany Her. Thus he had not been far off when word came of a foreign ship. Though the season was too sacred for combat, it had been only prudent for him and a few of his household warriors to arm themselves and go investigate. They must be back before dark.

As for how he came to know Latin, why, he laughed, that also was reasonable. Rome having conquered the Gauls and certain of the Germans, she was now the greatest power in

this part of the world as well as southward. Besides possible
diplomatic and military interaction, there was a growing volume of trade, thus far mostly with the mobile Danes. Why
should the Jutes not get a bigger share? Furthermore, Danes
venturing abroad, even serving hitches in the legions, had
picked up quite a lot of knowledge useful in war. Jutes had
better bestir themselves likewise.

Therefore Hesting had visited both Roman Germany and
northern Gaul as a young man. Later he had acquired a Latin-
speaking slave who kept him in practice. This man had lately
died of a flux, however.

Hesting had been hoping for the advent of somebody important. He and Memmius traded a glance which lasted for
several heartbeats after he said that. Oh, he knew already the
Roman was not merely a merchant, and the Roman knew that
the Jute knew, and they both smiled the least bit.

Let our leaders follow him on the sacred journey, he invited. It had just a few days left to go. Let them thereafter
come dwell as his guests at Owldoon, as long as they wished.
That was on the Great Road, an inland trade route which ran
many-branched from the Skaw on south through Iron Wood
into Germany. We would have no lack of passersby to ask
about things. Our goods could be carted there. If we wanted
to offer some at the seaside fair, he would arrange for their
storage in a nearby community.

"To be honest," Hesting said, "I'm afire to hear what
yarns you'll spin!"

I, seated humbly aside, was altogether charmed. Who
would have looked for alertness, humor, and curiosity in a
northland kinglet? Well, who, in the depths of northland winter, would have looked for the spring to blossom? Hesting
suffered from no more than the loneliness of his country, I
thought. In heart and brain, he was our kind of man—my
kind. I wondered if I would get a chance to recite him lines
of Sappho, no, Catullus, or tell him about Socrates and Alexander.

The passage of Nerthus reminded me of the rites of Cybele (and I would stare at the dolmen mounds which brooded everywhere over this landscape, and wonder half shivering what mysteries of a lost past linked the Midworld to the Boreal). Drawn by cows, Her wagon traveled from village to village. At each settlement the folk came forth shouting, singing, dancing, waving newly leaved and flowering branches, the girls garlanded. There followed rites, a feast, and a sacred orgy. Next morning the king and his men went on, to spread Her blessing further that the whole realm might be made fruitful.

Naturally, differences from the south were abundant, starting with those draft cows, which were tough little red beasts. Should one come in heat on the journey, she was bred in the very next place they reached. The bull was afterward killed by young men in a reckless chase and consumed, and great was the rejoicing because this year would surely be good.

The wagon was large, well carpentered, painted, and gold-trimmed; but the figures carved on it were too foreign to a Greek for me to see them as anything except grotesque. Only later would I find the powerful grace in the wood sculptures here. Upon the wagon stood a curtained shrine which housed Her image, that none might look upon save the king. He, white-robed, was the driver. His warriors were acolytes and honor guard, for no one broke the peace of the holy season, when even outlaws might creep from the moors and be given food and shelter.

The king was the priest of all vernal sacrifices and invocations. Those varied from stead to stead. In this thorp one gave a pig at the grave of its founder, in that hamlet a sheaf from the last harvest was burned—he knew each proceeding and conducted it with a dignity that made me, at least, feel Her veritable presence.

But immediately afterward the feast was spread, an extravagance of hoarded meats and breads and fruits, beer and mead and berry wine, for this otherwise lean period; and everybody, from the king on down, bawled in merriment. The jests, songs, and byplay got coarser as hours wore on, until at dark those who were married went by torchlight to a newly plowed field. There they formed a ring; and before their eyes, the king and a maiden chosen by lot disrobed, and he had her virginity; and each man and wife coupled in the furrows.

The girl was considered to be made lucky, a most desirable match. But she would thereafter know none but her husband. We were told that a woman's adultery was punished by her public scalping, clubbing, and living or half-living burial in a bog; she had tainted the blood of the clan. Even the bachelor youths were generally celibate, only a few rich households possessing female slaves whom their scions might enjoy.

"We seed our women upon the earth, that the seed in it may quicken," Hesting explained.

This was the day after we had been allowed to witness such a doing. I myself had been gripped by Her, oh, if only there had been a girl for me! Memmius had whispered dryly in my ear that he was glad this trip would soon be over and that Hesting had promised to include a concubine in his hospitality. I scarcely heard. The blood roared in me.

Now I saw Memmius lift an eyebrow. He knew better than to contradict, but his scoffing was obvious. I grew furious at him. The night before, in Hesting and the maiden I had looked upon raw beauty. That the king spoke in such a matter-of-fact voice did not lessen my respect for him. He went to his gods in the same unafraid way as he went about his daily work, or to war or sea or, at the end, death.

Not that I glorify the Jutes. They are uncivilized, unlettered, stolid save when drunk or in one of the fell rages that can come upon them, as close to the soil and waters as their own animals and therefore almost as far from the loftiest flights of the spirit. Though their craftsmanship is excellent and their art does have that primitive strength, both are limited by crude tools and scanty choice of materials. They think themselves free men, and are in fact the slaves of uncountably many traditions and superstitions. They have no concept of a better life than the labor and danger which are theirs, let alone any dream of a philosophy, a leader, or an empire that could make such betterment possible. They are physically admirable and keep themselves cleaner than I would have imagined after being in grimy Colonia; but their sports are clumsy and unorganized, their music a high-pitched keening, their dances ridiculous.

Typically, a house is a long one-room structure. Within a foundation frame of stones, walls and roof are turf supported by undressed timber, a firetrap if ever I saw any. Oriented east and west, the building has latticework doors but no windows, only a louver through which a little of the smoke off the clay hearth may escape. The gloom is hardly relieved by lamps. The floor is strewn with rushes or, on special occasions, juniper boughs. At one end are clay daises, wooden stools, a weighted loom, cooking gear, food hung from rafters, personal property—living space for the entire large family. The rest of the chamber is divided into stalls for cattle and horses, pens for swine and fowl. The livestock helps keep the place warm, and even I could get used to the stench; but it was disconcerting to rouse at dawn—after a night which had begun with unmistakable sounds of copulation— and see a boy trot past carrying a forkful of manure for the midden outside.

Ten or twenty such houses comprise a village. Around it lie the ancestral graves and the fields. Each family owns its land, but there is much collective effort, as well as a common. Nearby is a well or stream or other source of water, and usually a boulder or solitary tree or something of that kind to which small offerings are made.

As for religion in the larger sense, the Jutes worship primarily the Goddess, whom they call Nerthus, more in Her aspect of the Great Mother than of that inviolable Aphrodite Whom my heart serves. Her consort is Fro. The rough wooden images of either can be seen everywhere, to my mind grossly sexual until I remembered Diana of Ephesus and the Hermae in Athens. Only the idol which travels in the sacred wagon is forbidden to ordinary view. During the spring procession, the king is considered either to represent or to be Fro—the people are not inclined to draw fine logical distinctions.

They have numberless local divinities, tutelaries, and oracles. In addition, as I began to master the language and converse with folk, I heard about Danish gods and saw propitiations of them. These seemed to be principally the warlike three called by the Romans Mars, Jupiter, and Mercury. The Romans are forever making such naive identifications. I am far from sure that Tiwu, Thunarr, and Wothen really correspond that closely, not to speak of other deities. At any rate, Nerthus and Fro are the aboriginal Powers of land and sea, fertility and fisheries. The Danes put most of their pantheon in heaven and make them lords of war. As they and the Jutes come increasingly into contact, however hostile, more and more men on either side are deeming it wise to pay respects to the gods associated with the opposition.

This Hesting would not do. "I plain don't aim to truckle to Wothen Psychopompos," he stated. His manner was calm as ever. "Maybe, in time, we can reach an understanding of sorts with the Danes, and thus with their gods. Meanwhile I am Fro's, and Hers, and mainly my people's."

We were riding down the Great Road, approaching Owldoon, his home. The rutted, muddy, rain-puddled path was no legionary highway. Yet it ran for hundreds of miles to join ancient routes in the east of Europe, and along it had gone amber, bronze, furs, glass, slaves, hopes for more centuries than man has kept count of.

Here we were somewhat east of the middle of the peninsula, upon its spine. High banks on either side bore grass, daisies, ferns, dandelions like blobs of gold, briar, crab apple, blackthorn, wild cherry. Above was a thin forest, murky fir, palely budding willow, shuddering aspen. It was good to see trees again after the past days of empty immensity.

A drizzle enclosed my sight; mists smoked over the earth; my garments clung clammy to my skin. Memmius hung back among the guardsmen who followed the wagon and those sailors who accompanied us. The latter were few. They would transport our goods to Owldoon. On their return, the ship would raise anchor—no sense in letting her lie idle—to call for us a year hence. By that time, Memmius hoped to have founded a permanent trading post, with a factor responsible to him. Until then, he and I were the only ones whom it was worth keeping on hand. Wrapped in his cloak, he snuffled and sneezed, miserable from a cold he had caught. "Appreciate your youth while you have it, Philon," he had wheezed to me. Of course I didn't. I was merely not uncomfortable, and fascinated by Hesting's discourse as he drove.

Hoofs plopped, wheels groaned, often an animal puffed a weary snort. I couldn't see many birds but I heard them everywhere around, like an ocean which twittered and fluted. The damp air struck me in the lungs with greenness. Spring does not come this ardently to the Midworld.

"You do expect . . . war, then, . . . sir?" I dared ask.

The blocky eagle-nosed head nodded. "What else? We've had our spies and scouts out. Not that King Knui makes any deep secret of his intentions. He's already gathering ships. Right after hay harvest, we fight."

"But why?"

"Why not? For land, wealth, power, glory—do you Romans fight for anything different?" He turned a wry smile on me. "Except that you don't seem to get much fun out of it."

I thought of kings and heroes on both sides of the gleaming walls of Troy. Roman leaders used to go likewise in the van of their armies. However, Julius Caesar was more a player moving men around from his tent than he was himself a warrior, and as for his recent successors— Heat fluttered in my face, a pulse in my neck, and I cried, "I am no Roman, sir! I am a Greek!"

At once I was embarrassed at my outburst. Hesting put me at ease when he said, "Indeed? Well, tell me about that," and I knew his interest was perfectly sincere.

It became a long talk, followed by many more.

Hesting did not go directly home. At a crossroads, the folk of his own region met him, summoned by runners who had waited for sight of us. In a stately and, to me, quite moving ceremony, they bade the Goddess welcome back. Three female slaves were led forth, garlanded and gaily clad; a girl, a mature woman seemed numbed. The granny tried to comfort them both. So did Hesting, who spoke soothing words while he secured them to the wagon by thongs around their wrists. Thus they went along when he drove to Holy Lake, to return the image to its house.

"What will they do?" I tried to ask a guardsman when the solemnities had ended and we pushed on for Owldoon. He had as much trouble getting my meaning as I then had in getting his, but at length I worked out that they would help the king wash and anoint Her, dress Her in new clothes, and set Her in Her place.

Why should that terrify them? Awe? I didn't pursue the question, my knowledge of local speech being so rudimentary. Anyhow, new impressions were crowding in on me from all sides.

These folk were as intrigued by us outlanders as their kin were, though, living hard by the Great Road, they were more sophisticated. Anticipating a year in their midst, Memmius and I exerted ourselves to make friends. Among such open hearts, that was easy.

Owldoon is the largest village in High Jutland, probably on the entire Cimbrian Chersonese, and really deserves to be called a town. Nearly fifty houses hold a substantial population. That makes the outermost fields pretty far off, but their owners can afford horses, besides having sons who camp out to guard plows and teams or harvested sheaves. A number of men do no farming, being artisans or, in a few cases, full-time widely ranging traders. The latter bring in commodities like charcoal and lumber from distant forests, dried or smoked fish from the seacoast; they manage the annual fair which attracts merchants from as far away as Scrith-Finn Land or Burgundia; could the mucking Danes only be brought to heel, they grumbled, they would build ships.

It surprised me how much the ordinary dweller travels too, on hunting expeditions to areas where game is still plentiful, on visits to relatives or to religiously efficacious sites elsewhere. He works hard at certain times of year, but otherwise he is less homebound and has more leisure than the average Midworld rustic. To be sure, he has no standing army or swarm of officials whom he must sweat to support.

The houses sit in orderly rows. While swine, dogs, chickens, and naked children romp around freely in the unpaved lanes, each family is required to keep its frontage reasonably clean. Nobody minds, because gathered dung is good to spread on the fields. The buildings are not as drab as their turf construction would suggest, for rafter ends and doorposts are carved and gaudily painted, and in summer every sod roof goes wild with flowers. Many bear the nests of storks, a bird sacred to Nerthus. Indoors are apt to be considerable possessions, including some from factories in Gaul or Italy itself. Apart from utilitarian glassware, cheaply made and cheaply bought, the selections are generally tasteful.

Hesting's home showed little outward distinction. Inside, however, no animals were admitted save his hounds. Three hearths provided sufficient winter heating. Their clay had glass and stones inset, a quite clever imitation of Roman mosaic. He could be spendthrift with fuel, since a great peat bog lay nearby and his dwelling, well apart from the rest, would create no hazard to those if it caught fire. I found that a peat blaze is remarkably cheery, bright, and smoke-free.

Imported tapestries, polished shields and weapons, shelves full of workaday and ornamental articles lined the walls, above benches which ran the length of them. Household members and the frequent guests slept on those or, if low-ranking, on the floor. In the corners of the east end he had installed a Danish fashion, beds provided with sliding panels. They were so short that one must recline half sitting, but they did offer privacy to the master and mistress, and to especially favored visitors. Memmius got the spare.

The landscape around is rolling, often rising in stiff-backed hills or plunging into glens, every road marked by the burial mounds of a forgotten race. (The Jutes practice inhumation too, but make no dolmens and seldom a very conspicuous grave.) Most of what acreage meets the eye is intensively cultivated: barley, emmer, spelt, flax, plus plants we consider weeds such as nettles, black nightshade, buttercup, yarrow. Well-nigh treeless, it is dwindled by the sky and towering clouds, unshielded from the winds which boom down off a dimly seen northern heath.

In that wet country a well can be sunk almost anywhere, so men have no need to locate by water. A long lake shines about three miles southward. Separate from the sacred one, which is small and whose dense grove is not visible from Owldoon, this is free to everybody. The ground between it and the town is a common, where youngsters graze cattle, sheep, goats, geese throughout the endless summer days. Aspen, beech, and oak grow abundantly along its shores, making a sun-flecked rustling shadowiness where I often idled, plucked berries, chatted with folk, or dreamed by myself. Fishing boats lie at a dock. In fair weather the people like to go swimming. Ashore, adults are prudish about covering themselves; but nakedness of both sexes, laughing and romping in the water, does not count. How beautiful they are!

(My image of Greece—I have seen little of Greece, being born in Rome, my ancestors slaves since the destruction of Corinth; Memmius' multifarious businesses have taken him and me a few times to Athens, where my heart soared among the pillars of the Acropolis, and once unforgettably through the islands—my image of the soul of Greece is a boy, seated on a stone in a forest, beside a chiming stream. He is nude, deeply browned by the sun, the first signs of manhood barely upon him. He smiles as he plays a syrinx, whose notes twitter in tune with the brook's tiny cascade. . . . Since that Jutland summer, though I know it makes no sense, I see him as having blue eyes and flax-white hair.)

Barely discernible eastward is another strand of trees, which grow around the peat bog.

Hesting's wife was a tall woman, her gray-blond tresses coiled on a head whose face was too heavy and crag-nosed for my taste, but who greeted us gently. Her name was Ioran. Beyond his duties as Fro, or a twinkle when a pretty girl walked by, her husband showed no interest in others. I came gradually to learn that, in her barbarian fashion, she had a formidable intellect, including quite a sense of humor.

This was not immediately obvious, and not just because of my limited command of the language. Except when hostess at feasts, she was no "queen" in our sense, simply the hard-working mistress of a large household. For that matter, when he was not being priest or judge or president or general, Hesting's attention was on his private affairs. Besides farming and hunting, he had substantial shares in various trading enterprises. He plowed his own fields, did much of his own carpentry, took the lead in collective labors like threshing, even as did the kings in Homer.

At ceremonial times, Ioran flashed in golden torque and armrings, amber necklace, gown and cape of southland silk. But daily she wore a plain dull-colored dress, not unlike a peplos to which was added a rain hood. She herself took a hand in the numberless tasks she oversaw—milling, baking, brewing, cooking, cleaning, carding, spinning, dyeing, weaving, sewing, human and veterinary medicine, the rearing of everyone's children and the laying out of everyone's dead.

She and Hesting had six offspring who lived past infancy. The oldest, Walhauk, had become a man with house, wife, and first baby. The youngest was a girl-toddler. In between were two boisterous youths, two maidens quieter but no less independent, they having never been secluded like Midworld women. We fear for the virtue of ours; but those Jutish lasses carry knives just as their brothers do, and know how to use them for weapons as well as tools. I found their company delightful. All those siblings and I became good friends, who savored many an outing or jape or earnest conversation together. But I cannot write of that, it's blurred in my mind; what I remember in hurtful sharpness is their father.

He came home a day after Ioran their mother had received us, and for a while was unwontedly grave and withdrawn. In the complexities of getting better acquainted with him and his, I failed to notice that the three female slaves had not returned.

Memories, memories: they crowd around me, hungry to become real again, like the ghosts around Odysseus when he fared to hell. I too will give a draught of blood, now to this one, now to that one, that it may speak; but I must draw the blood from my heart.

The peat bog will not be denied, it must be first, however gladly I would drown it in its own mire.

I cannot even say that it looked evil (no, looks, far off in Jutland of my ghosts). Truly I clapped my hands and exclaimed when Hesting and I came upon it.

That was soon after our arrival at Owldoon. A spell of rain, day after day and night after night till earth dissolved, plashing broken by flare-ups when wind flung monstrous hailstones, lightning which turned clouds white-hot and thunder which rattled our bones, had driven its chill and damp into the cold Memmius already had. He lay in high fever for a week or more, barely able to get down the broth and herb tea which Ioran made for him. A month passed before he regained his strength. Meanwhile the weather turned good. Hesting went about his affairs, and he invited me along.

"Asrun will be disappointed," Memmius croaked, grinning a bit. She was the slave—taken as a child in a retaliatory raid on the Danes—whom Hesting had told to pleasure us in addition to her usual chores. A plump, freckled, not particularly intelligent redhead, apparently barren but altogether lusty, she routinely got such assignments and made no bones about enjoying them. "I'm scarcely in condition for her, and you're going away. . . . Ah, well, she'll doubtless find plenty of hayricks."

Hesting made numerous journeys, long and short, around his realm in the course of a year. His guardsmen he picked at each village and sent home from the next, for most settlements could not afford to feed many. Certain of the trips were official, to folkmoots where he presided and judged, or to a couple of festivals which the king traditionally attended. More of them were on his own, to look and talk and learn how went the land.

"I've gotten a lot of ideas, you see, mulling over what I saw in Roman territory," he told me. I being anxious to master his tongue, we spoke in it as much as possible; but often it, not I, lacked vocabulary and we resorted to Latin. He squinted across the hills, whose plow-rows were turning emerald as shoots grew forth. Above us the sun was a ball of fire, its light a cataract out of infinite blue. There were no clouds, but uncountable wings, up yonder. A breeze blew odors of earth, flowering, and the warm little horses which trotted between our knees. At our rear jingled the escort. Thrushes caroled, blackbirds whistled.

"My thoughts haven't come easy," Hesting went on. A shadow of struggle passed over the mirth-lined face. "I was a younger son, not expecting to succeed my father. Then he died and my brothers died, and there I was. I'd supposed I, who'd sought out the very Romans, couldn't be taken aback. Wrong. It's overwhelming when it happens."

"I think I can imagine, sir," I said.

He reached over. His fingers brushed lightly across my wrist. " 'Hesting' will do, Philon. We don't go in here for treating a plain leader like a god, the way they seem to southward." After a pause: "And yet, you know, every spring I am a god. It's not just having my image stuck in temples like Caesar's. I am the one She needs to quicken the earth, and hasten the sun homeward, and—well, at the same time, don't you understand, I've been abroad. I've seen how differently things can be done. And times are changing here also. More than the Danes coming in. I think we can handle them. But the trade stuffs, the foreign arts and crafts . . . gods, ways of living, even so innocent-looking a matter as our younger men getting interested in deep-water ships . . . I wonder what it all means, what it'll bring about. I suspect She" —he signed himself— "is readying a new fate for us. She may even intend to have us call Her nothing more than the wife of a he-god, as the Danes do—for Her own ends, for Her chosen centuries. I don't know about that. Yet change of some kind, the house of our fathers torn down and a strange dwelling built, aye, plain to see before us. We Jutes will ride that wave, or we'll be hauled under and drown."

He laughed. "Hoy! You'd call this a, uh, a mixed bag of metaphors, wouldn't you, Philon?" Seriously: "True, though. How glad I am to have somebody around who knows about the whole world." After a moment: "And, what's more, can think about it."

The road made a swing between its high, heathery, barrow-freighted slopes, and abruptly the view before us was new. Hesting laughed afresh. "At least the peat bog is reasonably permanent," he said in Latin.

The sight enchanted me. Afar glimmered another lake, tree-encircled, reedy, clamorous with ducks, geese, swans, curlews, herons, storks. It had no definite shore; the foreground, in this low valley, faded from water to quagmire to fen. Flowers had exploded over the uneasy soil, white daisy, tawny marigold, heaven-blue cornflower, girl-pink primrose, fiery poppy. A few yeomen were digging the turf with long-handled wooden spades. They took it out in rectangular brown chunks which they stacked on higher ground to dry for some weeks before they brought it in for fuel and building material.

Hesting drew rein and gossiped awhile. I admired how casual-seeming a way he had of probing their feelings, especially about the war he foresaw. They answered him with respect but not servility, using his name and no honorifics.

I noticed that, in spite of water oozing from the sides to make the workers splash barefoot on the bottom, this trench was considerably deeper than one several yards off. In fact, the latter had been partly filled in. As we rode on, I asked Hesting the reason.

He scowled. "They'd not want to grub up a dead body," he said. "The bog won't have let it rot away."

"Oh." I recalled what I'd heard earlier. "A lawbreaker buried there?"

"Yes, in this case. He was a thief. I hanged him myself." He pointed to a huge old ash on the marge of the fen, which I learned later was man-planted generations ago. "My single time as executioner, and I hope the last."

"It's kinder than crucifixion," I said, for his look was grim.

Turning eager, in that mercurial play which went ever across his basic calm, he said: "Oh, you misunderstand, Philon. This is no disgrace. Rather, it's the way the man gets his honor back. He's sanctified to Her, don't you see. His life goes to make the earth live, and his kinfolk can hold up their heads again. It's not necessarily a punishment, even. Once in a long while—" He grimaced. "Never mind. I didn't like seeing and feeling him struggle while I hauled him aloft. Let's make a wish it won't be needful anymore."

He leaned toward me. This time he clasped my wrist. His hand was hard and warm. I wasn't sure if I felt his pulse knocking in it or mine. "Maybe it won't be, Philon," he said, "not because men will get any better, but because ways will alter. I am glad you've come! You southerners—this writing you have—it gives you such a long view. You mentioned a Bronze Age before anybody knew about iron, and the rise and fall of . . . you called them republics? . . . and—so many things I have to ask you about."

My face burned like the sun. I stared at the mane of my
horse and mumbled, "I'll tell you what I can, . . . Hesting,
. . . but my patron knows far more."

He chuckled. "Aye, I expect to get considerable out of
Memmius. However—don't pass this on, no use giving offense—he strikes me as a narrow man. Sharp, but his cutting
edge strictly on business and politics. You may be callow,
but you think beyond yourself, and you're always trying to
learn. The night before we left, I watched you gaze long at
the stars."

"Well, they're different here—"

"You want to know them. And I'd like to hear about your
stars, Philon."

I will not seek to write down the discourses we had, hour
by hour as we rode or strode across those mighty hills, over
wind-scoured moors and down into wolf-haunted woods, or
at evening when low blue peat flames brought his face out of
shadow, and the hands he held forth to them. I dare not.

Let me say that we came to a oneness of giving, that both
our minds were widened by what we shared. I was learned in
books; he could read every leaf and spoor. I drew pictures of
the Parthenon or an athlete sculptured by Phidias, in charcoal
on skin; he took me to a hiding place where we watched a
family of otters at play, lovelier to see than I would have
believed. I recited verses which he said grabbed him by the
heart; he roared forth olden lays which shook me by the
throat. I spoke of exotic animals and physical laws described
by Aristotle; he made me familiar with the life around me
and in smiling patience taught me how to make a skiff on the
northern sort obey my will. I told him about theories of the
ideal state, deeds and misdeeds of historical statesmen; he in-
troduced me to the running of a here-and-now day-to-day
kingdom.

Memmius came along on some of our trips after he got
well. He was particularly interested when Hesting went on a
diplomatic mission to the Cimbrians, failed to make alliance

against the Danes but succeeded in winning their pledge not to side against the High Jutes—which he admitted to us was as much as he could hope for. "Our host's a fox of a bargainer," Memmius said to me. "If he'd been born a Roman, well, we might have a different Caesar. To be sure, we've not seen how he can fight."

That chance was soon forthcoming. Once cricketful eventide the beacon fires he had had made ready over the land blazed. I saw the nearest to Owldoon kindle afar, a bloody spark like the planet of Ares descended onto earth. Wildness erupted around me. Men ran forth yelling, the torch was put to our own heaped wood, iron and teeth gleamed in the dark, weapons dinned on shields. Inside two or three hours, warriors were arriving from outlying settlements. We set forth before dawn.

Ioran and her daughters bade Hesting and her sons goodbye with Spartan sternness. Yet I saw hands linger together, and my own ached to be among them.

At least I would be under his banner. Memmius and I had brought Roman gear for ourselves, in case of emergency. We could have stayed home, but that would have destroyed our repute and thus our usefulness. Anyhow, my patron wanted to observe events. "Observe only," he reminded me. "Don't get into combat if you can possibly avoid it. Barbarians have so feeble an idea of military discipline that we probably can hang clear without it seeming on purpose."

But these are my friends! cried in me.

A strenuous day's travel—most of the men being afoot— brought us near the coast. There the smoke of a burning village told us just where the Danes had landed. Hesting sent out groups of mounted scouts, leading one himself. I asked to go along, drew a scowl from Memmius and a cheery nod from the king. "Good lad," he murmured. I felt momentarily dizzy, then exalted beyond mortality.

Galloping across a ridge, we saw a few islands upon a bronze-calm sunset sea. These were not the wellspring of the lean black oar-driven ships, big enough to be named galleys, which lay beached in their scores or prowled the water on guard. King Knui, who led them, was the strongest lord on Zealand, across the strait from Scandia. Between it and the Chersonese, almost butting into the latter farther south, lay principally the other major island, Fyn.

They were more tall and fair than Jutes, the warriors who cooked, rolled out sleeping bags, took turns raping what women they had caught, near the ashes and corpses of the village. Mail and helmets were more abundant among them, too, though most had to be content with leather cap and doublet—if that—like most of our yeomen. They swarmed across miles. I estimated their number at three or four thousand.

Anguish twisted Hesting's mouth. He smote fist in palm. "I warned those folk to move," he groaned. "I begged them. They wouldn't heed, they wouldn't heed—"

That is the price of being free, I suppose. A Roman proconsul has authority to command evacuation. I have never decided whether it is worth it.

The Danes saw us. A beast-howl racketed from their throats. They ran toward us, arrows buzzed, but we riders left them behind and lost them in gathering dusk.

That night we camped on a high, defensible hill which Hesting had established as our rendezvous. From time to time, men would arrive in groups from remoter parts. The king did not sleep. He sat at a fire before a boulder engraved with sacred figures—the Sun Wheel, the Death Ship, the Goddess and Her consort coupling to renew the world—like a carven image himself. The light flickered over his countenance; so did the smile which greeted each newcomer band.

Between times, he was willing to talk. "How did you know the invasion would be here?" Memmius inquired. "Wouldn't your rival subjugate Fyn first?"

"No, that's too hard a nut until he's gathered much greater might," Hesting replied. "He has sworn oaths with some of the Fynish kings. They'll not help him—I've made arrangements of my own thereabouts—but they'll not fall on him either. He must break us, the High Jutes, before he can do anything else on the mainland. This is the best spot for a beachhead, especially if the Cimbrians swarm gleefully over our backs . . . as I've, hm, led him to think they will.''

Memmius wearied and dozed off. I myself listened throughout the night, utterly caught in his stories of spying, bribing, promising, weaving a net to catch the pike which menaced his people—tales harsh or suspenseful or even comical, each fascinating. This was no book by a long-dead Herodotus, Thucydides, Xenophon, Julius Caesar; this was the living stuff with which these men had dealt in their days. How they would have understood and respected Hesting!

Thus did I come to some knowledge of actual, as opposed to theoretical, statecraft. Soon I learned about actual war and generalship.

Hesting's plan had a simple skeleton. He knew the Danes would strike for Owldoon, but in leisurely wise, pillaging, butchering, capturing slaves along the way. When his whole force had assembled, it was a bit larger than the invaders', albeit inferior in equipment. He divided it in two. The first half engaged the enemy. In a running battle, they let themselves be driven up a valley which slanted inland from the sea between thickly overgrown slopes. Meanwhile he led the other half in a circuitous night march. They surprised the fleet, overran its guards, seized the beached ships, launched them, and cleared or put to flight those which stood out at sea.

Knui got word, naturally. In horror he brought his pack around. Cut off from home, they would be an irresistible temptation to the Cimbrians (who had not joined them), the Heruls, even more distant tribes, to hunt them down for their arms and loot. He tried to disengage, and failed. The Jutes followed, harassing his rear, sniping with bows and slings from the brush.

When he reached the strands, he found Hesting had rebeached the ships in formation and added stakes and thorntangles, to make a fortress which he must storm.

His men tried, roaring, battle-drunken, scarcely heeding

when their pursuers attacked from behind. They sought only to get at our livers, where we stood behind the dear hulls. We cast them back, sallied forth, and crushed them in the jaws of our twin hosts.

It is not easy to write of these things. It was not easy to be in them. I do not believe any other living barbarian could have done what Hesting did. Perhaps Vercingetorix himself could not have. Untrained, the northerners fling their bodies at a foe and think that that is war.

Hesting had spent patient years with the headmen of High Jutland—and more with their sons, and still more with humble folk who would be the backbone of what strength he could ever muster. He had explained, over and over and over, the concept of discipline and concerted action which had made Rome the mistress of half the world. He had orated, he had argued, he had browbeaten, he had gotten them to drill, and in the end he achieved enough organization that it was possible to execute an elementary strategy.

On this day his toil bore fruit. I wonder what seed he may have planted to sprout in later centuries.

Only in retrospect do I know what happened. The doing itself was tumult, terror, pain, exhaustion, and marvel.

Obedient to Memmius' orders, I had held back when we fell on the ships. That was not difficult, for the fight was short and most of us never got near a Dane. Nonetheless shame grew thick in my gullet, I could not meet anyone's eyes, I slunk about helping in the most menial parts of arranging our defenses.

When the tall golden-braided men boiled whooping from inland, I left Memmius' side. He clutched my arm. I struck his hand loose. "Let me go or I'll kill you," I heard myself say. He lurched back, appalled, to stand in the reserves at the center of our ring. I sped toward the floating banner of Hesting. It bore a stag.

Amidst shouts and chaos, he saw me and waved me to him. For an instant he squeezed my shoulder. I thought I could feel him through the loricae. Earlier, fear had dried my

mouth and given sight and sound an eerie, dreamlike quality—a dream from which I could not will myself to waken.
Now glory took me.

They came, they came, iron ablaze beneath the sun, to surf
against the ships. Arrows, spears, slingstones hailed into
them, they fell in windows, the sand squelched red. Yet they
came. I saw a warrior whose guts trailed out of his belly
crawl over a rail. When he fell inside the open vessel, a
gigantic comrade leaped to him, picked him up, cast him—
still grinning, still gasping his death-chant—against the face
of a Jute. The Jute staggered back. The Dane crossed the
hull, trampled him underfoot, and was among us, hewing.

Cool as a Roman, Hesting met that colossus. He fended
off ax blows with a shield and cut a leg open. When the Dane
went to one knee, Hesting smote his neck asunder.

I glimpsed that much before the attack reached me. They
had broken through at this point. They were not many who
did. We killed them and sent their followers reeling back.
But for a while it was wild around us.

There I slew my first man . . . most likely my only man,
peaceable clerk that I am. He was my age, I think, and had
cast off his garments in frenzy as northerners are wont to do.
His assault shocked in my shield, helmet, bones. He was
awkward, though, his sword already bent and blunted to a
mere club. I got under his guard, thrust home, and twisted.
The motion felt heavy.

He tried to run up the blade at me. I retreated while twisting, probing his entrails till he fell in a spout of crimson. At
the time it simply happened. I was not even conscious of
being Philon, a unique point in this vast thing. Strange how
often afterward I see my sword-thrusts, how white his skin
was, how handsome his face beneath its Medusa contortion.

Otherwise I mainly see Hesting flight. When the Danes
broke and scattered, the divine fury came on him too. But—I
might have known—for him it took the form of mirth.
Laughing through every yell and thunder, he hunted the mur-
derers of his people; and I, close behind, knew that he was

indeed the vessel of a Power, himself a god whom I longed
to adore.

The last Danes threw down their weapons. We bound them
to hold for ransom. They'd not make safe slaves, Hesting
said, calm again in a quietness whose immensity was hardly
touched by the noises from hurt men, the hush-hush-hush of
waves upon strand. Thereafter we gathered our dead and did
what we could for our wounded. Badly injured foes we left to
the village women we'd freed.

Then Hesting looked about in the yellow sundown light,
between green hills, metal-bright waters, darkening blue
heaven, over his folk who sprawled at rest too weary for
triumph. Into the peace he asked: "Where is Geyrolf?"

That was his second son. Walhauk, his first, came to him
and said, "Geyrolf fell. I think it took three of them to bring
him down."

Hesting stood moveless awhile, though I saw knuckles
whiten around his sword haft. At last he said tonelessly,
"Bring me to him."

His friends had already laid out the youth, swabbed off
most of the blood, bound the fallen chin. They had left it to
Hesting to close the eyes. He knelt on the sand to do so.
"Sleep well," I heard him whisper. He kissed his boy, rose
and went about his overseeing of the live men. I wondered if
he wept. We were all so sweaty that slow tears would have
passed unnoticed. I ran to him, seized his hand, and blurted,
"Oh, Hesting, I'm sorry—"

He could not keep pain from his voice. "It was a good
ending," he said, and broke from me. I imagined myself laid
out, my slain enemies around, wind in my hair, and he kiss-
ing me farewell.

Overhead, the gulls and ravens gathered.

Why are the greatest hurts, until the very last, set in the
greatest beauties? I can still hardly endure to remember one
light night.

The invasion had come shortly before midsummer. Soon

the exigencies of getting home, seeing to the injured, dickering out peace terms with Knui's successor, starting the next phase of work on the land—picking up life again—blunted the grief of those who buried their loves. They always live close to death, the northfolk. I wonder if they may not feel loss more keenly than Midworlders do; but they keep it mastered. And we had won our war, stamped out a threat, taken a booty of ships and arms, a ransom of more, which opened the way to our becoming unassailable. Considering the ferocity of the battles, our casualties were not excessive. Even those families which suffered them had cause to rejoice.

The midsummer festival lifted hearts in still more hope and gladness than was usual. It happened to fall in a spell of singularly fine weather—a good omen, as well as pleasurable in itself—yet this was no drought year and crops flourished. Nerthus smiled upon the world.

Though they have their solemnities, the summer solstice and the autumnal equinox are less portentous, more merry among the Jutes than the other two high holy days. Those concern themselves with the coming year. In the milder seasons, one knows fairly well what the Powers intend; one reaps the rewards of toil; it is meet and right to show appreciation of Their hospitality on this earth by feasting, dancing, singing, lovemaking, partaking of everything They give.

True, the moment was awesome when we kindled the balefire. From that hilltop where we did it we saw others come to life, wider than eye could reach, stars across the land. Robed and garlanded, Hesting bore among us the bowl of mingled milk and blood from Her cows, the bread from grain grown at Her shrine, that we might be nourished. As I knelt to receive it from him, I knew he was Fro (and Apollo of the Sun) and through him She entered me and I Her. Can the Orphic mysteries give more?

Nonetheless worship ended in revelry which continued for a week. They call this time Wink, because most parents turn an indulgent glance away from their half-grown children. Should something happen beyond a flirtation and kisses, it is not considered the deadly offense it would be anywhere else. If necessary, bethrothals are hastily rearranged, marriage dates advanced.

For this is the peak of the light nights, that we do not know around the Midworld Sea. The sun is down for a mere few hours, and true darkness never comes.

I had spent a day at the lake among people my own age or younger, for swimming, ball games, foot races, wrestling, loafing on moss and turf, yarning, joking, a stolen touch of nude bodies and cool lips in the water. It did much to ease my mind, which had kept imagining what sorrow must dwell behind the face Hesting wore . . . and Ioran too, though she did not really occur to me at the time. In truth, the day excited me, until I was relieved to see the slave girl Asrun at liberty when Memmius had already closed his shut-bed.

We needed no more than a look. She followed me from the town, onto the common. In systematic search for privacy— she didn't mind auditors—I had discovered a spot where bushes screened soft grass. She was eager and our passage went hastily. I got a bare minute to squeeze my eyes shut and put before me Wulf. He was a cousin-child of Hesting's whom I believed must resemble the king at age thirteen.

Afterward at peace, I meant to spend the whole night in love but felt no hurry. Raising myself on an elbow, the springiness of every moist blade underneath me, I drank of wonder.

In mild air full of earth, blossoms, green growth, the land reached to the lake, which glimmered like a misted mirror. Leaves were silver-hued beneath a heaven more silver than purple, where only a few tender stars dwelt. Dew glistened, fireflies swooped and darted, blink-blink-blink. On the far side of the water, a hill tall enough to be called a mountain upheaved itself, ghost-wan, unreal, seeming to float. Frogs chanted chorus to a nightingale's Pan-pipe. An owl passed splendid and soundless overhead.

Surely, I thought, Hesting let his own soul go free into all this. He did not speak of it, that was not the way of his people, but surely he too could come one with it, he and I and the light night of summer.

Asrun nuzzled me. I turned about, annoyed, for she was just a vehicle. Still, this was no hour to provoke a quarrel. "I like you, Philon," she sighed. "I like you real good. Better'n old Memmius."

"Thanks," I muttered.

Pale and clear in the moonless glow, she shook back her hair and giggled: "Not that he makes any difference to me. You know? Maybe twice a month, and hardly started when it's over." She stroked a hand across me. "You've not been such a stud horse either, sweet. You can when you want— oh, how!— but you don't want very often. Why?"

"I've many things on my mind."

"Awww, now. You ought to unload'm." She nibbled by earlobe, rubbed my belly, and tittered anew.

That sound was abruptly irritating. I wanted my own thoughts, my own dreams, until at last I grew ready— "Let me be!" I snapped.

She bridled. She was not spiritless; Hesting and Ioran treated their slaves decently. "What's the matter? Aren't you up to more, lover boy?"

I swung on her, lifted a hand to cuff, let it drop but spat in a shivering rage: "You'll do what you're told, which is keep quiet till I lay you again. Or must I tell my host he's lent me a useless mare?"

She choked down a shriek. The terror upon her struck into me. I rolled about, scrambled to my knees, caught her arms, and exclaimed, "What's wrong? I didn't mean— What happened, Asrun?"

She cowered from me. "Y-y-you . . . won't, . . . Philon," she got forth. "You won't, you won't. Please, please, please. I'll, oh, no, *plea-ea-ease*—"

I have seen underlings in Asia actually grovel. They know how. She didn't, which made it hideous.

I slapped her to cut off the hysterics, held her close to lessen the sobbing, and asked for her dread. She stabbed me:

"If he doesn't think—I'm good—I know I'm not a good housemaid, and I'm barren, and if, if, if men don't want me for fun—he'll drown me! He will, next spring, he'll drown me!"

"Nonsense. Why in the world—"

"Nerthus! She takes three each spring . . . girl, woman, carline . . . th-th-they see Her, they handle Her, and then he, he holds their heads under . . . Holy Lake's full of their bones—Oh-h-hh, Philon, darling, don't tell him!"

I remember little more until the moment when I stumbled past his house. I must have raved around for some while, because my bare feet bled from thorns and stones, my weeping had gone dry and hurt my ribs, dawn stood white in the east where we had been victorious.

He came out. To this day I do not know how that occurred; it was always too hard to ask. Maybe he chanced to be awake, for one sleeps very lightly in those nights. Maybe a watchful servant roused him to something unusual, and was told to stay behind. Maybe the Goddess had Her will, whatever it is. I do, ludicrously, know that this stretch of trail was lined with blackberry bushes, and that a silence had arisen between the nightingale and the lark.

Suddenly, there he was, in a wadmal tunic whose roughness scratched my bare skin when he cast an arm around my shoulders. "Philon," he murmured, "what is your trouble?"

I wrenched free of the embrace. "Let me go, you murderer!" I may have screamed. A dog got excited and started to bark. From afar came an answering wolf howl.

"I don't understand," Hesting said. The first rays of the still hidden sun made a halo in his hair.

I fell to hands and knees, beat my fist on the ground, and cried, "A girl, a woman, a granny. Every year!"

"Oh." He was long silent. The light strengthened. I do not know if others came from the houses or the meadows and saw us. It was never spoken of; they have a sense for what is sacred.

At last he nodded. "Philon," he said, word by word, "this must be, that the land may live. Do you imagine I like it?" He lifted crook-fingered hands to the sky. I saw that his mouth was stretched quite out of shape. "It's hard to drown them—and yet, Philon, that's a release, an ending, a thing I can leave behind till next spring. Harder is putting them through their duties first, while I try to calm them, make them happy, make them drunk. . . . Hardest is to choose them, to choose them. Can you see that?"

Agamemnon and Iphigenia . . . Achilles who butchered the Trojan captives for dead Patroclus. . . . Maybe the gods, if they exist, do not demand horror of us; but we always do of each other.

I rose and laid my head on his breast. He held me close, ruffled my hair, and said shakenly, "I've been thinking of you as a son, Philon. A son in the stead of him we've lost."

Why was I shocked?

Well, he had been so relaxed, curious, jolly, the whole first while that we knew him. Had he shown any reluctance when he drove off to Holy Lake, those three bound to his wagon like cows, I might have guessed the truth earlier. After all, the Gauls and Britons practiced human sacrifice till Rome conquered them and suppressed their Druids. I had heard of it among German tribes.

Slowly I came to know that I had not wanted to know. From the outset, my mind covered the fact up. Memmius took for granted I had made a deduction obvious to him, and didn't think the matter worth discussion. He is a Roman who enjoys the arena. I went just once, and fell vomiting. Whenever I pass a crucified felon at a roadside, I turn my eyes and cover my ears. I cringe a little when I see slave gangs stooped in the fields of a latifundium, their foreman passing among them with his whip.

However, I savor the fruits of their toil, and admit that criminals must be disposed of, and take pride in having killed an enemy. Thus I struggled toward a vantage point from which I might see the world as Hesting did. Before long I believed I had succeeded.

A kindly man at heart, he hated this duty, therefore dismissed thought of it until the ineluctable annual moment. Nevertheless, to him it *was* a duty, along with many others. The Goddess must be served, yet Her mysteries might not be profaned, lest death come over the land. It would not even be proper for him to show distress over his obedience.

Philon, I scolded myself, you've been stupid. You blindly assumed that he, the father of his rugged people, the incarnation of their male god, shares your squeamishness.

I wondered if he could be won from his superstition. He had seen that different ways are possible. . . . No, it would be no favor to change his belief, when his folk would never let him change his act.

Was it a superstition, indeed? The Goddess has uncountable aspects. Aphrodite, She is not only that grave beauty whose image stands at Milos; She is the foam-born Virgin of Cyprus, She is the Mother of Eros, She is Our Lady of the Weddings, She is the foolish slut Whom Homer mocks. Artemis, She is the moon-crowned maiden huntress, and She is the Ephesian, many-teated and fecund as a sow. She is Cybele the inspirer of madness, Hecate the terrible, Hera, Ceres, Athene, Persephone Queen of the Dead. . . . When She is Nerthus, can it be right that She takes lives? So gaunt a land may need them.

Can it be wrong what they do, these people who still adore Her while a weary Greece and a corrupted Rome relegate Her to consorthood, turn more and more to Oriental he-gods or to no gods at all?

I had felt Her nearness, my first evening upon these shores.

Thus did I assure myself it was not wrong to love Hesting and be his—son. Meanwhile summer waned, days shrank before nights, hasty clouds and spilling rains warned of on-coming winter.

My reconciliation to the facts may well have been speeded and strengthened by an absence of almost three months. Memmius, having gotten considerable knowledge and made considerable contacts among the high Jutes, wanted to do the same in other tribes, albeit less thoroughly. When the fair at Owldoon broke up, mid-July, he joined a party from the southern end of the peninsula who would hawk their wares at similar, lesser gatherings elsewhere. Perforce I went along.

Our companions were Heruls, Angles, a couple of Teutons, a Saxon, and a Longobard, whose partnership was years old. Despite their uncouth ways, this mixedness, this partial uprooting from home soil, made them somehow familiar to us. Memmius was more cheerful in their midst, and won more friendliness, than he had among Hesting's uncosmopolitan folk. I liked them well enough, and in a way enjoyed being on the road again, new sights, each day unforeseeable. But a weight lay always on my heart. I recognized it when we watched the autumnal equinox being celebrated in a tiny fisher settlement and I felt nearly ill at not being elsewhere. I was homesick for Owldoon.

Our course took us north through Cimbri and Vandals, then down the bleak west coast nearly to Chaucian territory. There Memmius and I said farewell, hired a few local men to accompany us, and rode back up the middle of the country. This was at the end of September. We had seen much of interest, accomplished no little of value or profit. None of it is worth my writing down.

I will see him soon, it sang in me: soon, soon, soon.

Thus I was dashed when we entered the town and Ioran informed me he was away on one of his circuits. She expected him presently, however. I composed myself and settled down to record our results in orderly fashion. Memmius dictated most of this, then let me interpolate what I wished as I transcribed from wax tablet to paper. So passed a few days.

Asrun approached me; but though we'd had no women on our journey, I said the house lacked privacy and outdoors was now too cold. "Not really," she sniggered. "Go!" I commanded, and she crept off in fright. I'd not spoken badly of her, but neither had I been able to bring myself to praise her talents to the king as she had begged.

"I'm afraid we have another dreary winter ahead of us," Memmius sighed. "Worse for you than me. I'll at least be conducting interviews, looking for somebody who's got sufficient wit and will that I can make a factor of him. You—well, of course you can inquire too. Maybe you'll hit on a promising man. However, I do suspect we want one of mature years, perhaps too old or handicapped to risk his neck in these silly little wars. I can't expect you to become intimate with that class of person." He smiled and patted my shoulder. "Amuse yourself as best you can till we sail. On the whole, you've earned it, Philon."

We chanced to be alone, in a turf-and-wattle shack Hesting had lent us for the storage of our goods. These were gone, in trade and gifts, replaced by native products. We were taking inventory, subsequent to this latest venture of ours. Light seeped through thick clouds and wicker door, forcing us to illuminate the dusk within by four lamps which had also made the space fairly warm. His hand continued down my side till it rested on a flank. The aquiline head drew near to mine. "You have been a good boy," he breathed. "No flutter-brain slave. You're better-looking than Asrun is . . . by a long shot . . . did I ever tell you?"

I stepped back. Confusion whirled in me. "Is something wrong?" Memmius asked.

"I feel a little sick—the smell of that burning blubber—"

His eyes narrowed. I'd never voiced objection to odors before, as he occasionally did. At last he shrugged. "Well, let's knock off, then. Jupiter knows we've ample time between here and our ship."

When the trestle tables were set up in the house for the evening meal, I merely picked at my food; later I drank but a few sips of the winelike beverage brewed from berry juice and honey—though my appetite and thirst were normal. This made it plausible for me to sit apart, and stretch myself early on a bench. Not that Memmius would have invited me to his shut-bed. Such would have outraged custom, we knew. It might even require death in the peat bog. The Jutes are as narrow in that respect as other Germanic tribes. I have declared before that I do not idealize them, and try to see their failings as well as their virtues.

What I couldn't afford was to let Memmius realize that I had repulsed him.

Why had I? The question kept me long awake and found no answer. My dreams were troubled.

When in the morning I asked leave to take a walk, he agreed. "You look poorly," he said. "Fresh air may help. I hope so. The nearest proper physician is quite a ways off."

Can even Aesculapius heal the spirit which keeps wounding itself?

After a night's rain, morning had been born in beauty. Many women were about in the town, taking this chance to air bedding, butcher and pluck fowl, and otherwise batten down against winter. Some men worked on their houses. Most had gone off before dawn with nets and club-headed arrows, to the fen after migratory birds. I met few on my northward tramp, none by the time I stopped for a bit of bread and cheese.

I tried to lose myself in the land. This had been a lingering fall, as if She were reluctant to take summer's ghost from us. Across the high heath I had reached, the ling still bloomed, purple billowing beneath a wind which smelled of it and of distances. Southward whence I had come, plowland rolled brown, black, tawny, till brilliance flared on lakeside woods. The air was loud and swift but unutterably clear. I could see every barrow along roads and fields, Owldoon like a ranking of little hedgehogs. Somehow today the mountain across the water did not look humble beside my memories of southland peaks; it sailed blue and gold into heaven. The hugeness of that sky was broken only by last flights of geese and storks, by a sun which swung pallid and low.

I should have made nature my medicine, as wise Vergil advises. But I kept thinking of the winter ahead. The Jutes hate it. True, they have sports like hunting, sledding, or ice-sliding in the normally short period when the weather turns cold enough; they have games at home, visits with friends, a week of festival after the sacrifices at solstice. But the sun-lessness! More than one had admitted to me that hope wears as thin as the stocks of food, that quarrels among penned-up wretches are much too apt to bring manslaughter. How was I, Greece's child, to endure a thicker murk than in Colonia?

Why, there would be Hesting . . . and never a minute to be alone with him, in a crowded and ever more foul sty of a house. And when spring brought back light, cleanliness, free-dom, Memmius would take me away.

Long lean shadows reminded me that not much time re-mained till dark. I shook myself, sprang erect, and started back at a brisk gait. Maybe that would flog the sadness out of my blood.

It seemed to, a little. After a mile or so, regardless of the chill streaming over my skin, I grew thirsty. I recalled a brook which ran past a barrow I recognized. It wasn't far off the trail. I turned, picking a careful way through stiff heather and prickly gorse.

Rounding the mound, I slammed to a halt. My temples drummed. Two hobbled ponies cropped what they could find. The single man showed that one beast was a remount. He had undressed to wash off the grime of travel. Against dappled luminance in the brush, sun-darkened face and arms, his body shone white as a girl's.

I stood amidst a roaring and a soaring.

He sensed me, whirled, snatched for his sword. How the muscles flowed! Across their hardness was strewn the same ruddy hair as hung loosened around his cheeks. I had never seen him naked before. The king must maintain a degree of aloofness.

He knew me at once and straightened. "Philon!" he cried gladly.

A far-off part of me decided that he must have dismissed his last set of warriors several miles back, to let them reach home before nightfall. In the peace he had wrought, he need not fear to end his journey alone. And it was like him to stop here first, that he might meet us clean.

"Hoy, what good sprite brings you?" he called through the wind. "How went your trip? Come!" He spread his arms wide.

I ran to them. He hugged me. How powerful he was! Under the wetness glowed warmth. Our hearts beat together.

"I've missed you so—" I began.

He stepped back, but the hands still rested on my shoulders. "You're weeping, lad," he said. "Why?"

"For joy and—sorrow—I know not," gulped from me while the tears whipped forth. "The, the Goddess has me, and I must leave you, Hesting—" I sank, hugged my knees, lowered my face to them.

The brook rang over stones. A horse whickered. Wind sighed under the heaven, soughed in the heather. I shuddered and fought for air.

The warmth descended on my neck, clasped me by the left upper arm, touched my right ribs and thigh. I raised my head. He had sat down beside me, laid that arm around. His free hand turned my face to his. "Philon, be glad again." His smile was shy and, oh, very near my lips.

I kissed his.

There was an instant which was eternal, when my tongue and my hands sought, when my whole being tried to say what words cannot. And then, and then—

I lay sprawled. Blood ran from my mouth. The bruise of his fist would remain for days. I did not feel the pain. I looked up to him where he stood crouched, fingers bent into talons as they had been when he asked for my forgiveness. Behind him reared the barrow, helmeted by its dolmen.

His teeth gleamed. Amidst the chaos in my skull, I saw that Dane who had run my sword into his guts as he strove to get at me. "What in death's name were you doing?" he screamed.

I rolled over, dragged myself to my knees, reached out, and stammered, "I love you, Hesting."

He stood quiet for a space. His hair tossed in the wind. At last he turned, beat fist in palm, went to the stream, and likewise knelt. He rinsed his mouth several times, scrubbed his body, stared forth at earth and sky.

"Kill me if you want," I said into his silence.

Rising, he shook his head. "No." The voice was flat. "It was a . . . surprise. I'd heard about Greek ways, but never thought you— You were like a new Geyrolf to me."

"*Was* I?" I yelled, and stretched my neck for the mercy of his sword.

He gasped.

Presently I opened my eyes. He had toweled himself dry and was scrambling into his clothes. "Speak to none about this," he slurred, never looking my way. "It's the bog if you do."

"I might welcome that," I said. A leaden steadiness had come upon me.

"Then I must be your hangman. I'd rather not. Even now."

Dressed, he fetched his horses and rode off at a hard trot.

I followed afoot, so slowly that it was night before I arrived. Walking, I worked to reconcile myself to this latest truth. I had been a fool again, had reached too far and thus lost what had been mine. Well, at least I could take it like a philosopher. At least I could spare him a scandal and the pain of making me, for whom he once had cared, sprawl choking on a rope. We could both endure the winter. I would lie about the cause of my injury, and contrive an excuse to move elsewhere. When spring resurrected the world, I would leave his sight forever.

Dogs clamored until they recognized me. Nobody seemed roused by that brief noise. I groped to the king's dwelling and stealthily into its gloom. Fires banked on the hearths threw enough light for me to find a clear floor space to try to rest on.

From the royal shut-bed drifted a whisper. He must have supposed that everyone else was asleep, that none save Ioran heard his hoarse, agonized curses.

By day the lakeshore trees stood skeletal athwart water and sky that were iron-gray. But day was turning to the shortest of glimmers in the middle of night.

Through gifts and glibness I wormed out an invitation to stay with a yeoman named Sigern who dwelt at the opposite end of town. Memmius arched his brows when I asked his permission to accept. The oldest son and I are good friends," I said. "I'd have a better time, and maybe gather more information, than here."

"You would that," he agreed. "This house has become a tomb." He peered closer. "Have you any idea what's wrong?"

"No. . . . Winter's influence. . . ."

"Not this early. It's the king and queen. As moody and curt as they've become, they cast a pall over the whole company." His eyes ransacked me. "You've not been any comedian yourself of late, Philon."

"For that same reason."

I did not quite tell a falsehood. Mainly, however, it was the trouble in Hesting which picked and picked at my own wound.

What was his, though? I couldn't imagine. Very well, I'd shocked him, much as knowledge of the vernal sacrifice had done me. Those slayings went on, and I could live with them. As for him, nothing he would call untoward had really happened between us, nor ever would. We scarcely spoke anymore. Each time his vision chanced to cross me, straightaway he looked elsewhere. That attracted no attention, because he had withdrawn his comradeship from the entire world.

So I had disappointed him. He must be able to shrug that off!

Something else, then. What? Often I saw Ioran his wife touch his hair or the back of his hand. Her mouth had grown pinched and she was liable to start at loud sounds or to shrill at her underlings. Meanwhile she could not always refrain from showing him in public that tenderness which hitherto she had saved—I suppose—for the shut-bed. And he, he seemed to tauten when she did, as if to keep from flinching.

His face was a mask these days, save when anger livened it and a word barked forth more likely than not to be unjustly harsh. He went about his duties, including his duty to be a fairly courteous host, like Talos the automaton. Otherwise he drank heavily and joylessly, or went for long solitary gallops.

"Hesting, what is your pain?" I wanted to cry. "Can I ease it? Hang me aloft if that will help." Of course I could speak nothing.

When I told him and Ioran that I wished to move, and thanked them for their hospitality, he closed fingers on knife haft. I had seen him grip his sword that hard, on the strand after the last battle. For an instant his gaze touched mine, then snapped to the dusk beyond. "As you will," he said. "Yes, it might be best."

Ioran's reserve broke briefly in puzzlement. I knew he had not told even her what happened at the barrow. Nor would he. She would be certain to get me slain, if not by denunciation and formal execution, then by inciting some ruffian to pick a death-fight. I, who betrayed her man's faith!

The house of Sigern enfolded me. They were glad to lighten winter's burden by hearing my tales, recitals, translated songs, whatever I chose, whether or not they had listened to it before. In entertaining them and their neighbors I found a measure of comfort.

Zeus knows we had little else to do. Darkness, and raw chill which could bring inflamed lungs if we ventured too much outside, caged us. Food must be hoarded, to see us through till the first catches of spring, the first reapings of summer. Solstice and equinox would see feasting, but this heightened the need for parsimony at all other times. Cheese, butter, honey, preserved meat and fish, dried apples, stored nuts were scarcely more than seasoning for flatbread and gruel. The latter was made out of grains both cultivated and wild—bindweed, rye grass, burdock, whatever could be picked by the children while it grew.

Chores like caring for beasts or bringing in fuel became outright welcome. One slept as much as possible.

A day in late November or early December (I'd long lost track) happened to be comparatively warm. I went for a walk. Beneath an overcast which it seemed I could reach up and touch, the woods stood bare, shadowless, above steely waters. No snow had fallen thus far. Dead leaves lay sodden, plowlands stiff and black. Now and then a flock of crows mocked me. The sound was soon lost in dank stillness.

It startled me to come upon Asrun. She wore her usual drab, soiled gown, but in this bleached universe her hair was a shout. I stopped, reminded of Hesting, though his locks were bronze and it seemed to me that each time I glimpsed him there was more white in them. I doubled my fists, determined not to be overwhelmed.

"Philon!" she piped. "What a nice surprise!" Reaching me: "Where've you been? I mean, you've moved, but you could drop in on your old friends once in a while, couldn't you, naughty?"

"No doubt. What are you doing?"

"I got sent to empty the weir, if anything's in it." She dropped her basket and laid hands on my waist. "Nothing moves fast in winter. I could stay here a little and nobody'd notice."

I glanced around at trees, lake, desertion. She simpered. "Sure, it is kind of wet and cold here, Philon. If we're, you know, quick—"

"I'd better be getting on."

"Really? Awww." She rubbed her breasts against me.

"I've missed you. You're always gentle, and you know what a girl wants and care that she gets it." When I didn't respond, she grew sly. "After the letdown, yes, the fright I've had, you might be nice to me."

Somehow that didn't suggest idle chatter. My stomach tightened. "What's this?" I exclaimed.

"I mustn't tell."

"What is it?"

"No. Honest. I swore and— You wouldn't want me flogged, would you? Or killed?"

I grabbed her. She watched me, made her shallow calculation, and breathed, "The king? What of him?" I shook her till her teeth rattled. "Tell me! Tell me, or, or by Fro, I'll be the one who kills you, you bitch!"

Frightened now, she whined, "You'll hear soon anyway," and, "Let go, you're hurting me, how can I talk when you hurt me?" and, "M-m-m, well, for a *friend*—" And perceiving that I had no wish whatsoever of that kind, "You too, ha? At least friends give gifts. Don't they?"

In my wallet I generally carried some Roman coins, which northerners value as amulets. I offered her one. She demanded three. "All right!" I yelled, and cast them at her dirty feet. She collected them before she confronted me, fluttered her lashes, toyed with a braid, and dragged it out:

"Well, you know, us girls . . . the queen's sent us each by each to his bed. . . . He wouldn't have me. I don't know why. He—" Fear crossed her again. "I thought he'd murder me then and there. I, I, I ran away, and— The rest of the slave girls he did try. From different houses, too. We were told not to talk, and we don't, 'cept 'mongst each other—" She relaxed back into self-importance.

"What do you talk of?" My hand rested on my knife. Earthquakes went through my head.

I wonder if she guessed something. Why else should such spite dwell in her grin? Perhaps it was just the slave's unending impotent hatred.

"They'll get them a new king soon, I bet. He can't be Fro anymore. Not with anybody."

She dared laugh before she saw my face. Bleating, she fled. I caught her, hurled her to earth, nearly slashed her open. Mastering myself in bare time, I stabbed the nearest tree instead, again and again, while I wept.

None but men, heads of households from all High Jutland, might attend the abdication. It took place on the mountain across the lake, in darkness. That night was clear, numbingly cold. A rare aurora shivered among the Boreal stars. My eyes were only for a crimson gleam upon the unseen peak.

None spoke about it afterward, not that I would ever have asked. I can but imagine him as he stands on a great boulder before their eyes. A balefire roars below, flames whirling red and yellow to claim from the northlights their right to show him forth. He is clad in his best—silks, linens, furs, chased leather, massive gold and amber. To his breast has been fixed a sprig of mistletoe as if piercing the heart behind. In his upturned hands lies a drawn sword.

He says, iron steady: "Nerthus has taken Her blessing away from me."

He does not hear the horrified calls, the wild questions as to why. Maybe there are none. Maybe the folk accept that Her will is alike beyond cruelty and pity. He says—he will give those who love him as much of his self— "I had not looked for it. Not at my age. I hoped, as every man does, to die before She wearied of me. That could not be." Duty comes back, takes every softness from his voice. "Choose then your next king, and give Her that which She will have."

He casts the sword down into the fire. Sparks rain upward. And suddenly he smiles.

He smiled.

He walked among us and our griefs, through those last sleety days, in more than the mirth-underlain serenity we remembered. Often tears met him, a harsh "Landfather, abide!" He stilled the outbursts and proceeded to order affairs, give counsel, make everything ready for his son who would follow him. When there was a small child, he liked to hold it on his lap while he talked and jest it into laughter. He went off by himself many times, though, hours and miles upon end. I think he wanted to be one and of his land, however stark a look it wore, before he must sink within it. And he no longer sat in the royal house. He and Ioran dwelt apart, in a cottage borrowed from a peasant: a lowly place, suitable for two who had scant need anymore of earthly goods.

She could not help showing how hard was her fight to match his peace. No doubt he consoled her when they were alone.

"What is this barbarian lunacy?" Memmius stormed at me. "Can you comprehend it? He's gotten his virility back—"

"How do you know?"

"How do you think? I slipped out after sunset and listened. These flimsy doors—"

"What made you do such a filthy thing?"

"What ails *you?* Listen, Philon, we've spent some nine unrecoverable months in this hole, and now the baby we hoped would come to term . . . won't. Walhauk isn't like his father, he's more interested in enlarging the kingdom than its trade, he's suspicious of Rome, you know that. When he succeeds, he won't encourage any permanent outpost. Everything we've done could be wasted!" Memmius drew breath. "Anyhow, about Hesting, his recovery is common knowledge. Owldoon knows him, sees it shine. You must have heard gossip."

I nodded unwillingly.

"Then why must he die?" Memmius demanded. "If he can carry on the rites at spring as before, why must he die when I need him?" He leaned forward. "You and he were pretty close once, Philon. I don't know what happened—I never did quite believe you tripped and landed on a rock—still, lately I've seen him greet you quite pleasantly when you chance to meet. Can't you learn, and maybe talk him out of his idiot aim?"

If I could . . .

Like a cat at a mousehole, save that the fear and entrapment were mine, I watched. Hitherto I had not dared trail him on his lonely stridings. Now Midwinter Day was so near that nothing remained for me to lose.

I caught him at the edge of the heath. The first snow of the year, no, the last snow of the old year had fallen overnight, a fine whiteness and silence across dead plowlands. Barrows and leafless bushes reared above. Their shadows were blue, under a pale sky and dim, low sun. The air was heavy with chill.

"Hesting," I called, and stumbled to overtake him.

He stopped, leaned on his spear, crinkled upward his lips and the crowsfeet around his eyes. "Hail, Philon," he said in Latin.

I stopped before him. My lungs burned from running. "Speak your own speech," I pleaded.

"If you wish." The breath smoked from him and vanished.

"Hesting, you— Is it that—I mean, what I did, if that brought a curse . . . or if Nerthus wants a death for any reason, I'd gladly, gladly—"

Had his tone carried scorn rather than politeness I could have borne it easier. "It is well thought of you. However, I am the one who is wanted. She would not be appeased, might well be angered, by a different offering." Altogether levelly, he uttered it: "What if She did not call the sun home?"

"But the curse was lifted!"

"That makes me doubly sure of Her will. She did not smite me—not the little while wherewith She punishes most men who offend, but week after week— She did not smite Her Fro for nothing. Nor is it for nothing that as soon as I vowed myself to death" —all springtime broke forth in his tone— "She made me whole again!"

I could not ask what he meant; my tongue locked. Nor can I to this day follow his thought, nor reach that final haven he shared with Orestes and Oedipus. The Goddess has never touched me since; my world is a drumskin above a void which has no ending.

He finished in a kindliness as impersonal as if already it spoke from the grave: "Don't blame yourself. Now, if you will forgive me, I have only this one night left with my wife."

He turned and walked off across the snow.

At dawn he went alone to the shrine of Nerthus. They tell me he took along just a bowl of hallowed gruel to eat. I wonder what his musings were on the shore of Holy Lake.

The day after was Midwinter. It had warmed, snow melted in soft little gurgles, the sun swung red behind overcast. Somewhere I heard a rook caw.

I must stay in town, of course. None but the heads of households, and Walhauk his son, might meet him when he returned down the forbidden road.

They accompanied him to the peat bog. I never asked what the ceremonies were. I could not help overhearing talk of them—whatever was known to everybody, whispered in darkness. He undressed, stood naked until they gave him a leather cap to cover his head from the light and a leather belt to hide the scar of his birth. Of leather, too, was the noose his son laid around his neck. Not being an evildoer condemned to slow strangling, he himself ascended the ash tree. He secured the other end of the cord to a lofty branch, smiled upon them, and stepped free.

They buried him there, with no grave-goods save the rope and his honor. Owldoon would not sacrifice a bullock this year. It had given Her a king.

Nonetheless the winter turned hard, winds whistled down from the Pole Star, cold rang in the earth. The time grew long before our ship was able to come and bear me back to people I can understand.